Take a Chance

SHELLEY SHEPARD GRAY

Take a Chance

BLACK STONE
PUBLISHING

Copyright © 2018 by Shelley Shepard Gray
Published in 2018 by Blackstone Publishing
Cover and book design by Alenka V. Linaschke

Printed in the United States of America

First edition: 2018
ISBN 978-1-5384-4087-2
Fiction / Romance

1 3 5 7 9 10 8 6 4 2

CIP data for this book is available
from the Library of Congress

Blackstone Publishing
31 Mistletoe Rd.
Ashland, OR 97520

www.BlackstonePublishing.com

For Tom, for more reasons than I could ever name

Letter to Readers

Thank you for picking up *Take a Chance*. I hope you enjoy Kurt and Emily's book!

I came up with the idea for the Bridgeport Social Club series years ago, during a conversation with my husband one morning after his monthly poker game. To be honest, when Tom first started playing poker one Friday night a month, I couldn't figure out what the attraction was. The games were held in a buddy's garage, which was hot in the summer and cold in the winter. I knew they played cards, ate a lot of junk food, drank beer, and smoked cigars, sometimes until late in the night. It sounded crowded, noisy, and kind of smelly, too.

Truthfully, I was kind of annoyed about the whole thing.

Then, one Saturday morning, instead of complaining about his smelly poker clothes, I asked my husband who he had talked to the night before. That's when Tom started telling me about the guys' kids. And recent vacations. Who had a new job and who was still looking for one. Who was dating someone new and who was about to celebrate an anniversary.

And that's when it clicked.

Those Friday-night poker games weren't actually just about poker. They were a chance for a group of friends to get together.

Now that, I could understand! I have the same connection with my writing buddies. Yes, we write and edit each other's work, but we also value our friendship just as much. Our monthly meetings are always about so much more than the books we are working on.

I decided right then and there to stop complaining (as much) about Friday-night poker.

So, that's the story of how *Take a Chance* and the whole Bridgeport Social Club came to be. I hope you enjoy the book. But more importantly, I hope that you, too, have found your own group of family or friends who you believe in and who also believe in you.

That's worth everything, I think.

With my blessings and my thanks,
Shelley Shepard Gray

CHAPTER 1

FROM LES LARKE'S
TIPS FOR BEGINNING POKER PLAYERS:

Avoid becoming too emotional. Bad bets will happen.
Losing sessions will happen. Annoying opponents will
happen. Live with it.

Kurt Holland walked into Bridgeport High feeling a bit like he'd just entered a prison. Honestly, who would've ever guessed that visitors would need to have their pictures taken in order to enter a public high school? It was almost as disconcerting as getting a call that his brother—who he was now guardian of—had gotten into a fight and was in the principal's office.

When the call had come, he'd been knee-deep in a drainage ditch at the convention center. That meant that while he had on a fresh white T-shirt and washed his face and hands, he probably still looked and smelled like he'd just crawled out of the mud.

It was not the way he'd hoped to make his first impression, but what could he do? It wasn't like Sam getting in a fight was any better.

"May I help you?" the matronly receptionist asked, making him realize that he'd been standing there for a good twenty seconds, lost in thought.

"Yeah. I'm Kurt Holland. I'm here to speak with Mr. Hendrix about my brother, Sam."

"Oh. Yes. We've been waiting for you."

Kurt caught the vague note of disapproval in her tone, but he shook it off. He wasn't going to apologize for his brother, his appearance, or the fact that it took him an hour to get over here. Instead he signed his name where she directed. "Where do I go now?"

"Go to the first door to the right. And clip this on your … ah, T-shirt."

Looking at the plastic name badge that proclaimed he was a visitor loud and proud, Kurt wondered if there had ever been a more fitting item to symbolize how he felt. Though they'd been in Bridgeport for almost two months, he and Sam weren't any closer to feeling like they were a welcome addition to the sleepy town than the first day they'd driven up in his truck.

Clipping the badge to the collar of his shirt, he nodded his thanks and walked to the door she'd indicated.

He noticed his seventeen-year-old brother right away when he entered the cool, carpeted office. Sam was sitting on one of the brown-and-orange plastic chairs that lined one of the walls. Both of his elbows were resting on his knees and one of his hands was holding an ice pack on his eye.

When Sam spied him, he sat up abruptly. The ice pack fell away, revealing a good-sized knot on his cheek and the beginnings of a black eye. His expression flitted from disdain to relief to apprehension in seconds.

He scrambled to his feet. "Sorry you had to take off work." His West Virginia accent was out in full force. The kid was nervous.

This was why Kurt had decided to pull Sam out of Spartan. The kid needed a future. He also needed something more than what he'd been getting at home lately, which was a front-row view of their father's descent into grief and bitterness.

Sam was a good kid. Better than he'd ever been. Actually, Sam was everything that Kurt had never been. Friendly, clean-cut. Smart. Really smart. But more than any of that, he'd had their mother's goodness. It shined through his heart and always had.

Kurt shrugged off Sam's apology. "You all right?" he asked. Seeing the kid's face bruised did not make him happy. An old, familiar tension rose in his chest as he wondered what had happened and who he was going to have to talk to in order to make sure Sam was taken care of.

Sam shrugged. Staring at a spot right behind him, he mumbled, "I don't know."

Kurt was just about to ask what that meant when another door opened. In walked a woman about five years younger than his own thirty-one years. She was wearing a black slim skirt, three-inch black heels, and a pink sweater. As his gaze traveled upward, he noticed that she had pearls in her ears, her dark brown hair was confined to a ponytail, and she had dark brown, kind-looking eyes.

And a pair of perfectly formed lips that curved upward slightly when they turned to him. "Mr. Holland? I'm Emily Springer. Sam's English teacher." Glancing toward Sam, her voice warmed. "And his advisor."

"Hi. I'm Kurt." When he heard Sam cough, he tried again. "I mean, it's nice to meet you, Miss Springer. Call me Kurt."

"And I'm Emily."

He held out his hand to shake hers, realized that he hadn't gotten all the dirt out of his nails, and considered pulling it back. Instead, he clasped her hand gently, not wanting to inadvertently hurt her. "Sorry about my hands. I, uh, well, I've been working in the mud all day."

"Nothing to apologize for," she replied as a door he hadn't noticed in the back of the room opened and a slim man in a polo, khakis, and shiny loafers stepped out. A couple with a boy about Sam's age stepped out of the office behind him. The couple looked at Sam then him warily. The boy's face was flushed. He was also sporting a good-sized bruise on his face and his nose looked swollen, like it had been bleeding recently.

To Kurt's surprise, the kid stopped in front of Sam. "Sorry about earlier."

"Yeah," Sam mumbled as the other kid's parents shuffled him out.

When the door closed again, the principal strode forward. "Hi. I'm Terry Hendrix. I'm the principal of Bridgeport High."

"Kurt Holland, Sam's brother."

"I believe you're his guardian as well?"

"Yeah. Our father is back in West Virginia. I'm legally in charge of Sam."

"Good to know. Let's go talk in the conference room, shall we?"

Kurt raised an eyebrow in Sam's direction as they followed the principal and Emily, the pretty teacher who shouldn't have such good legs.

After asking them all to take a seat, Mr. Hendrix folded his hands on the top of the conference table. "So. We had a fight today. I don't know what Sam has told you so far?"

"He hasn't told me anything. I just got here."

"Ah. Well, then, Emily, will you please fill Sam's brother in?"

Kurt didn't care for that. Sam was too old to be forced to sit and listen to some teacher's play-by-play when he could speak for himself. Kurt considered mentioning that but decided it probably wouldn't help Sam's predicament. Therefore, he held his tongue, but he didn't attempt to hide his irritation.

Obviously sensing his mood, Emily cleared her throat. "Sam, I'm going to let you share your thoughts too. But from what I understand, there was an issue in the hall by the lockers. Garrett freely admitted that he threw the first punch. Sam threw the second, then the girl they were fighting about stepped into the fray and managed to calm things down."

Of all the situations that could have brought on this fight, it hadn't occurred to Kurt that a female would have been the reason. "You fought over a girl, Sam? Don't you think you have a bit much at stake to be getting all hot and bothered?"

Heat flew up Sam's face. "It wasn't like that."

"What was it like, then?"

Sam glanced around the table. Stared at the principal, at his teacher, at him. Then finally spoke. "Garrett Condon was talking trash about Kayla." After that statement, he pressed his lips together like that was the end of the story.

It wasn't. Not by a long shot. "You better start talking, Sam. Maybe even tell me who this Kayla is."

"She's Kayla Everett. She's a cheerleader."

"Uh huh?" He didn't even try to hide the sarcasm in his voice. He might be over thirty now but he still remembered crushing on a certain high school cheerleader back in Spartan. But even though he remembered what a crush like that feels like, it didn't excuse his brother fighting over her.

Sam scowled. "She's a nice girl, Kurt. A good girl."

"And?"

"And someone took a picture in the locker room of her in her bra. Somehow Garrett got it on his phone and he forwarded it to everyone else. Now everyone's seen it. She's been really upset."

Kurt felt bad for the girl. He really did. But even he knew kids were sharing far worse things than that. Why was Sam acting like the girl's defender? "I don't understand how Kayla's bra pics got you and Garrett so spun up."

When Sam's expression turned mutinous, Emily spoke. "Maybe I should step in here. From what I have understood, Sam and Kayla have been talking quite a bit. And seeing each other some, too. When Sam heard Garrett talking about her with other boys, he um, let Garrett know he wasn't happy about that. Garrett didn't take kindly to being told what to do. This discussion escalated, and Garrett hit Sam."

Sam folded his arms over his chest. "Yeah, he hit me. And I wasn't just gonna sit there and take it, so I hit him back." Before anyone else at the table could comment, he rushed on. "And

Kurt, don't start telling me that you wouldn't have done the same thing. Because you would have."

Heck, yeah, he would have hit Garrett back. Their father didn't raise his boys to stand still and get beat on by idiots. If he wasn't so stunned about the reason for the fight and the girl, Kurt knew he would have expressed himself a whole lot better.

Now, all he wanted to do was get Sam out of there. He turned to the principal. "Is Sam in trouble or not?"

"While I don't exactly disagree with Sam's viewpoint, we have zero tolerance for violence in the school. Because of that, he is going to be suspended for one day."

Suspended for a day. Because of a skirmish in the hall over a girl. Glancing at his brother, Kurt realized that Sam had shut down. He didn't expect Kurt to fight for him. All he was doing was waiting to get out of there. Though Kurt knew that was all Sam had known from their father, it still hurt. Dad had been distant on his best days, uninterested on most.

Which was one of the reasons he was sitting in this room with Sam instead of their dad.

Leaning forward in his chair, Kurt said, "This punishment seems a bit much, don't you think? Nobody was seriously hurt or anything. And what about whoever took the photos in the first place? I'm guessing it was some creepy girl in the locker room. Have y'all discovered who that was?"

The principal folded his hands together on the table. "We're still sorting that out."

"I hope you finish sorting it real soon, seeing as she's taking secret photos and all."

"Kurt, stop," Sam hissed under his breath.

Thinking about his brother, the new kid in school, getting hit while standing up for a girl, then getting suspended for it, made him fume. So he talked right on through. Looking directly at Mr. Hendrix, he said, "At his old school, what just happened wouldn't have drawn much more than a day's worth of gossip."

The principal pursed his lips. "I don't know what things were like back in West Virginia, but we handle things differently here. It's for everyone's safety."

"Is it? 'Cause right now it seems like the only people who are getting hurt are the ones who are trying to do the right thing."

Miss Springer turned to face him more directly. "Kurt, you see, if we let this go, it could set a bad precedent. We can't let that happen."

Set a bad precedent. Educational talk for they weren't going to budge. Kurt was just about to sign whatever he had to, take Sam, and get them out of the school. A day's suspension wasn't the end of the world. He'd get the whole story on Kayla when they didn't have an audience.

Plus, Sam looked like he was about to start edging toward the door with or without him. He should put the kid out of his misery.

But then he remembered his dream for the kid. College.

A college education could practically guarantee that Sam would never see the inside of a coal mine. Or do half the things Kurt had had to do to get his landscaping business off the ground. Those things meant he was going to have to swallow his pride and do whatever he had to do to ensure his brother's future. He had to.

"Sam is real smart," he blurted.

Sam squirmed. "Jeez, Kurt ..."

Emily smiled at Sam. "Yes, he is. His test scores were impressive. So far, he's been doing very well in my class, too. He's in my honors class. Other teachers have shared just as good reports about him."

Though he wasn't Sam's father, he felt a burst of paternal pride swell inside him. "So, he's college bound."

"Of course he is." Emily lifted a hand like she was about to squeeze Sam's arm or pat him on the back or something. Then, as if she realized what she'd been about to do, she clasped her hands back together.

Her actions were real sweet. Caring. When was the last time that boy had been on the receiving end of a woman's comforting touch? Far too long.

He turned back to Mr. Hendrix. "I'm not real sure how all this works. Is this suspension going to present a problem with college applications?"

The principal looked taken aback. "That would be up to the admissions offices ..."

"Come on, you have to know. I mean, Sam can't be the first kid who let his temper get the best of him."

"Kurt, stop," Sam moaned.

"The suspension shouldn't come into play for all of them," Emily interjected.

Though Sam was sending him death glares, Kurt asked, "What does that mean?"

Emily looked uncomfortable. "Well, um, Sam will receive automatic zeros for any assignments he misses during his suspension. And some universities do ask if applicants have ever been suspended. But there's also places for the applicant to explain." After a pause, she continued. "And then, well, there are scholarship applications. Some of those might be affected."

Kurt couldn't imagine his brother writing paragraphs about how he'd been attempting to protect Kayla's honor. "So, what you're sayin' is that being suspended could cause Sam some harm. It could interfere with getting into college, or even paying for it."

"Technically?" Emily's doe eyes filled with remorse. "Yes, I'm afraid it could."

Kurt looked around the table. "That's gonna be a problem, then."

Principal Hendrix stiffened.

"It's okay, Kurt," Sam said quickly.

"No, I don't think it is." Feeling for the first time in his life like he was on the right side, he added a new thread of determination in his voice. "After all, I wouldn't be doing a very good job as a guardian if I didn't point out that nothing can interfere with Sam getting into college."

Mr. Hendrix frowned. "I can see that you are concerned. However, Garrett received the same punishment. I can't very well give one boy one punishment while Sam gets a different consequence."

Finally, Kurt felt like he was on even ground. He might not know much about college and scholarship applications, but he knew plenty about fighting and how life was hardly ever fair.

"Sure you can," he said easily. "Garrett threw the first punch. That matters, I know it does. Plus, he was the one sharing pictures and talking trash about Kayla, correct? That seems a lot more worrisome to me. Don't you think so?"

Miss Springer bit her lip like she was trying to stop herself from chiming in.

Feeling encouraged, Kurt continued. "I don't know how you treat women here at Bridgeport High, but back in West Virginia, we are taught to treat women with respect. You might not agree with the way Sam handled things, but he didn't take the picture, he didn't share it, and he was obviously trying to stop it, too. Which, frankly, someone on staff should've done in the first place."

For the first time since Kurt arrived, Sam's expression turned hopeful.

His teacher looked even more uneasy. "Your points are valid, Kurt. However—"

"However, we moved here so Sam could get a better education. I know he's going to get that in Bridgeport. Now, I know he wants to do well here. He's gonna work hard and be respectful of the staff. But my little brother here is more than just a smart kid. He's a good man. If you think I'm going to let him start throwing everything out that our parents instilled in him, you've got another thing coming."

"Of course we don't want him to ignore the values he was taught," the principal said in a rush.

"I'm real glad to hear you say that. Because I really don't want to have to explain to my father about how you're wanting him to throw out his morals just to fit in around here. Our father would be real disappointed if he found out that Sam walked away when other boys were mistreating his girl."

"Of course he would," Emily said.

Sam kind of choked. "She ain't my girl, Kurt."

That "ain't" chewed on his last nerve. "You talk like you're supposed to, kid."

Abruptly, Sam jumped to his feet. He stood up straight and tall. Proud. Looking directly at the principal, he said, "The one-day suspension is fine, sir. When do I start?"

The principal shuffled some papers. "It could be effective tomorrow."

"I'll take tomorrow, sir. Thank you," Sam blurted.

Kurt grabbed hold of his brother's arm. "Hey, now. Wait a minute."

Sam jerked his arm away. "You aren't my father. I'm also not a kid. I'm seventeen and a half."

In Kurt's mind, Sam was a kid. And the fact that he'd added "and a half" to his age pointed it out perfectly. "I realize that, but I'm trying to do right by you."

"I know, but it's okay." His brother turned and stared at him. A dark smudge was now staining the tender skin under his eye. But what drew Kurt's attention the most was the steady look of resolve in Sam's eyes.

It was the same look their mother had in her last days before the cancer took her. It was the same look in their father's eyes when he'd confided to Kurt that he wasn't capable of doing any more for his youngest child than he already was.

And it was the same look that Kurt had seen in his own reflection when he'd realized that he was going to move to Bridgeport and grasp hold of a life that he'd only seen in television shows.

Turning back to the principal and Emily, Kurt sighed. "Looks like Samuel will be taking his suspension tomorrow. What forms do you need me to sign?"

CHAPTER 2

FROM LES LARKE'S
TIPS FOR BEGINNING POKER PLAYERS:

Pay attention to the game. You'd be surprised at the number of people who miss key pieces of information because they've let their mind drift to things that don't matter.

Emily loathed hot yoga. She hated how it was seventy minutes long and how it felt even longer than that. She hated how she found every single position the instructor attempted to put her in to be painful and awkward. She hated how the five o'clock class felt like it was simply one more thing to get through at the end of another long day.

She especially hated how she always ended up looking like a sweaty rat by the time she walked out of the nondescript studio in the middle of the biggest shopping section of Bridgeport. A sweaty rat with way too much frizzy hair, thanks to the humidity that filled the air from everyone's sweat.

Actually, about the only thing she did like about the class was the way it made her look. Because of this class, she could wear her slim skirts and tailored slacks without worrying that some part of her was jiggling too much. Then there was the fact that because she subjected herself through this torture, she could eat ice cream two nights a week.

It turned out that ice cream and clothes that fit were powerful incentives.

But tonight, she was also glad that she could concentrate on holding that plank position for another thirty seconds instead of thinking even more about the meeting that she'd just walked out of. The way it had ended had left a sour taste in her mouth … and a whole lot of feelings she wasn't sure how to deal with. Though she hadn't been teaching all that long, this was unusual.

First of all, she'd felt bad for Sam Holland. He was the type of student that made her job wonderful. He was inquisitive and bold. Funny and feisty. He was smarter than he realized, and she loved how any compliment seemed to surprise him. He wore his heart on his sleeve, too. He didn't just like Kayla Everett. He *really* liked Kayla Everett. Her grandmother would have described it as smitten.

She'd vowed to herself that she was going to personally talk to every one of the teachers on his schedule to see if they could give him a break on the zeros. Kids like him were the reason they'd all gone into education. If he suffered because of the fight today, she'd take it as a sign that she hadn't done enough for him. He needed someone to fight for him.

Well, besides his big brother.

"Downward dog," the instructor called out in her sweet, singsong voice.

With a grunt, Emily switched positions. And, as she settled into staring at the mat, she made herself admit the other reason she was suddenly tolerating the class for once.

Two words: Kurt Holland. A man who was too much of everything. Too handsome. Too sexy. Too much for a girl like her.

But boy, it was sure hard not to imagine how things would be if she ever had a reason to be around him again. His voice had a slight drawl. His features were hard and chiseled and supremely attractive. He was a six-foot, three-inch hunk with dark brown

13

hair and dark blue eyes. What was even more disconcerting was that he wasn't even off-limits. He wasn't a parent. He was a brother.

She'd never thought to add brothers of students to her Do Not Date list.

"Runner's pose."

Should he be? Maybe she should add an addendum to that list. For her own good, of course.

"Runner's pose, Emily," the instructor fairly ordered in her ear.

Hurriedly, she tried to move her right foot into position … and then promptly fell.

Campbell Weiss, her best friend, fellow teacher, and second cousin, snickered. "Better get your mind on the game before you hurt yourself, Em," she whispered under her breath. "You don't want to go to school saying you twisted your ankle doing yoga."

Emily didn't bother to look at her. If she did, she'd be treated to a perfect rendition of a runner's pose as well as a blinding white smile. As much as Emily hated this class, Campbell thrived on it.

"Warrior one."

With a grunt, she glanced at her cousin, forced herself into position, and started thinking about vanilla ice cream and her navy pencil skirt. If she survived this class, both could be in her future.

Twenty minutes later, she was guzzling water outside her car and trying her best to evade her cousin's questions.

"What was going on with you in there?" Campbell asked as she lightly ran a towel over her shoulders, that perversely, didn't look either sore or like she'd sweat all that much.

"You know how much I hate this class."

"Oh, I know. What I don't know is why you go at all."

"You know why," Emily said.

"There are other activities to do that would allow you to eat ice cream and still fit into your skinny jeans."

"Not really. I've tried everything. I hate running, got injured last time I attempted weight training, and made a fool of myself doing aerobics."

"Does anyone even do aerobics anymore?" Campbell teased.

"That's beside the point."

Looking at her carefully, Campbell said, "I'm beginning to think that there's something more here than just two scoops of Graeter's chocolate–chocolate chip ice cream. What is the point?"

"That I'm not going to let this class get the best of me. I'm going to master it. Sooner or later."

"That is so you," she murmured, not exactly sounding impressed either. "You are a girl who is determined to keep to your lists and goals, no matter what."

"Don't knock them. Those two things keep me on track."

"They also limit your life." She softened her voice. "One day you are going to realize that no matter what that jerk Danny says, you are just fine how you are, Em."

She inwardly flinched at the mention of Danny's name. "I can't talk about Danny."

"I know, and I don't want to make you. I'm just trying to get you to see that things might be okay if you take some chances every now and then."

That was so Campbell. Her best friend in the world had a faith that was as strong as her steadfastness. Emily admired it, she really did.

But that didn't mean that she was going to be able to do that very easily. However, before Emily could argue that point for about the two hundred and seventy-sixth time, Campbell opened her car door.

"Sorry. I'd talk about this all some more, but I've got to rush home and shower. I've got a date tonight."

"With whom?"

"Hunter Carvelles."

Emily grimaced. "Oh, Camp. Really?"

Though she looked more than a little embarrassed, Campbell jutted out her chin. "There's nothing wrong with him."

"There's nothing right either."

"That's not true," she replied in a rush. "Hunter's nice and he has a good job. Plus, he thinks I'm pretty."

That was all it took for Emily to stop holding her tongue. "Hunter's kind of slimy, I bet everyone hates him at his job, and you are pretty."

Campbell pursed her lips. "I know I just said that we're all like we're supposed to be … but sometimes I wish I wasn't built like a 1950s pinup girl."

Only Campbell could make her hourglass figure sound like a bad thing. "For the last time, your figure—"

Holding up one hand with perfectly pink manicured nails, her girlfriend shook her head. "Uh, no. I am not going to start discussing this with you. Again. Say bye and wish me luck."

"How about I tell you bye and that I hope you have fun?" No way did she want Campbell to end up with Hunter.

"Thanks," she replied before opening up the sunroof on her spiffy silver Mazda and driving off.

Still feeling too damp and thirsty to step into her trusty Corolla, Emily sipped her water and tried to think of someone better for her girlfriend. No one came to mind, but that didn't mean much. She hadn't had a whole lot of luck in the dating department herself.

All that did matter was that Hunter definitely wasn't the guy for Campbell. He was crazy smart—rocket-scientist smart. But he had an awful sense of humor and had somehow adopted Campbell's parents' passive-aggressive way of treating her.

Sure, Campbell was heavier than Emily by about forty pounds. But she wasn't fat by any means. She simply had curves—in all the right places. She also had thick long brown hair that she took the time to put in hot rollers every day. But while most other women's curls would fall in a saggy heap by ten every morning, Campbell's hair stayed perfectly curled all day long. It danced along her shoulder blades when she walked down the halls.

Even all the teenage girls envied her hair! Really, it was beautiful. Then, of course, she had bluebonnet-blue eyes and was something of a computer genius. And she was a gourmet cook. Emily wasn't a guy, but she was pretty sure that Campbell had a lot of attributes that most men liked a lot.

All she had to do was drop Hunter like the clod he was and set her sights elsewhere. On someone who could appreciate her package, because it was a pretty amazing one. Surely there was a man like that somewhere in the vicinity?

Just as she finished her water bottle, a large silver Ford truck pulled in to park two spaces down. She absently smiled at the driver, intending to hop in her Corolla and finally go home. Then the driver's door opened … and out came Kurt Holland himself.

When he turned to her, his gaze drifted over her body. She caught a look of surprise as he took in her sweat-dampened body and frizzy hair. He quickly hid it, but not quickly enough for her to not wish she'd driven off about five minutes before he'd arrived.

Suddenly, she felt out of place and incredibly awkward.

Kind of like seeing him in a yoga parking lot. Kind of how she couldn't ignore how attractive he was, and how her mind was turning to mush around him. Again.

This wasn't good. She needed to get away from him, stat. After she said something friendly and polite. And, perhaps, smart-sounding. She just had to hope he liked working out. Then, maybe, just maybe, he would be able to somehow appreciate her efforts to stay in shape.

Yeah, that could do it. Maybe.

As long as he was standing downwind.

CHAPTER 3

"Poker is...a fascinating, wonderful, intricate adventure on the high seas of human nature."
—DAVID A. DANIEL

"Miss Springer, right?" Kurt asked, feeling pretty proud of himself for acting like he was trying to place her name. It was a lot better than her discovering the reality, which was he hadn't been able to stop thinking of Sam's drop-dead gorgeous teacher and the many ways he would have liked to have gotten to know her … if she wasn't off-limits.

Which Emily Springer was.

"Yes. That's me." She paused awkwardly, looking like she needed to take a second to come to grips with something important. After another second went by, she stepped forward, pulled her shoulders back, and smiled. "It's nice to see you again, Mr. Holland."

He was slightly disappointed she didn't offer her hand. He would have liked to touch her again. But she probably had a whole lot more practice than he did keeping her students' families a firm distance away. "You know, I can only think of about two people who've ever called me Mr. Holland, and one of them was my sixth-grade teacher. Do you think you could continue to call me Kurt?"

"I suppose I can, if you call me Emily."

Feeling successful though he really shouldn't be feeling anything at all, he smiled. "I can do that, Emily."

Looking awkward, she shifted her weight. He took in her outfit again, noticed that her leggings showed off better legs than he'd imagined. And the black sports bra with a damp white tank over it accentuated the rest of her attributes. Which he shouldn't have noticed.

Realizing that she was watching him studying her intently, he mentally cursed. She'd seen him checking her out. Nothing creepy about that. His mother would have slapped him upside the head.

He needed to give her space and not make her uncomfortable. Taking a step backward, he attempted to sound politely bored. "Sorry, I was just wondering what you've been doing." Letting out a little moan, she pressed her hands to her cheeks. "I know. I look terrible." She wrinkled her nose. "I think I smell, too. I'm really sorry."

He would have started laughing but he was pretty sure that would hurt her feelings. "I wasn't thinking that you look bad or um, smell, Emily. Only that you looked a lot different than you did at school."

"Oh, I know I look different. There's only one thing that makes me look like this." Pointing to the sign above one of the stores, she explained. "I've been at hot yoga."

Looking up, he frowned. "What's that?"

Her brown eyes widened. "You don't know?"

"Nope." Though he'd heard of yoga, of course, he'd never paid a lot of attention to it. He never paid any attention to the latest workout craze since he earned his living working outside. But her interest in it might make him change his mind.

Finally giving in, he smiled softly as he leaned against the side of his truck. "Never heard of it."

"Oh. Well, it's a class where everyone does different yoga poses in a room that's a hundred degrees."

"Why would you want to do that? It was over ninety today."

"It, uh, is supposed to encourage sweating."

He almost mentioned that she could probably get a good sweat just by going for a walk outside, but he kept his mouth shut. "Looks like it did a good job."

She pulled at her tank top, which gave him a peek at even more bare skin that he wasn't supposed to be noticing.

Her lips pursed. "I can't believe I'm talking to you looking like this. I need a shower in a bad way."

Emily. Plus. Shower.

Shoot. There he went again. Thinking about her in a really inappropriate way. When he noticed that she was blushing, he knew it was time to say something and put her at ease the way his mother would have expected him to do.

No, actually, he needed to salvage this conversation before she transferred Sam right out of her class because his older brother was a creeper.

And that was why he said one of the most embarrassing things he could remember speaking in his entire life. "Don't worry about it, Emily. I'm used to damp clothes."

Her eyebrows raised.

"You know, since I do landscaping." Feeling dumber by the second, he blurted, "I mean, what I'm trying to say is that I already sweat a lot."

"Ah."

Ah. Crap. Now he sounded just plain gross. Afraid that if he looked at her directly she would get all uncomfortable again, he averted his eyes. "Sorry. I usually don't talk about sweating and showers."

She slapped a hand over her mouth in an obvious attempt to not laugh. "Thank you. The moment I saw you, I was feeling mortified."

"Which means my fumbling around made you feel better."

She giggled.

"Mission accomplished." He smiled.

"I promise, I actually try to give a better impression than this."

"If it's any consolation, you made a good impression on me today. Thank you for everything you did for Sam. We both really appreciate it."

"Sam is a good kid. Though he might not realize it, we're all on the same team. We all want him to succeed and do better."

"I'll pass that on to him. Thanks." He needed to go now. Leave her alone and let her get on home.

"Hey, are you settling into Bridgeport okay?"

He shrugged. "Well enough."

"Good."

She looked relieved. He wondered why. Did hc look that out of place … or was she concerned about something else? But no matter what, he didn't think it mattered, anyway. "I'll let you go. I only stopped here to grab some Mexican food to go."

Emily lit up. "Oh, El Fenix is really good. You should try the Santa Fe burritos."

"Will do." He smiled at her then, pleased when she smiled back.

Twenty minutes later, after he had gotten fajitas, enchiladas, and a Santa Fe burrito, he wondered why he had done such a thing. It wasn't like he was going to see her anytime soon. In fact, it would be best if he didn't see her much at all.

When he walked in the door, Sam was sitting on the sectional playing Xbox like he didn't have a care in the world. "Hey," he said over his shoulder while he continued to press his thumbs on the controller.

"Hey, come on over to the table and eat."

"Why?" he asked suspiciously. "We usually just sit on the couch."

"We don't usually get to have a meeting at school either. Turn that off, or whatever you have to do, and join me. And grab some plates and silverware for us, okay?"

Sam looked like he was going to argue. But then he turned off the television and joined Kurt in the kitchen. After he grabbed the plates and a pair of forks, he pulled out a chair at the kitchen table. "What did you get?"

"Fajitas, cheese enchiladas, and something called a Santa Fe burrito," he said as he unwrapped it and cut it in half.

Sam eyed it suspiciously. "What the heck is that?"

"Not sure."

"Why did you order it then?"

"Why not?" Kurt replied, because, well, he didn't have an answer to that. It wasn't like he could tell his brother that his teacher recommended it after her hot yoga class.

"Um, okay," he said as he dug in.

Kurt did the same. When he cut into the burrito and discovered some freaky green sauce, black beans, and chicken, it took everything he had to give it a try. Surprisingly, it was good. Would he get it again?

That would be no.

Sam raised his eyebrows at it but didn't say a word.

Finally, Kurt knew they couldn't put it off anymore. "So, about today. You okay?"

Sam leaned back. "Yeah. I guess."

"Any fallout from the kids?"

He chuckled under his breath. "Not really. Most are pretending it didn't happen. A couple acted like I should have gotten into bigger trouble, but nothing else."

"What about Kayla?"

"Kay?" His expression softened. "She didn't say much, but she didn't act like she hated me hitting that kid, either." Looking pleased, he said, "She said I could call her later. We're going to talk tonight."

Kurt knew that tone of voice. He used to sound like that about Becky. Well, he did until she'd gotten a scholarship and moved to

Morgantown and found herself a guy with a future.

His mother had said good riddance, but he'd remembered every harsh word Becky had said. About how she wanted something more. Something more than what he was. More than what she imagined he could ever be.

And just like that, all the disappointments he'd ever felt about himself rushed forward, both embarrassing him and frustrating him at the same time. He'd been hurt and Becky had dropped him like an unwanted bug clinging to her shoe.

Back then, he'd been just a guy starting his own landscaping business. He'd known that he wasn't much of a catch. But he still resented that she'd felt the need to stomp on his heart, too. He'd thought he'd loved her. But she? Well, she hadn't. Not even close.

No way did he want Sam to go through that. "You know, we moved here so you could get into college. Not so you could start dating some girl who was going to get you into trouble." When Sam swallowed hard, Kurt realized that he'd sounded harsh. And yeah, he sounded pretty judgmental, too.

What was wrong with him?

Sam put his fork down. "I know that."

"Then you know you can't mess this up. Keep your head on straight and don't get into any more fights."

"I didn't intend to get into one in the first place," Sam snapped.

Though he knew he should shut up, Kurt just kept talking. "If you need to distance yourself from this girl so you can concentrate on what's important, then that's what you need to do. We pulled up both of our lives for this. *Both* of our lives."

"You don't think I realize that?"

"I'm not sure if you realize what I did for you."

"What you did for me? Is that how it is now? Because when we first talked about moving here, it was because both of us needed to take a chance. Both of us had something we wanted to do."

"Don't make this fight about me, kid."

Sam raised his eyebrows. "Well, how about this. Do you think some asshat sharing half-naked pictures of Kayla and making stupid remarks about her ain't important?" Before Kurt could attempt to defend himself, Sam continued. "Was all that stuff you said in the office at school just talk?"

"Of course not. And of course what happened to Kayla was bad. It was really wrong. But what I'm trying to tell you is that it wasn't your problem, Sam."

"She's sixteen and Garrett was showing all of his friends her boobs."

Kurt winced. "She could have handled it on her own."

Sam shook his head. "No, she couldn't. She was crying."

Kurt felt his insides clench. He'd never been able to handle girls crying, either. "That's too bad, but that doesn't mean you had to get in that guy's face."

"Don't give me that," Sam said, his eyes looking like they might start watering. "He hit me first. You wouldn't have just stood there."

It was time to back down, and maybe even tell the truth, too. "I hear you. You're right. I wouldn't."

His brother kept talking. "Besides, someone had to stand up for her. It needed to be me."

It needed to be him. Well, there was further proof that nothing about Sam's relationship with Kayla was casual. The kid was in deep. Forcing himself to remember just how much of a loser he'd felt when Becky had tossed him out of her life, Kurt cleared his throat. "Sam, all I'm trying to say is that sometimes a man has to weigh what is important in his life. He needs to prioritize. For you, that needs to be college."

"I was college bound when we lived in West Virginia, Kurt," he retorted, his voice louder. "I got those test scores after Mom died! I made straight As while you and Dad were always working and I was playing football. I can do more than one thing at a time."

"Things are different here, though."

"Yeah, they are. Most of the kids are stuck up. All of my real friends are six hours away. And you ..."

"And me, what?"

"You're riding me like a horse."

"Come on."

"And you're stressed out and in my face all the time."

"Of course I'm stressed out. I've got a mortgage and a business and a brother to raise."

Sam slapped his hand on the table. "Don't you get it? I already am raised."

"Not completely." The kid needed him. He knew it. He knew it as surely as if he was advising him on what card to pick up in a poker game.

"Okay, how about this? I may still need you, but I don't need to be supervised. I don't need you to ride me about grades or test scores. I don't need you remind me about how much college costs or how lucky I am to even think about going to some Ivy League school. I know I'm lucky. I know that."

"Then?"

"Then what I need you to do is back off. I swear, half the time I think you're going to ask me if I did my homework."

"If you don't want more conversations like this, then you need to behave."

Sam glared at him. "Did you even mean all that stuff you said in the principal's office?"

"Of course I did."

"Then you know I did the right thing, Kurt." Softening his voice, he said, "Sorry, but I think your problem is that you aren't thinking about yourself."

"I just told you that I'm working ..."

"I mean for fun."

"Sam, life isn't—"

"Kurt, all you do is work and hover over me. You don't do anything here that you used to do."

"I'm not really the golf and tennis type of guy."

"Then go fishing," Sam said in an exasperated tone. "There's a big lake that's fully stocked just outside the town's limits. We've got a river that runs through downtown where you can kayak. There's hiking and biking trails."

"You sound like a brochure."

"Maybe I need to, since you haven't explored Bridgeport much." Sam held up a hand. "And, before you start telling me that you don't want to go on a ten-mile bike ride, I bet there are other men in Bridgeport who like to sit around and drink beer too. Maybe even play cards. Go find them."

"Thanks for the tip. I'll get right on that."

Ignoring his sarcasm, Sam said, "You need to get back to how you used to be. Call up Troy. He's from Spartan and is half the reason we're here. Call up Ace."

Kurt was about to blow off that suggestion when he realized that the kid was right. "I'll give them a call."

Gathering up his plate, Sam gave him a steady look. "Good. Now that this real fun convo is over, I'm going to go call Kayla."

"Sorry for asking, but did you do your homework?"

Humor lit his eyes. "Yeah."

"And tomorrow, for in-school suspension. Do you have stuff for that?"

"Yeah, Kurt. I'm bringing stuff to do."

He gritted his teeth. "You sure? You got the right books to read?"

"I do. Both *Romeo and Juliet* and *The Rise and Fall of the Roman Empire* are in my backpack. So is *Alive*." His eyebrow rose. "Any more questions?"

"No."

Sam just laughed as he rinsed his plate and walked down the

hall. Grabbing a bottle from the fridge, Kurt opened it and thought about calling their father.

But the time wasn't right. What would he say, anyway? That so far, Sam had gotten in a fight and he was currently crushing on his teacher.

Dad would be real impressed about that.

CHAPTER 4

FROM LES LARKE'S
TIPS FOR BEGINNING POKER PLAYERS:

When in doubt, play it straightforward.

Holding her books close to her chest, Kayla Everett darted down the English wing on the third floor of Bridgeport High. She hated how far her last class was from the bus. Hated it almost as much as riding the bus after school. Her mom had promised that she'd be able to have a car to drive her senior year, but that hadn't happened.

It wasn't like she could complain about it, either. All the money Kayla had saved to help pay for a car had gone to school fees, clothes, and uniforms for cheerleading. It also had to help pay her cell phone bill. And all the other things that a girl in high school needed.

"Hey, Kayla. Wait up!"

Turning, she saw Shannon striding toward her in the way that only a girl who was five-foot-nine could do. "Hey."

"Need a ride? I can give you one, if you'd like."

Shannon was a friend, but she was also one of the biggest gossips on the team. And, well, she wasn't above cashing in favors either. Since she also already took Kayla to practice on the weekends, there was no way she was going to be even more indebted to her if she didn't have to. "Thanks, but I'm good."

"Are you sure about that?"

Kayla nodded as she kept walking. "Yeah. I'm like the second stop. The bus isn't any big deal."

"All right," Shannon said as she adjusted her designer bag. It was the Tory Burch that Kayla had spied at the mall just last week. "So, see you tonight?"

Brent Holloway was having a bunch of people over for a bonfire. "Yeah. Maybe."

"Maybe? But—"

"I gotta go or I'm going to miss my ride. Sorry." She attempted to smile before turning down the stairwell and picking up her pace. Shoot! She only had like two minutes before the bus rolled out of the parking lot.

Glad she had on tennis shoes instead of her usual flip flops, she trotted down five steps, turned, then grabbed the rail and rushed down another seven. Out of breath, she turned again—

And ran right into Sam Holland. Just as she was letting out a little cry and attempting to juggle her armful of books, notebooks, and purse, he held her arms to steady her.

"Hey," he murmured as he rescued her Shakespeare anthology from free-falling onto her foot. "What's going on?"

Just like always, she turned breathless whenever she was around him. Only it was worse now because (a) he'd seen that picture of her in her underwear and (b) because he'd beaten up Garrett for showing it to a bunch of his buddies.

He'd even been suspended for it.

Snatching her heavy book from him, she said, "I'm sorry but I can't talk. I've got to catch the bus."

His eyebrows rose like he was surprised. After the briefest pause, he smiled. "No, you don't. I can take you home."

"I don't think that's a good idea." Too flustered to say another thing, she turned to race through the door.

He reached it before she did and held it open for her. Then he continued walking by her side. His legs were so long that one of his steps equaled three of hers. Seeing that he was real aware of that was embarrassing.

Knowing that she still had to turn the corner around the building, she said, "Sam, I was serious. I've gotta hurry. I can't talk."

"I know you're serious. But can't a guy even walk you to the bus?"

He wanted to do that? In front of half the school? Gaping at him, she stopped. "You don't have to do that." And then, there went those books again. Hating herself, she fumbled them.

He held out his hands. "Let me carry your books, Kay. That Shakespeare book alone has to weigh almost as much as you."

"You don't have to—"

"Stop arguing and start walking. Otherwise, if you ain't careful, you're gonna have to let me take you home after all." His eyes warmed. "Give the books to me, okay?"

Without a word, she handed them to him and started walking fast. When the buses were finally in sight, she released a breath. Her bus was fifth in line. None of them had left yet. She wasn't going to have to walk home or explain to her mother why she was getting a ride from Sam Holland.

Gazing at the Shakespeare book's cover, he whistled low. "This book is a beast. Do you always have to carry it around with you?"

"It's my last class, so kind of. It's easier to carry it with me home than put it in my locker at the end of the day. Some kids have it on their iPad, but I like writing in the margins." She also didn't have an iPad. Feeling self-conscious that she was walking with Sam Holland and talking about homework, she blurted, "Um, where are your books?"

"In my locker."

"You don't have any homework?"

"I had in-school suspension today. I had nothing but time to read and study."

She flushed. That was her fault. "I hope it wasn't too bad."

"Nah. I don't know what Miss Springer told all my other teachers, but none of them made a big deal about it. And they stuck me in the conference room. Half the staff came in to shoot the breeze."

"Wow." She'd been envisioning him in some little closet next to the principal's office all day.

"Yeah. I didn't see that coming, either, but I went with it." He paused, then spoke again. "Hey, Kayla?"

They were almost at her bus, but she had enough time to stop. "Yeah?"

"Why don't you want to look me in the eye?"

For a second, she was tempted to lie. To say that she had looked at him. But he deserved better than that. "You know why," she whispered.

"Is it 'cause of the picture? Or is it because I fought Garrett about it?"

There was his twangy accent again. It made her feel like smiling and melting, all at the same time. "It's the picture," she whispered. "I'm so embarrassed."

Shifting her books in one arm, he reached out and lifted her chin with his other. She had no choice but to stare up at him. "You have nothing to be embarrassed about."

"That's easy for you to say."

"Kayla—"

They were standing in front of all the buses. She felt like every freshman in the school was watching them. "I need to go, Sam."

"Can I come over later?"

"Why?"

His lips curved up. "'Cause I want to talk to you. You going to be home later?"

She wasn't sure what her mom would say. "You can call me if you want."

"All right."

She nodded as she reached her hands out. "I've got to go now."

31

"I'll text you later," he said as he gently placed her books back in her arms. "And I'm going to ask if I can come over."

She nodded as she finally climbed up the steps of the bus.

"I didn't know if you were going to get on or not," Eddie, their seventy-year-old bus driver said to her good-naturedly.

"Me, neither," she admitted as she took her usual seat right behind him.

When Eddie closed the doors and pulled forward, she leaned back and tried not to think about Sam Holland. How was it possible to like someone so much but not want to see him again?

She sure wished she could figure it out.

***

"Hey, Sam," Anthony called out. "You coming to the lake with us?"

Turning, Sam did his best to act like he wished he could. Anthony was cool enough. He was friends with everyone and had an easy, happy personality that was contagious. He was on the basketball team, too. He wasn't one of the best players, but he was good enough to have played on varsity for three years. He also just happened to be one of the few guys in Sam's AP classes that wasn't a complete nerd.

But he had other things on his mind, mainly fixing things with his brother and convincing Kayla to let him come over to her house. "Hey. Sorry, I gotta go home."

"How come?"

"I had in-school today. My brother's pissed."

Understanding lit Anthony's eyes. "Oh. Yeah, I guess he would be. My dad would have grounded me for a month. But it's good you only got a one-day suspension, huh?"

"Yeah."

"Did it suck?"

"Yeah. But not too bad." Actually, it had been a whole lot better than he'd been expecting. It had also given him a break from all the questions he would have gotten if he'd been in his classes.

"At least it's over."

Sam nodded as he headed toward his truck. It was black, old, had chrome bumpers, and looked completely out of place in the high school parking lot filled with shiny foreign sedans and tricked-out SUVs. But that was why he liked it, he supposed. It reminded him of home. Of smaller houses, friends that he'd known from practically birth, and everything that was easy and comfortable.

It had been everything he'd ever known, until he'd come to Ohio.

Anthony was still by his side. "Garrett got a two-day out-of-school suspension. I heard his parents are pissed you didn't get the same punishment."

"He deserved it." As far as Sam was concerned, Garrett deserved to get the crap beat out of him, but he knew better than saying that out loud.

Anthony eyed him carefully. "What's going on with you and Kayla?"

"Nothing."

"Sure? I saw you walking her out." He grinned. "And I could be wrong, but I'm pretty sure you were carrying her books."

Anthony was commenting on that? Was he in the middle of some chick flick? "Her books weighed like a hundred pounds. She needed some help."

He laughed. "Oh. Yeah. I'm sure that's why you were walking with her."

"Why do you care?"

Holding up his hands like he was fending off an attack, he laughed again. "Don't get mad at me. I think she's great."

Sam stared at Anthony hard, wondering if the guy meant something by his words that wasn't innocent at all. Like that he, too, had taken a good look at her without a shirt on.

But Anthony's expression was completely innocent. Or maybe he just didn't want to get hit. Knowing it wasn't going to help him or Kayla if he got in another fight, Sam shrugged. "I better get going before my brother starts blowing up my phone. See you around."

"Yeah. See you tomorrow." Anthony slapped him on the back and trotted off.

Getting in his truck, he smiled when it roared to life, earning a couple of startled glances from some girls two rows over.

After giving them a little salute, he pulled out, absently looking at the school's well-sodded and well-lit ballfield. Then at the auditorium and gymnasium in the distance. Next to the school was a state-of-the art natatorium.

His school has its own swimming pool. Who would have thought?

It also had its own swimming and dive team. He'd met a couple of the swimmers, and they lifeguarded at the pool and gave lessons in the spring to the little kids in town.

As he drove on, he passed a couple of new Volkswagens and Hondas and even a couple of sweet-looking trucks. From what he'd heard, they were all kids' sixteenth birthday presents. New cars and trucks for turning sixteen.

When he'd first gotten to Bridgeport, he'd stared at the cars everyone was driving. It had seemed like every other person was driving an Escalade or a Mercedes or a BMW. Not only was he not used to being around so many expensive cars, but no one in Spartan bought any vehicle that wasn't proudly made in America.

Yet again, he wondered what Dad would think about it all. He figured Dad would either think he was joshing him or go on some tirade about how spoiled everyone was. Every time Sam said something about Dad to Kurt, Kurt shut him down. Sam didn't know if he was still angry at Dad for everything or for something that he was keeping to himself.

Just as he was about to pull into his driveway, his cell phone chirped. When he saw who was calling, he clicked on and set the truck in PARK.

"Coleman. Hey."

Sam's best friend Cole—who pretty much everyone called Coleman—laughed. "So, you do remember us poor guys stuck back in Spartan. I was beginning to wonder."

"Why wouldn't I?"

"'Cause when I called you last night you didn't pick up."

That was because he'd been on the phone with Kayla. "I picked up now. What's going on?"

"Nothing. I was just talking with everybody and we agreed things aren't the same without you here. It's boring as hell."

Sam grinned. "That's your fault. You've got to pick up the slack and stir up some excitement."

"I would if I could. But I got no time for that."

As if his tight control finally loosened, he exhaled. When he spoke again, his accent matched his buddy's. "Oh yeah? What's going on?"

"We're all tired and sore. First game is on Friday, you know."

"You starting?"

"'Course. So are Anton and Burl."

Opening up his door, Sam let one of his legs swing out and he leaned back in his seat, letting the familiar trash talk and complaining wash over him like a warm towel after a cold shower in the locker room. It was because of Coleman that he'd been able to leave without a lot of hard feelings. Instead of feeling resented because he was moving someplace better in order to get into college, pretty much everyone was counting on him to do it.

It was a pretty amazing thing when a ton of people had your back.

After a good five minutes, Cole finally took a breath. "So, that's what's been going on around here. What about you? What have you been doing?"

"Nothing. Going to school."

"That's it?"

"I just got here. You know how it is when you're the new kid. I'm trying to keep my head down and get through it."

"You making friends?"

"I don't know. Maybe. It ain't like there's some welcome wagon."

"Oh. I guess not." After a pause, he said, "What about the girls? Any of them pretty?"

Thinking of Kayla, Sam smiled. "Oh, yeah."

Coleman's voice warmed. "Now we're getting somewhere. Well, who is she? What's she like?"

No way was he going to say anything about Kay. "I'm not seeing anyone serious. Not yet, anyway." Sure that Coleman wouldn't let that go, he switched topics fast. "Now tell me about practice. Burl puke yet?"

"Only every day." And sure enough, that was all it took. Coleman was off and running again, talking about football practice, their buddy who always ate too much before practice, and Coleman's longtime girl, Annabeth.

"You give her your ring yet?"

"Oh, yeah," Cole said, his voice warm. "Anna had to wrap it with a mess of tape, but it looks good on her. Real good."

Sam felt his body relax. He loved hearing about everyone, and felt that familiar ache that never seemed to go away whenever he thought about West Virginia. Back there, he knew how to act, knew what to expect, and felt good.

It wasn't as fancy, but it was home.

As far as he was concerned, it was also a whole lot better than where he was now.

Getting out of his truck, he leaned against the side of it. "Well, don't hold back. Fill me in on everybody else."

"Want to hear about how Anton made an ass of himself at last week's field party?"

"Oh, yeah."

"Then settle in and hold on tight. This is a good one."

As Coleman started talking, Sam leaned his head back and grinned in a way he hadn't since last time they'd talked. It felt good. It felt perfect.

Almost like he was home again. Almost ... but not quite.

CHAPTER 5

*Be aggressive when in play ... but selectively
aggressive. Good players learn when to jump forward
and when to hang back and let things happen.*

Emily Springer was double-checking her grocery list on her smart phone in the middle of Kroger when she ran smack into Kurt Holland's impressive chest. "Umph!" she kind of yelped, just as she pressed her hands on that chest.

It was solid. It was warm. And groping her student's brother next to an arrangement of honeycrisp apples was a mistake. "Sorry!" she blurted as she shot her hands in the air.

Which made her drop her phone.

It clattered to the floor just as Kurt placed two strong hands on her waist to steady her. "Hey. You okay?"

Actually, no. No, she was not. She was mortified.

"I'm fine. I'd be better if I could learn to watch where I'm going." When he chuckled, she raised her chin. And found herself looking into the best set of blue eyes she'd ever examined at close range. Luckily, they were filled with amusement and not annoyance. "Sorry I ran into you. Are you okay?"

Kurt bent down and picked up her phone. "It takes a bit more than a bump in the grocery store to do me much harm."

She laughed. She wasn't sure if that was a line he'd used before or if it was the honest truth as far as he saw it. "I really am sorry. I was double-checking my grocery list." She tapped the phone's surface a couple of times and showed him the list.

"I'm not much into lists, but I guess they would come in handy." It was kind of obvious that he thought scribbling on a scrap of paper would work just as well.

"It's a side effect of working with teenagers. You get used to adopting all kinds of new apps because they do."

"You're making me even gladder that I carry around plants for a living."

Oh, that drawl! Smiling at him, she murmured, "Trust me, there are some days I wish I did the same thing."

He raised his eyebrows. "Yeah?"

"Those plants don't talk back to you, do they?"

He caught onto her comment and grinned. "Only a couple," he replied as he shifted his weight to his other foot. "Sometimes the Boston ferns get mouthy, but I shut 'em down fast."

She giggled, and finally took the time to look him over from head to toe. He looked different than he had back in that confer- ence room. Tonight he was dressed in a button-down, dark jeans, and scuffed, tan cowboy boots. He looked like something out of a George Strait video. "You look nice," she blurted.

He looked down at himself as if he'd forgotten what he was wearing. "Do I? Thanks. As you can see, I'm not always covered in mud."

No, he was not. Actually, he looked really handsome. And that was saying something because he'd looked awfully good coming from a job site. Realizing that she was checking him out ... and that he was watching her do that checking, she took a step back. "Well, I had better let you go. I'm sure you've got things to do."

He gestured to his cart. "Not so much. Tonight's highlight

involves grabbing a frozen pizza for me and about a ton of junk food for Sam. You aren't interrupting anything but a night in front of the TV."

She would have thought that he would have had a busy social calendar. Or at least was following Sam's. "You're not going to the game?" Pretty much everyone in town went to the Friday-night games. This was the first game all season she was missing.

He shook his head. "Nah. I went to Sam's games when I could back in Spartan, but he's not playing here."

"I bet that's hard on him."

Instead of offering some kind of breezy comment, he took the time to consider her words. "I thought it was going to be a whole lot harder on him than he acts … but so far he seems to be taking it in stride. 'Course I think it might have something to do with Kayla."

"I saw him talking with her the other day. They seemed happy." Actually, Kayla had been glowing and Sam had looked like he was going to hurt anyone who looked cross-eyed at her.

Kurt shook his head. "I tried to tell him to back off a bit and concentrate on school."

She inwardly winced. "Let me guess, that didn't go over real well."

"Not even a little bit." Lines around his eyes crinkled. "I'm learning that being his guardian instead of just his big brother takes some getting used to. I'm making mistakes right and left."

"Something tells me that you'll get the hang of it." Kurt Holland looked like he could do just about anything he set his mind to.

He shrugged. "We're gonna continue to take it one day at a time. That's why tonight I'm home with pizza and beer, and he's sitting at the game watching his girl cheer."

It struck her then that Kurt had given up a lot to enroll Sam in Bridgeport High. He'd left his entire social network and gained a ton of responsibilities.

How many thirty-year-olds did that? She couldn't think of many.

It made her feel even warmer toward him than she already did.

It also gave her an idea that was no doubt dangerous. But how could she ignore it? There was something about Kurt Holland that struck her as lonely. And maybe it was because she had a soft spot for his brother, or maybe it was her nurturing nature. But she couldn't just say goodbye and leave him to his pizza.

Or, to be brutally honest, maybe she didn't want to say goodbye at all.

Before she lost her nerve, she said, "You know, I only ran into Kroger's to get a couple of ingredients for dinner …"

His expression shuttered. "Right. I'll let you go, then."

"No, what I'm trying to say is that, well, would you like to come over for dinner? I'm no gourmet, but I can cook a decent meal."

"Tonight?" The look on his face would have been priceless, if she wasn't suddenly so embarrassed.

And, there she went, fast as lightning. She'd now turned the corner from embarrassed and was racing toward being officially humiliated.

Holding her hands up, she tried to laugh off her offer. "Hey, it was just an idea. Don't worry. You don't have to say anything. I'll just be on—"

"I'd love to."

"Really? Gosh, I forgot to tell you what I'm making. It's—"

"Anything is fine. Do you drink? I could bring the beer." Looking at her sandals and simple black knit dress, he frowned. "Or, ah, I could get a bottle of wine, if you tell me what you want. I don't drink much wine."

"I drink on occasion. And thank you, beer sounds good. Want to come over in about an hour?"

"I can do that." He pulled out his phone from the back pocket of his jeans. "Now I better get your phone number."

"You want my number?" Oh, Lord. Did she really sound as breathless as she feared?

Confusion filled his gaze. "Yeah. So you can text me your address."

"Oh. Of course." Her brain really was disintegrating to a teen-ager's. And a shy, awkward one, at that. Slowly she gave it to him. Heard it ping when he texted her, so she'd have his number, too.

"See you in an hour, Emily."

Her name sounded growly and really good on his lips. "See you then!" she replied. Way too enthusiastically. Sheesh. He probably thought she was desperate. Maybe she actually was.

He grinned and shook his head slightly before walking away.

Looking into her basket, she mentally figured out how long it was going to take her to finish her shopping, run home, start cooking, and clean her place.

It was never going to be enough time. Especially since he no doubt saw the two boxes of cookies in her basket. And the container of Graeter's chocolate–chocolate chip. He was probably thinking that now he understood why she went to those hot yoga classes.

***

Kurt barely remembered getting through the checkout line. Wasn't even sure how much he'd paid for everything, he'd just swiped his card.

Now, though, the reality of what he'd just said yes to hit him like a ton of bricks. He needed some advice, stat.

After weighing his options, he swiped his thumb over his phone's screen two times then pressed the phone icon.

The Lord must have known he needed all the help he could get because his best friend in the world answered immediately. "Kurt?"

"I need help," he blurted as he started piling all his bags in the cab of his truck.

"What's wrong?" Before Kurt could answer, Ace started firing off more questions. "You got a problem with Sam? Or the house? Or is it your dad? Do you need me to stop by your dad's house?"

Kurt exhaled as the muscles in his neck slowly eased. The rapid-fire questions gave him a new perspective that he had needed. "No, it's nothing like that." Gathering his courage, he blurted. "The thing is … I think I've got a date."

"You're callin' because you got yourself a date?" His confusion was so strong that Kurt could practically see his best friend's dark eyes shut in that pained way he adopted when something hit him off guard. "Kurt, you know it's Friday night, don't you? We're tail-gating right now."

Of course he was. Unless there was a real good reason, everyone in town tailgated in various parking lots around town then went to the game. And that game would be the high school game. Where he and Ace had their share of glory days and where half the supper crowd at the diner still talked about from time to time.

"I already feel like a loser for calling you about this. You don't need to make it worse."

Ace chuckled. "What's going on? Do you need tips on how to get to first base or something? 'Cause I had that down pat by the time I was thirteen at Krissy Miller's bonfire."

Kurt shifted as he stared at a family walking to a minivan two parking spaces over. "I'm going to ignore that because I don't have time for your jokes. I've got to be at her house in an hour. She's cooking me supper."

"Sorry. What do you need?"

"I need you tell me if I'm making a big mistake. This gal is great. Sexy and sweet." Thinking of some of the comments Sam had made about her, he drummed his fingers on his steering wheel. "She's smart, too. And kind of classy."

"What's the problem, then?"

"She's also Sam's teacher. Am I breaking some kind of teacher-parent dating rule?"

"I doubt it. I mean you're not Sam's dad."

"I know. But I'm his guardian."

"She knows this, right?"

"Well, yeah."

"Then don't worry about it. Or ask her if it's an issue. She'll tell you. Teachers know about that stuff. They have to."

"Yeah. I guess you're right."

"I know I am." He paused. "So, Sam's okay with it? He doesn't care that you got the hots for his teacher?"

"He doesn't know about it."

Ace laughed. "Well, there you go. Are you going to tell him?"

"Of course I am." Of course, Sam's reaction had been the last thing on his mind when he'd been talking to Emily at the store.

"Then it sounds like you've got nothing to worry about."

Pulling out of his parking space, he headed back down the windy two-lane road to his house. Hearing Ace's matter-of-fact tone eased his mind and underlined how he really didn't have anyone in Bridgeport who he could count as a good friend.

Just as quickly, he felt like dunking his head in cold water or something. Anything to gain some perspective. He was a man, not an insecure woman. What was he doing, thinking about how he needed some good friends to hear all about his insecurities?

"Hey, buddy, you still there?"

"Yeah. I was just sitting here thinking that I shouldn't have been calling you to whine like this. Sorry."

"No problem. It's good to hear your voice."

"Same."

"Hey, I was thinking maybe I'd come up your way soon," he said with a new thread of tension in his voice. "I need a break from this place. You got anything going on in the next couple of weeks?"

"Beyond Sam and work? No."

"'Kay. Maybe I'll head up next weekend."

That soon? Something was definitely going on with him. But figuring that out would have to wait for another day. "Plan on it."

"I'll call in a couple of days. If things are going hot and heavy with your teacher, I can postpone it."

"Yeah. That ain't going to happen."

"I'm just saying that if you get too busy and don't want company, just let me know."

"I will, but there won't be anything going on. Thanks for calming me down."

"Anytime."

After he clicked off, Kurt pulled up in the driveway, grabbed his groceries, and hurriedly put them away. After tossing the six-pack in the freezer to get nice and cold, he headed to the shower for the second time in three hours.

Yeah, all that fussing might be unnecessary. But something inside told him that this night just might be the start of something good.

And if that was the case? Well, he sure wasn't about to ruin it.

CHAPTER 6

"It's not whether you won or lost, but how many bad-beat stories you were able to tell."
—GRANTLAND RICE

The doorbell chimed just as Emily finished brushing out her hair. Looking at her reflection, she hesitated. She'd been planning to pull it back into a ponytail, but now there was no time to do that.

She'd have to let it rest against her shoulders and back. Just as she was going to have to let her indecision about wearing skinny dark jeans and a flowy tank top go, too.

After checking that it was definitely Kurt, she opened the door in a rush. "Hi! Sorry, I was double-checking something." Then she tried desperately not to notice how good he looked in faded jeans and a moss-colored T-shirt. "Come on in."

As he followed her to her kitchen, a six-pack of beer bottles in his hand, he looked around her condo with interest. "Your place is real nice."

"Thank you. It's a work in progress. I just bought it last year."

He ran a hand along one of her kitchen's granite countertops. They had been her parents' Christmas gift to her. "You did a good job on it. These are pretty."

Pleased by the compliment, she smiled back at him. "Thanks." Running her hands on her jeans, she said, "I'll take one of those beers. And then you can have a seat while I cook."

"I can do that." After he popped the top on both of their bottles he lifted his in salute. "Cheers."

"Cheers to you." After she took a sip, she smiled. "This tastes perfect. Especially on a Friday night."

"Did you have a hard week?"

Emily took a minute to slice the chicken breasts into thin medallions while she thought about how to answer. "Not really. It's just the normal give-and-take of dealing with teenagers and a demanding principal."

"I don't know how you do it. Those kids would drive me crazy."

"I love working with teenagers. Being with them is my favorite part of the job. It's everything else that's exhausting."

"Like those demanding principals?"

"Yes. And the other people on staff." Getting out a fresh knife, she sliced mushrooms and onions. After seeing that he looked interested and not bored, she continued. "Not everyone is always on the same page. Usually I try to get along with everyone, but that isn't always easy to do."

"I guess that's the case with any big company. Any time you get a lot of people together, you're gonna have problems."

"Is that what you did in West Virginia? You worked with a lot of people?"

He smiled. "No. My, uh, father has told me stories his whole life about office politics. Even though his weren't actually in an office building. He worked at the coal mine."

"Wow. I can't imagine what a hard job that is."

"Imagine it being a whole lot harder than you can imagine."

"It's work to be proud of." Hard work that made her wish she hadn't just complained about working at a suburban high school.

"For sure. But even so, I knew before I was sixteen that I wasn't cut out for that."

"I think I would miss being in the daylight."

"I would miss a lot of things." He shrugged. "It's hard, but my father never complained about it. It's what he knew. And his dad and grandfather, too."

"So your family has worked the mines for generations."

He nodded. "It used to be a pretty good job, believe it or not. But now, with all the cutbacks and changes in energy …" His voice drifted off.

"There's not the future in it that there used to be," Emily said, studying his expression. Kurt looked reflective … and more than a little sad, too. "Is that why you moved?"

"For me? No. If it was up to me, I probably would have stayed. I don't need a lot. I moved for Sam."

Emily swallowed. "I don't mean to turn this into another school discussion, but for what it's worth, I think you made the right call. Sam is really smart, just like you said in the meeting. He's going to do well in college."

"I hope so." After he took another sip of beer, he motioned to her hands, which had been motionless for the last five minutes, she realized in dismay. "Can I help you?"

"Why? So you don't eat at midnight?" she joked.

"I'm not opposed to that, but me being here so late might cause talk."

Emily stilled, unsure whether he was joking or not. But when she caught his gaze, she noticed that while his lips were set in a firm line, there was a warmth in his eyes. An answering warmth pooled inside her.

Before she started doing something like blush, she held up a knife. "In that case, come over here and chop a cucumber for the salad."

"Yes, ma'am." While she turned on the burner and started

heating up oil, he washed his hands. "So, it just occurred to me that I don't know all that much about you. Are you from here?"

"I am. Well, close enough. I grew up in another suburb of Cincinnati but I always wanted to live in Bridgeport. When the position opened three years ago, I jumped at the chance to teach at the high school."

"Is your family nearby?"

"Yeah. I'm one of three kids to Jack and Erin Springer. My sister, brother, and I all live near them. We actually go over every Sunday for dinner."

"Sounds nice."

"It is. It's kind of crazy now, too, on account of the fact that both my sister and brother are married." She lowered her voice. "I think my sister-in-law is pregnant, too."

He grinned. "Is there a reason you're whispering?"

Now she really was blushing. "Only because I'm goofy. Brenden hasn't officially told us yet. I think because Samantha hasn't told her parents. I'm so excited though. I can't wait to be an aunt."

Kurt grabbed the tomato she handed him and started cutting it into neat wedges. "I bet." After a moment, he said, "I'm kind of surprised you don't have a man in your life, too. Or do you?"

"No. No man." And didn't that just make her sound so interesting and cute?

He smiled. "Glad I wasn't wrong." As he continued to slice and dice, he said, "I don't mean to get too personal or anything, but back home you'd be the kind of girl any man I know would be dying to take out."

And just like that, all the memories of Danny came flooding back, stirred with a good dosage of regret and shame.

Emily knew enough about Kurt to realize that if she changed the subject he'd drop it. But if she didn't address it then she knew she was going to have to in the future. Especially if he ever met any of her family or friends. It was going to be like the big elephant in the room.

"Um, well, there's a story there. I did have a boyfriend. We were serious, we dated for three years."

"What happened?"

"He, uh, Danny, he couldn't really handle things after college."

"How come?"

"I don't know. Maybe he wasn't sure what to do? Maybe he just didn't want to work." She shrugged. "Whatever the reason, he started drinking a lot, then he got even more restless and angry."

"And you stayed with him?"

"I guess I did. Now, I don't know why." She paused to think about it. "Maybe I stayed with him out of habit? Anyway, I was teaching and thinking about marriage, but Danny wasn't." She paused again, knowing that she could probably end her story there and he would never know the difference, or wouldn't pry. But she didn't want to do that with Kurt. "We started arguing a lot. Then, one night, after he had way too much to drink, he hit me."

Suddenly the air in the kitchen felt like they were in the eye of a hurricane. It was that tense and still.

With methodical movements, he set his knife down and turned to her. "He hit you?" He swallowed. "Were you hurt?"

There was that accent again. Pronounced in a tone that was now two octaves lower. "Bad enough for me to never want to see him again."

"I hope to hell not."

Now she felt stupid, like she should've been smart enough not to date a man like that in the first place. "Danny, he wasn't always bad. He just had an addiction, you know?"

He shook his head. "That doesn't excuse what he did, Em. Where I come from, men don't hit girls. Not when they're drinking. Not when they're in trouble. Not ever."

A little shiver went through her. Kurt sounded like he really cared. Sounded like he cared about her. Though she didn't really know him, she liked how that made her feel.

50

"Does he still live around here?" he asked, interrupting her thoughts.

"Danny? Yeah. Every once in a while, I'll run into him at the grocery or see him from a distance on the bike trail."

His blue eyes were scanning her face. "Does that go okay?"

"Okay enough. We pretend we don't know each other."

"I wish I would've known you then. I would've taken care of him for you."

"There was no need. He felt bad about what he'd done. Plus, Brenden and my brother-in-law, Chris, paid him a visit."

"Good."

She blew out a deep breath. "I'm sorry. I sure didn't intend to talk about my ex." What a way to ruin a perfectly good first date!

"No, I'm the one who asked about your past. And for what it's worth, I'm glad you told me."

"Really?"

He nodded, his blue eyes staring at her in such a way that she felt like there wasn't another person in the world who mattered to him. "Oh, yeah. Because now I know."

Now he knew.

Emily couldn't say exactly why, but those three words felt important. Fighting a blush, she turned away from him and pressed a hand to her stomach.

She was feeling things for Kurt Holland that she hadn't felt for any man since Danny. Yes, she was attracted to him, but it was something more than that. It was like she wasn't able to concentrate on anything else but him whenever he was nearby.

No, it was like she didn't *want* to. For better or worse, she had developed a full-on infatuation with this man in her kitchen.

She couldn't help but wonder what was going to happen between them next.

CHAPTER 7

FROM LES LARKE'S
TIPS FOR BEGINNING POKER PLAYERS:

Don't base everything you do on something that you saw on TV. Those poker players on television are not only professionals—but they know they're being filmed. Real-life poker is messy and complicated.

Kurt had the urge to either wrap his arms around Emily and promise her that no one would ever hurt her again … or take off in his truck and pay a visit to the loser who'd dared to lift a hand to her in anger.

Neither of those actions made sense.

Once again, Sam hadn't been wrong. Kurt would've hit Garrett, too. Fact was, he'd never been the type of man to shy away from making his point. And while he was real glad Emily had her brothers' support, there was a small, jealous part of him that wished he'd been the man to have helped her back then.

He would have been more than happy to have taken care of that loser ex of hers. Heck, if he came across this Danny guy now, he'd probably get in his face.

But he was more than sure that she wouldn't have appreciated the gesture. She wasn't his. Not anywhere close to being his.

He also had no business attempting to try to comfort her in the middle of her kitchen. She'd probably send him straight for the door.

Therefore, since neither of those ideas were an option, he looked around for something to do. "You got anything more for me to cut up?"

She sighed in obvious relief. "Ah, no. But if you'll sit down, I'll finish up the last of this. We should be eating chicken marsala in ten minutes, tops." After glancing at the clock on her stove, she frowned. "I really didn't think it was going to take this long."

He had no idea what chicken marsala was, but it sure smelled good. "Take your time. Like I said, I didn't have any plans tonight. And it's been a real long time since I've had a home-cooked meal beyond burgers and chili."

Pulling out a wooden spoon, she stirred around the onions and mushrooms in the pan. "Why don't you tell me about what you've been doing since you moved here? Have you gotten the chance to explore much of Cincinnati?"

"Not really. My buddy Troy took me down to a Reds game when I came out the first time, but other than that, I've been trying to get my business going."

"I bet." She smiled at him before returning to her dish. "What about Bridgeport? Do you like it so far? I mean, what you've seen of it?"

"It's nice. The river's pretty." He frowned. Even to his own ears, his appreciation was lacking.

"A lot of my students' dads play golf. Do you play?"

"Uh … I'm not really the golfing type."

"I see." After taking a sip of her beer, she said, "Well, now I have a new project. I'm going to help you find your niche around here."

"No offense, but I don't think there's a lot for a guy like me to do around here. But that's okay. I mean, I didn't move here to make friends."

She turned off the burner and set the wooden spoon in her hand on a plate on the counter. "What do you mean, a guy like you?"

Now he felt like more of an uneducated hick than he already was. "I'm just pointing out that there are a lot of country clubs and fancy gyms with juice bars around here. I'm not that type of guy."

After taking another sip of beer, she tilted her head to one side. "What type are you?"

Was it his imagination, or had her tone altered slightly, turned suggestive? "More of the hunting, fishing, and poker-playing type of guy."

"Ah. Now I understand."

What did she understand? Kurt was beginning to get the feeling that they were having the same conversation but were talking about two different things. Taking a closer look at her, he noticed that her pretty brown eyes were sparkling. "What did I say that amused you?"

"Nothing." Gesturing to the serving dishes, she murmured, "Will you help me carry these to the table?"

Turning, he belatedly noticed that behind the bar was a small table set for two. White linen napkins were folded into neat rectangles on the left of each plate.

She'd gone to a lot of trouble in an incredibly short amount of time.

As he picked up one of the dishes, a burnt-orange-colored dish, Kurt decided that things like that were yet another aspect of femininity that remained a mystery to him. Where did women pick up the idea that serving dishes and cloth napkins were items that needed to be on hand in the kitchen? He was lucky if he and Sam had plates that didn't have chips in the rims.

After Emily joined him at the table, she smiled. "I hope you will enjoy everything, Kurt."

He already was. It was nice not sitting at home by himself. He liked being around a pretty woman, especially one who was as smart and kind as Emily. She was the type of woman who his mother would have paraded in front of him if she'd had the chance. A marrying girl, she would have called Emily Springer.

Realizing she was still waiting for him to comment, he forced himself to step up his game. His momma had taught him his manners, he'd just gotten lazy over the years. "It all looks delicious. Smells like heaven."

"Thank you."

Moments later, he knew the food tasted as good as it looked. He actually had to force himself to eat slowly. Sitting across from him, Emily ate more than he thought she would. She kept their conversation easy and low-key, too, mainly sharing some of her funniest mishaps in the classroom.

After he had a second helping, Kurt was just about to share a story about him and Ace, back when they were both on the high school football team, when there was a knock at her door.

Emily frowned at it. "I'm sorry. I don't know who that could be."

As she crossed the room, Kurt got to his feet, stopping himself before he cautioned her to look to see who it was first.

When she half-moaned and half-giggled, she said, "I'm going to apologize for this in advance, Kurt." And with that, she pulled open the door.

Kurt took another step closer, then stopped when a man about his height and woman with short blond hair entered. They greeted Emily with hugs then abruptly drew to a stop the moment they spied him.

"Huh. You have company," the guy said.

"Oh, my gosh, Em. You've got a date!" the blond exclaimed.

"Now that you've completely embarrassed me, come on in. I'll introduce you to my guest. And it's not a date."

The guy stared at the table. "Looks like one."

Emily's cheeks turned even pinker. "It's just dinner. No, I mean, I have a new friend over for dinner." Turning to Kurt, she cast a nervous glance his way. "I'm really sorry, Kurt," she muttered.

The guy stood a little straighter. "Your name's Kurt?"

Feeling awkward as hell, Kurt stepped forward to her side.

Emily began a stilted round of introductions before he could take care of it himself. "Brenden, Samantha, please meet Kurt Holland. Kurt, this is my brother and his wife."

"Good to meet you," Kurt said as he shook hands with both her brother and sister-in-law.

"I'm sorry we barged in like this," Samantha said.

"It's okay," Emily said. "So, is everything all right?"

"Oh. Yeah," Brenden replied. "We were out and thought we'd come by and say hello. Sorry to interrupt," he added, though his expression looked like he wasn't especially thrilled to find Kurt there.

Samantha rested a hand on her husband's arm. "We should go. Like Brenden said, we were just out nearby and thought you were home alone. You know, like usual."

"Kill me now," Emily moaned.

Samantha bit her lip. "I mean, um, I'm glad that wasn't the case."

"Me too," Kurt said.

Emily cleared her throat. "Well, thanks for stopping by, but I bet you need to get on home."

"Not really," Brenden said. "How did you two meet?"

Emily might have been embarrassed, but after her sharing how the last man in her life had hit her, Kurt completely got her brother's cool greeting. "My little brother Sam is in one of your sister's classes."

Her brother slapped a hand on his forehead. "Emily, you're dating a student's parent? That's not allowed, is it?"

"To be clear, Kurt is one of my student's brothers, not his father. So it's pretty different. Therefore, yes, it's allowed."

"Huh." Brenden stepped forward. "How long have you known each other? And what do you do?" He looked him up and down. "Do you work?"

"I own a landscaping business."

"Is that right?"

"We're not going to play twenty questions any longer, Brenden," Emily said, with a sharp bite to her voice.

Walking over to Emily's side, Kurt pressed a hand to the middle of her back. "Don't worry, Em. I'm fine." When he felt some of the tension leave her, he dropped his hand and gazed at her brother. "What else do you want to know?"

Brenden raised his hands. "Emily's right. Your life isn't any of my business. I didn't mean to offend."

Kurt shook his head. "You'd have to ask more than that to offend me."

Samantha edged toward the door. "Come on Brenden. We're making a mess of things."

After glancing Kurt's way, Emily said slowly, "Guys, we're done eating. Do you want to sit down and join us? Kurt brought some beer."

Brenden glanced his direction. "Is it all right with you?"

Suddenly Kurt realized Emily's brother was growing on him. He cared about his sister. Obviously, he took time to check on her on a regular basis. "It's fine."

"Thanks. We'll join you but we're fine, Em. Go finish eating."

Emily rolled her eyes. "Samantha, since my brother didn't even ask, can I get you anything? Water? Juice?"

"I'm good. And I can serve myself. I know where everything is. So that's fun. I didn't know Emily had much cause to meet her students' families."

"My brother had some trouble. I came up to a meeting."

"He's new. Kurt and Sam just moved here from West Virginia." She smiled suddenly. "He was just telling me that he wasn't the country-club type. I was going to tell him about Lake Isabella. Turns out you came at the right time."

Brenden's expression turned far less judgmental. "You haven't been out to the lake yet?"

"I didn't even know there was a lake nearby."

"It's nothing real special, but there's good fishing."

"We used to hang out there," Emily explained. "We went walking."

"Lots of kids used to also go parking out there," Samantha said with a laugh. Looking at her husband, she grinned. "Us included."

"Sam and Brenden have been together forever," Emily explained. "Since high school."

Kurt sat down on one of the barstools, liking how easy the siblings got along with each other. "I'll have to go out there sometime."

"Poor Kurt has been telling me that he didn't think there was anything to do around here but join the country clubs."

"There's nothing wrong with that," Brenden said. "Our sister Violet and her husband Chris belong to a golf club. They love it. But I never saw the point of chasing a little white ball around."

"We should go out to the lake tonight. All four of us," Emily said. "Want to, Kurt?"

"I'm game."

She turned to her brother. "Brenden?"

He glanced at his wife. "You up for it, Samantha?"

She nodded. "I think a walk will do me good."

"Let's go, then."

Kurt held back. "What about the dishes? Let me help you with them."

"I can do them later."

"You worked all day, then made all this. No way am I going to make you face a stack of dishes when you get home." Already picking up two of those serving platters, he started carrying them to her small kitchen.

"You do dishes?" Brenden asked.

"Yeah." Kurt eyed him. Wondering if he'd just opened himself up to get teased for caring about dishes.

But all Emily's brother did was nod. "Good," he said. "I'll help, too."

Kurt had a feeling he'd just passed some sort of test. And though he wouldn't have thought he'd ever care about that, he felt a small measure of relief.

CHAPTER 8

FROM LES LARKE'S
TIPS FOR BEGINNING POKER PLAYERS:

*If you don't have a good poker face, don't attempt to
bluff. You'll get burned every single time.*

"Thanks for getting me out of there," Kayla said to Sam as he
pulled out of the high school parking lot. "I can't believe those
girls were so mean."

Glancing her way, he shook his head. "Don't thank me, Kay.
You know I wanted to see you. I spent most of the last month trying
to figure out a way to ask you out."

And just like that, Kayla felt like her night had gone from absolutely horrible to amazing. Sam Holland had a way about him that
was so different than all the other guys she knew. Not only was he
really cute, he was humbler and more honest, too.

She couldn't think of another guy who would ever admit to
trying to get the nerve to do anything.

"Where do you want to go?" he asked. "I would take you over to
my house, but my brother's out on a date. I bet your momma would
have a fit if she found out I was taking you to an empty house."

She laughed. "That's kind of an understatement, though since it's
you, she might make an exception. She thinks you're pretty great."

He looked pretty pleased about that. "So, where to?"

Even though her parents might be okay with her taking him to her house, she wasn't up for that. They'd probably send her little sister down to be with them. Brianna was in seventh grade and loved acting like she was sixteen. It was beyond annoying. She would likely either spend the entire time talking about her hair or attempting to flirt with Sam.

"How about Lake Isabella? There's a path there around the lake. We could walk on it, if that sounds okay to you?"

"It sounds good. So, you hungry? We could go to a drive-through if you want."

Her stomach had been in knots from the moment she noticed some junior boys leering at her while she was cheering. She might have been imagining things, but she was pretty sure that even though her picture was supposed to be off those phones, not everyone deleted it.

"Maybe just some fries and a Coke?"

He turned his truck down Bridgeport Avenue. "I can do that. Just tell me where you want to go."

She watched him drive and loved how confident he was. Only his left hand was on the wheel, and it was resting on the top of it like he'd been driving forever. Whenever she drove her mother's car, her hands were still glued at ten and two. "I guess you've been driving a while."

"Yeah. I got my temps at fifteen, but my dad had me out on country roads way before that. Probably when I was thirteen or so."

"Thirteen? That's hard to believe."

"It wouldn't be if you lived where I used to. There's a lot of open spaces out there in West Virginia."

He sounded wistful. "I guess you miss it."

"Sometimes, but then, there are some things about Bridgeport that aren't so bad, you know?" he drawled as he glanced her way with a smile.

Butterflies fluttered in her stomach as she realized he was talking about her. Gosh, he was dreamy. "I know," she said at last.

"So, Burger King or McDonald's?"

"For french fries? McDonald's, of course."

He laughed as he pulled into the drive-through lane. There were four cars in front of them, so they settled in to wait. "Want anything else?"

"No. That's plenty." Bending down, she reached for her purse.

"I got it."

"I'm not going to make you buy my food."

"My brother would skin my hide if he found out I was taking you through a drive-through and making you pay," he said.

"Sometimes it sounds like your brother raised you. Did he?"

He shrugged. "No. But he's kind of intense about things like that. A lot more than my dad." His expression looked pained before he shook it off again. "So put your money away, Kay. It's just fries and a Coke."

"Thank you," she said as he pulled up again then rolled down his window.

"I'll have two orders of fries, a Quarter Pounder with Cheese, and two Cokes," he said into the speaker.

She raised her eyebrows. "I guess you were hungry, too?"

"Yeah." He shifted, taking his wallet out from a back pocket and pulling out a twenty.

Kayla couldn't help but notice that the twenty-dollar bill wasn't the only one in his wallet. There had to be at least two others, along with a couple of fives and ones. She couldn't remember a time when she had so much cash. "Do you work?"

"Yeah. My brother owns his own landscaping company. You're looking at his number one grunt."

She laughed. "Sounds important."

"Real important. I get to do all the crap none of the other guys who work for him want to do," he joked after he paid the lady at the window and pulled the sack and drinks into the cab of his truck.

"Mind if I pull into a parking space and eat right here?"

"Not at all. We can do whatever you want," she said softly.

He laughed. "Didn't your mother ever tell you to not say things like that to boys?"

She started, then giggled. "Sam, you're funny."

Smiling at her, he opened the bag and pulled out one of the cartons of fries and handed it to her. "Nah. What I am is hungry. Here you go, Kayla."

Digging in, she popped a french fry into her mouth. Like always, it tasted piping hot and perfect. Sam maneuvered his truck into a parking space at the edge of the lot, rolled down both of their windows, and turned off the engine. Then, he was biting into his burger like he hadn't eaten in days.

As she picked at her fries, she was suddenly conscious of the quiet between them, and the sounds drifting up from around the parking lot toward them. In the distance, she could hear teenagers laughing. Two cars over, some parents trying to get their toddler into his car seat. Music from a handful of cars mixed together as they sped down the street.

Not a bit of it was unusual or particularly noteworthy. But all together, here, while the sky was darkening and she was sitting by Sam Holland's side? It felt amplified. Almost different.

Maybe because she felt so happy to be with him? Or, maybe it was because while she couldn't help being aware of everyone around them, the guy next to her didn't seem aware of it at all. Instead, it was as if the only thing that mattered to him was in his truck.

"Hey, you okay?" Sam asked as he crumpled up the wrapper of his burger.

Instead of answering, she asked a question of her own. "You finished it already?"

He grinned. "It wasn't that much."

"Not for you, I guess." She looked down at her cardboard container. "I still have half of my fries left."

"I'm a guy. We like to eat lots ... and don't have to fit into cheerleading uniforms," he added with a wink.

She didn't know what to say to that. "I was just listening to all the sounds around us."

"Really? I didn't notice anything." He craned his neck, looking out the windows. "Did you see somebody you wanted to talk to?"

"No." Feeling self-conscious, she shrugged. "Forget it. I don't know what I was thinking."

He popped a fry into his mouth before sipping on his drink. "Ready to go to the lake?"

"If you still want to."

He put his truck into reverse. "Let's go on, then."

Kayla smiled at him as he headed out of the parking lot, then followed her directions to the lake. About fifteen minutes later, they were getting out of his truck and throwing their paper sacks in a metal trash receptacle.

It wasn't completely dark yet, but the sun had almost disappeared over the horizon. The lake was a good size. Big enough to put in a little boat and fish or to stand at one of the docks on the side and cast a line.

Vintage-looking black iron lights were situated every fifty feet or so along the path around the lake. There were about thirty people scattered in the area. Some were families barbecuing, others were couples like themselves who were obviously out for a walk. Still others were groups of men fishing. But the best part, for her, at least, was that no one was paying them the slightest bit of attention. After feeling like she was living in the middle of a snow globe, where everyone was staring at her and analyzing what she did, Kayla felt fresh and clean. Freer than she had felt in days.

"This is nice," Sam said. "It kind of reminds me of back home."

"How so? Did you used to live near a lake?"

"No," he said as they started walking on the gravel path that bordered the water. "Not really. But back home, everything is spread out. There are a lot of long roads with nothing around but fields. You feel like you can see for a while and breathe. That's what this makes me feel like." After a second, he glanced her way. For the first time that evening, he looked a bit hesitant. "Does that even make sense?"

"More than you know. At least to me. These last few days have been terrible. I've been so upset, my mother started talking about me going to see a counselor."

"Is that what you're gonna do?"

"I don't know. I don't want to," she admitted. What would he say if she confided that she might want to talk to someone? Would he think she was overreacting?

Looking down at her, his usual easy expression tightened. "I guess we should talk about what happened."

She couldn't think of anything that would be more awkward. What could they talk about? The state of her very plain, very virginal-looking white bra? Or the fact that she didn't have a whole lot to fill it out in the first place? "No way. Believe me, we definitely do not need to talk about that picture."

He reached for her hand. Before she could fold it over her chest, he linked his fingers through hers and rubbed his thumb over her knuckles. "Come on, Kayla. It's just me."

Just him? "It's embarrassing."

A soft smile played on his lips. "Not so much." Before she could ask him about that, he spoke again, his accent turning thicker. "I think it might be a good idea."

A fierce rush of emotions flowed through her, settling into that spot just under her ribs. She wanted to be mad. To be mad at him, even though all he'd done was try to help her.

But how else could she feel? Here, they were alone, he'd just taken ahold of her hand … but instead of being able to enjoy this moment, he was making her think about stuff she was trying so hard to never think about again.

"Come on, Kay. Trust me not to make things worse."

Hesitantly, she said, "What, exactly, do you want to talk about?"

He leaned back. "Maybe we could start at the beginning. Do you know who took the picture?"

Relieved that this question, at least, wasn't embarrassing, she nodded. "Yeah. A girl named Elizabeth."

"I don't know many girls. Is she on your squad?"

"Oh, no. She's not a cheerleader. She, well, it turns out that she was playing some truth-or-dare game with a couple of her friends. She was supposed to take a girl's picture when she was in the locker room. I think the girl was supposed to be naked or something. But she chickened out and just sent that picture of me." Emily tried to keep her voice matter-of-fact, but she wasn't sure she was succeeding. Because, really, it didn't matter *why* Elizabeth had done it. Just that she had.

"So it wasn't personal."

"I guess not. I just happened to be standing nearby." Giving in to her emotions, she said, "And you know what? I don't even know if that makes it better or worse."

"Because ..."

"Because it still happened. And get this—my mom said that one day I'm going to realize that there was a reason this happened to me. Like having a half-naked picture of me on social media is all part of God's plan," she continued in a rush. "Like I'm supposed to assume that God wanted everyone to see my boobs?"

Sam's face turned carefully blank. "Ah, maybe He let that happen for a reason only He knows."

That was Sam. Instead of cracking a joke or rolling his eyes, he gave some thought to her comment. It calmed her down. "Maybe. But it was still awful."

"I know."

"It really was. Then it only got worse because she sent it to one of the girls in her crew and she sent it to Garrett."

"What a bitch."

Kayla privately agreed, though so far she'd never come out and talked about those girls that way. For some reason, her parents and friends all expected her to take the high road and shrug it off. Even though she was completely innocent in the whole thing.

She squeezed her eyes tight. "So it's all stupid, really."

His voice was hard. "Did Elizabeth ever apologize? Shoot, did she even get suspended, too?"

"Yeah, she got an at-home suspension like Garrett. And she and her parents came over to my house and apologized."

"Good."

Remembering how it had felt to stand there, knowing that Elizabeth's parents had probably seen the photo, too, Kayla felt that knot under her ribs expand. "She was crying, like she'd been having a really tough time. It was so stupid."

"Shit," he murmured, drawing out the one word until it was two or maybe even three syllables.

She took a breath, intending to stop, but suddenly everything she'd been feeling came pouring out. "So it's all over. But I feel so gross now. I wouldn't exactly call Elizabeth and me friends, but we didn't hate each other. But she ruined my life. And now Principal Hendrix acts like it's over. He even told me that I should forget about it, because this whole episode was going to blow over soon."

"I got the feeling he was hoping if he pretended it wasn't that big a deal it would all go away and he wouldn't have to do anything besides give me and Garrett suspensions."

"But it hasn't," she said, hating that her voice sounded shaky. Of course, that was exactly what she was on the verge of doing—dissolving into a mess of hot, bawling, ugly tears. "Nobody seems to care that my body was on that phone. It's me who everyone was talking about." She'd even heard one of Elizabeth's friends laughing about her underwear looking like an old lady's.

Sam looked down at his feet. "I'm real sorry, Kayla. I'd go beat them all up if I could."

"You better not." After giving him a watery smile, she swiped her eyes with the side of her hand. "I just want it to be over. People keep bringing it up. A girl on my squad even told me at halftime that she thought I shouldn't have made such a big deal about it. She didn't know what the problem was."

Sam grunted. "No way."

"Yeah, that my bra covered up a lot more than most bikini tops, so it wasn't any big deal. And that … that I'm thin, so I don't have anything to be embarrassed about besides, you know, my small boobs. But I am."

He squeezed her hand.

They had stopped by one of the lights. Because of that, she could see that Sam was gazing at her. So sweetly. But it also seemed like there was something else going on, too. Fearing the worst, she knew she had to ask this question. "Did you look at that picture?"

For a second she thought he wasn't going to answer. But then he did. "Yeah."

"Oh." Now her humiliation was complete. Yeah, she assumed he probably had … but she'd been holding out hope that he had been the one decent guy at Bridgeport High.

Just as quickly, all her insecurities rushed forward. Hating herself, she realized she was actually waiting for him to comment on how she looked.

What was wrong with her? "Look, I'm gonna go."

When she attempted to pull her hand from his, he held on tighter. "Now, hold on. Listen to me."

"Sam."

"No, stop," he retorted, his voice firmer. "Will you listen to me?"

"I don't think I want to hear what you have to say."

Impatience flared in his eyes before he visibly tamped it down. "It wasn't like you're thinking. Garrett handed me his phone and then, there you were."

She closed her eyes.

"No, look at me. Please, will you look at me?" When she looked at him again, he continued. "Kayla, that's why I got so mad at Garrett. I didn't know what he wanted me to see. I thought it was some pic of a football game. I mean, it could have been anything. It caught me off guard."

Closing her eyes, she allowed herself to try to imagine being him. And she could. Everyone was putting up YouTube videos or random memes and stuff on their phones. He was right. It could have been anything. "I believe you."

He sighed. "I hope so, 'cause once I realized it was you, I told him to take it off." Turning red, he continued. "I wasn't um … staring at your picture or anything. I'm not a perv, Kayla."

He sounded so appalled that she would think that, in spite of how upset she'd been, she started laughing. Maybe it was the relief. Maybe it was just the way he'd sounded, like he was offended that she'd think he was the kind of guy who did stuff like that. "Oh, Sam."

"It's true."

His cheeks were so red it looked like he'd been in Florida for a week. And that just made her laugh harder. And while she did, she realized that she felt better. At last, instead of holding everything in, she admitted everything that she was feeling. Yes, what had happened had been awful, but in the grand scheme of embarrassing situations in high school, she figured she got off kind of lucky. "You know what? All of a sudden, I feel a whole lot better. Thanks for letting me rant."

"Anytime." He smiled at her, then tugged her closer and kissed her cheek. When she giggled again, he pressed his lips to her cheek again. But this time the action was a whole lot slower and a whole lot closer to her lips.

Was he about to kiss her? Did she want him to kiss her? With a burst of awareness, she realized that yes, yes, she did.

Her breath hitched as he reached for her other hand and linked their fingers together. "Kayla, you don't know how—"

"Sam? Sam, what are you doing here?" a voice called out.

He jerked away and turned. And then his whole body stiffened.

Kayla felt off balance. "What's wrong?" she asked as she tried to figure out who he was reacting to.

"You are never going to believe this, but my brother is here. With Miss Springer."

She dropped her hand. "Miss Springer from school?"

"Yeah. If I'm not mistaken, my brother is out on a date with my English teacher." Mumbling something under his breath, he groaned. "I'm sorry, Kayla. I think things are about to get weird."

CHAPTER 9

"There is more to poker than life."
—TOM MCEVOY

"Sam, what the f—heck?" Kurt called out, hating that he had almost started cussing like a redneck who didn't know better. But he couldn't help himself. What were the odds that both he and his younger brother would be at Lake Isabella at the same time? Until an hour ago, he'd been barely aware the lake existed.

Thanks to the many muted lights that had been set up at regular intervals around the park, Kurt watched Sam lean down, say something to the pretty girl he was holding hands with, and then head his way, glaring at him and Emily the whole time.

"Uh-oh," Emily whispered.

"Yeah, this is going to be awkward," he mumbled before bypassing Sam and directing his attention to the girl. She was following Sam, a wary expression on her face.

He needed to fix this pronto.

Taking care to keep his voice gentle, he said, "Hey. I'm thinking you're Kayla."

After glancing at Sam, she nodded. "Hi, um ..."

"His name is Kurt," Sam supplied. He didn't exactly look or sound pleased by the fact.

"Hi," she repeated. After a pause, she mumbled, "And Miss Springer."

"Hi, Kayla. Sam," Emily said in that pretty voice of hers. It was light and airy and sounded as if coming across each other was a great surprise. "How was the game?"

"We won," Sam answered, his voice verging on surly.

Kurt wasn't sure how to handle this whole situation, so he decided to fake it. With that in mind, he figured it would be better to focus on Sam and his girl instead of the fact that Sam had caught him and his teacher out together. "Sam, I thought y'all were going to go to a field party or something after the game."

"I didn't want to," Kayla supplied. "And since we couldn't go to either of our houses, I decided to show Sam around here."

"I did the same thing," Emily said with a smile. "Kurt had no idea that we had a good fishing lake here in Bridgeport."

Looking more at ease, Kayla stepped closer. "I was telling Sam the same thing."

"Smart girls think alike, I guess," Emily said.

Kurt relaxed slightly. Maybe everything was going to be fine after all. He could tell Sam he'd see him later and go on his way.

But Sam didn't seem to be of the same mind. "You didn't tell me you were going out with Miss Springer tonight."

"Well, we should talk about that later."

Sam puffed up like a bantam rooster. "Maybe we should talk about it now."

"No," Kurt said, his voice hard. "Emily and I are meeting her brother here so we're gonna to let y'all go. Come home by curfew."

"Will you even be home by then?"

The question caught him off guard, probably because he hadn't thought that far ahead. "That's none of your business."

But instead of backing down, Sam raised his chin. Almost like he was hoping to air all their laundry right there in front of God, both women, and a good portion of Bridgeport, too.

Kayla's eyes widened. "I have to be home before midnight," she said as she leaned toward Sam.

"Then that's when we'll get you home," he told her gently before hardening his voice when he turned back to Kurt. "I'll be home after I drop Kayla off."

"Good." Feeling foolish and as awkward as he'd ever felt about anything, Kurt raised a hand. "See you later."

"Good to see you, Sam," Emily said.

To his credit, Sam smiled slightly, and nodded. "You too, Miss Springer." Then he reached for Kayla's hand again. "Want to keep walking?" They started off in the opposite direction before Kayla could do anything more than nod.

After a second, Kurt pressed a palm to the center of Emily's lower back and maneuvered them off to the side. "Well, that was fun."

Emily grinned. "It wasn't so bad. And I'm pretty proud of you. You hardly sounded embarrassed to be seen with me at all."

That surprised him. "I wasn't embarrassed to be seen with you. I guess I'm still trying to get used to looking out for him. And having our lives intersect so much."

"In other words, you're used to having your own life."

"Yeah. I'm almost thirteen years older than Sam. Until recently, I did my own thing and assumed that our parents would look after him."

"And they did, yes?"

"Yeah. Until Mom got sick." Until she died and their father decided he was done doing much of anything.

She touched his arm. "That's what should have been happening, right?"

He shrugged. Why did it sound like he was betraying his father by admitting that?

"I mean, I'm guessing your father looked after you."

Her hand was still resting on his arm. He liked the feel of it there. Liked her reaching out to him. Touching him. "He did. My mom did, too. But then, I didn't need as much looking after as my brother."

"Really?"

It was awkward as hell, feeling like Emily was digging up all the thoughts and memories that he'd been suppressing for years. "I, well, I wasn't anything special. I mean, I wasn't smart like Sam." Hating that he sounded pitiful, he cleared his throat. "What I'm trying to say is I was just an average kid."

"Ah."

Half afraid to see her staring at him with distaste—because what kind of man actually shared his weaknesses?—he forced himself to continue. "Anyway, I made the call to make sure my brother got what he needed. So here we are, for better or worse. I was so sure that pulling Sam somewhere new was the right thing to do. But what if it isn't?" Of course, what he was really wondering was what if this place wasn't the right place for him.

"Maybe you're worrying too much, Kurt. With the exception of Sam not being real excited to see his older brother and teacher show up in the middle of his date, things seem to be working out."

He smiled at that. Just as he was about to wrap an arm around her shoulders and pull her close, Emily grabbed his hand. "Here's Brenden. Let's go enjoy the rest of the night."

Before he turned around, he scanned the area for Sam and Kayla. "Emily, you know teenagers. Is this place okay for them to be hanging out?"

"I think it's safe, if that is what you're asking."

He wasn't sure what he was asking. "I guess I feel like I should have been offering some kind of words of wisdom or something." Or be telling him not to disrespect the girl. "I don't know, I guess I feel like I should be telling him to take care with her."

"He was holding her hand and walking with her in a public park. I think he's doing a pretty good job so far."

"Yeah. I guess so."

"Come on. Looks like my brother and Samantha brought a cooler and stuff for s'mores." She smiled. "I'm warning you now that s'mores are kind of a weakness of mine, so don't make fun of me when I get melted chocolate and marshmallow all over my mouth and fingers."

"I'll try to hold back the comments," he murmured. Actually, he knew he would be trying to take his own advice and not do anything that he'd later regret, like offering to help clean up that mouth with his own.

Sheesh. When was the last time he'd been looking forward to something so simple? He couldn't remember. After joining them and having a good-natured laugh with Emily and the others about getting caught on their date, Kurt grabbed a beer and helped Brenden start up the charcoal fire in one of the picnic areas off the main area. There was plenty of space to spread out and enjoy a barbecue. And since it didn't seem as if any of the other folks who'd come to the lake were interested in sitting by a campfire, it felt almost like they had the whole area to themselves.

The women had gone back to Brenden's truck to get some blankets.

"I bet this is a pretty tame night for you," Brenden said.

"Nah. It's a good one. Well, despite running into my brother and all."

"And you ran into Emily's brother, too."

Kurt wasn't sure where he was going with that. "Like I said, it's all good."

Brenden studied him a moment before seeming to come to terms with something. He nodded. "Good. Now let me tell you about the fish I almost caught here."

As Brenden launched into a convoluted fish tale, the girls got back and set up chairs next to them. Minutes later, all four of them were sitting down, the girls wrapped in blankets, and chuckling about Brenden's fish that got away. Conversation meandered along as they opened another round of beers, and ate way too many s'mores.

Around ten o'clock, Samantha was yawning and they were cleaning up. "We should get together again soon," Brenden said. Winking at Em, he added, "I didn't know going on my sister's dates could be so fun."

Kurt had an idea. "My buddy from home, Ace, is coming here next weekend. We were thinking about getting a poker game together in the garage."

"In your garage?" Emily wrinkled her nose. "Why there?"

"We smoke cigars. We don't smoke them in the house even back in West Virginia."

"So you want to sit in a garage, smoke cigars, and play poker?"

"And drink beer. Don't forget that."

"Sounds like a bunch of smelly, smoky guys," Emily teased. "I'll remember to keep my distance."

Brenden turned to his wife. "What did you say you have going on next Saturday night, Samantha?"

"My mother has tickets to a play downtown."

Brenden brightened. "That means I'm free, right?"

"It does," she said slowly, "though I thought you said you were going to winterize the backyard."

Kurt noticed that Emily was trying very hard not to laugh about that. He took another bite of his last s'more and leaned back on his hands, letting the beer and the company soothe him.

"Can I bring a buddy over to play, too?" Brenden asked. Samantha grinned. "Brenden, you sound like a little kid wanting to come to a birthday party."

"Sorry, but I want to know."

Kurt grinned. "Yeah, sure. The more the merrier."

"Great. I'll see if Chris wants to go, too."

"I'm sure he will," Samantha said drily. "I can't see our

brother-in-law saying no to a garage full of men, beer, poker chips, and cigars."

Emily winked at her sister-in-law. "Sounds like trouble."

Kurt realized it sounded like something far different than that. It sounded almost like home.

CHAPTER 10

FROM LES LARKE'S
TIPS FOR BEGINNING POKER PLAYERS:

Stop worrying about what everyone else is doing. Pay attention to the cards in your hands—usually that's plenty to worry about.

"I had a good time tonight," Emily said when Kurt parked in front of her condominium complex. "Actually, I don't remember the last time I had so much fun with my brother."

Kurt grinned as he set the car in park. "As compliments go, I'll take that as pretty good."

Belatedly, she realized that she'd just talked about her brother on their date. She wrinkled her nose. "I guess that sounded pretty bad, didn't it? I only meant—"

He chuckled. "No reason to explain, Emily. I know what you meant." When she released her seat belt and reached for the door handle, he pressed a hand on her knee. "Hold up. I'll come get you."

Then he got out of his side of the truck's cab before she could tell him that she was perfectly capable of getting out of a truck on her own.

When he opened the door and held out a hand to help her down, she started thinking that maybe she'd had it all wrong after all. Feeling his hand in hers, and his other around her waist? Well, it was enough to make a girl think taking care of herself 100 percent of the time was overrated.

After closing the door, he clasped her palm again and started walking. "Is your tongue bleeding?"

"Hmm? Uh, why?"

"Most women I know these days get irritated when they aren't allowed to do things for themselves. I thought maybe you were working on keeping your opinion to yourself."

She looked up at his profile. Even in the dim light, she took the time to admire his strong jaw, the way he was holding her with care. And how he wasn't apologizing for his actions, only for the fact that she might have fault with them. "No, I was just thinking it was nice to have you help me." She'd liked touching him, too, but didn't feel brave enough to share that.

After wondering just how honest she should be, she decided to admit something else. "I was just thinking that it's been quite a while since a guy put forth so much effort. It was nice."

"It wasn't anything. Some habits are hard to break, I guess."

"Did your father teach you to open all those doors?"

"Oh, yeah. And what he didn't get into my head, my mother did. We weren't fancy around our house, but my parents made sure I didn't act disrespectful around women. It stuck."

"For Sam, too?"

"I hope so." He winked. "Otherwise, my father's gonna kick my ass for messing him up." Stopping in front of her door, he held out his hand. "Give me your key so I can help you get in. Then, I'll head on home. I promise."

She realized that he said that to keep her fears at bay. "You must have done a real good job on your gentleman lessons," she teased as she pulled out her keys and dutifully handed them to him.

A muscle ticked in his jaw as he unlocked her door, then opened it and helped her turn on the light. "Don't know if I did or I didn't. But, uh, well, I just wanted you to know that I've been thinking about what you told me about your old boyfriend."

And that felt like a splash of cold water. "I didn't tell you about Danny so you would stew on it."

"Of course I'm stewing on it." He scowled. "Look at you, Em. You're gorgeous. Sweet, too. Pretty damn near perfect."

"I'm not any of that."

His voice lowered as he stepped closer. "Don't do that. Don't shrug off my compliments. Don't act like I don't get to have an opinion."

"I … I'm sorry. I just meant that I never thought of myself as all that."

"Well, to me you are," he murmured, linking a couple of his fingers through the ones on her left hand. "And even if you weren't, it wasn't okay for him to mistreat you."

She knew that. "I just don't want you to feel like I heaped too much on your shoulders …"

"No, don't you apologize for sharing. I'm glad you did. And I took it to heart, too." He turned so she could see his expression in the ray of light streaming out of her tiny entryway. "I don't want to presume that, uh, this is anything more than a good night for you. But if, by chance, it does move into a real date, or maybe something else, well, Emily, I need you to know something. I would never lay a hand on you. Never."

His expression was serious, and his voice? That drawl was thick with concern. It practically made her insides melt. "I wasn't worried about you hurting me, Kurt."

He looked at her intently, like he was trying to read her expression. "Good. I'm glad. I don't want you to worry when you think about me." He inhaled. "I mean, if you do think about me." His breath hitched. "Oh, hell. I think I'd better tell you goodnight."

Tilting her head up, she smiled at him while her heart beat a little faster, waiting for him to lean down and at last brush his lips against hers. "Goodnight, Kurt."

But instead, he ran his thumb along her cheek. "Night."

Then he turned away and headed back to his truck. "Lock up safe, 'kay?"

No kiss. She swallowed her disappointment.

"'Kay," she whispered as she walked inside and shut the door. Then, when she was finally alone, she leaned her head against the wall and sighed. She didn't know what was going to happen between the two of them, but she did know that Kurt couldn't have been more wrong.

Because she knew that (1) she most certainly was going to be thinking about him, and (2) she was definitely going to hope that he called her soon and that he'd come over again. Or that he would drive her around in his truck and open lots of doors for her, too.

Because then she could smile and get to know him and try to figure out how to convince him that there was more to him than he believed.

And that she really, really would like to kiss him very soon.

After kicking off her shoes, she turned off the downstairs light and went up to bed. She wanted to think about their night and sit and dream about him.

Just like all those silly girls she taught. Who, she now realized, might not be all that silly after all. They might have been right on the money.

CHAPTER 11

FROM LES LARKE'S
TIPS FOR BEGINNING POKER PLAYERS:

Don't play drunk. Enough said.

"When's Ace supposed to get here?" Sam asked from his spot on the couch.

"The same time I told you ten minutes ago," Kurt said.

Sam looked at the screen of his cell. "That time passed two minutes ago."

Kurt was real close to either cussing out his brother, telling him to stand outside until Ace arrived, or taking away the cell phone when the reality of the situation hit him hard. Sam was acting like a kid again. An excited kid.

He hadn't done anything like that in weeks. Maybe not in months. Try as he might, Kurt couldn't remember the last time that Sam hadn't acted like he had the weight of the world on his shoulders.

And that allowed him to take a deep breath and give the kid a break. "You're looking forward to seeing Ace, aren't you?"

Getting to his feet, Sam nodded sheepishly. "Yeah."

"You miss him that much?"

"I don't know. Maybe." He looked down at his feet. "Or maybe it's that he's from home."

That was it. Kurt had once heard it took people a full year for a new place to feel like home. He'd only paid half attention to it, thinking that Spartan, West Virginia, was going to be his home forever. But now, well, yeah. He got it. No matter how nice their house was or how much money he was making or how much better the schools were, Bridgeport didn't hold a candle to the way things were back in West Virginia. That was where his roots and his heart were.

Realizing that Sam was standing there, half waiting for him to either say it was okay or to make fun of him or something, Kurt gave a little of himself. "I get it, Sam. I think that's why I called Ace in the first place. I've been looking forward to seeing him, too."

Sam stepped closer. "You have?"

"Yeah. I've known the guy since I was five. Of course nobody here is going to be like him."

"Do you think Miss Springer's brother is really going to show up here tonight?"

Remembering the look of interest in Brenden Springer's face, he nodded. "I do."

"Do you think that's weird?"

"No."

"How come?"

"So far, what I've learned from life here in Bridgeport is if a guy wants to have a good time, he's got to head down to the city. That involves money and getting an Uber or something. Why would a guy want to go to all that trouble if he just wants to play some poker and have a couple of beers?"

Sam laughed. "That is so typical of you, Kurt."

"What do you mean by that?"

"I mean that you're always sure you're right."

He was feeling a little offended. "That ain't a bad thing."

"It ain't for you." He laughed. "For the rest of us, though? It kinda sucks."

Not sure if he was offended or amused, Kurt stood up. "Hey, I swear I'm not that—"

"He's here." Sam threw open the front door and walked outside, his face looking like he was seven years old again and finding out that they were going to Gatlinburg.

Shaking his head, Kurt followed, then was pretty sure his expression matched his little brother's when he caught sight of the old black Chevy truck … and Ace.

Ace, with his short-cropped blond hair, brown eyes, and permanent tan looked the same as ever. But there was an air about him that felt different. Was it relief? Or was he merely putting that emotion on his buddy's shoulders because he was feeling that way? He had a feeling it could have been partly both.

"Hey," Ace said to Kurt after he hugged Sam. "How are you?"

"I'm good." He held out his hand, then grunted as Ace gave him a one-armed hug. "You?"

"Better now. It was a haul. Tons of traffic." Looking up and down the street, he whistled low. "Y'all are living the life of Riley here. This is quite a place, Kurt."

"It's all right."

"It's better than that."

He supposed it was. The house was an older one for Bridgeport. Unlike most of the houses in newer subdivisions that were made of brick, his was wooden. It was painted a pale yellow and had white trim and a dark green door. He and his team had planted a variety of trees and redone the flower beds. All in all, the house looked well-kept and comfortable.

Thinking of how it compared with the house he grew up in, he had to admit that it was a step up.

"Kurt has turned into a neat freak," Sam griped as he led the way inside, Ace's rolling duffel bag trailing behind him. "We clean all the time now."

"Hardly that," Kurt said.

"Feels like it."

"It ain't like you have much choice, kid," Ace said. "There's no one else around. I mean, it's just you and Kurt, yeah?"

A shadow passed through Sam's eyes before nodding. "Yeah. It's just us now, and even that isn't going to last real long. I'll be at college next year, so it's just gonna be Kurt here in Bridgeport."

Kurt braced himself, ready to hear Ace say something about how he needed to move back home as soon as Sam went to college. But instead of doing that, his buddy just shrugged. "Maybe. Maybe not."

And that set off an alarm. What did that mean?

Catching his gaze. Ace shook his head, letting him know that they'd talk later. That was good enough for him.

"You want the tour or to go get something to eat?"

Ace clapped him on the back. "Let's get that tour, then eat. Then, we'll catch up."

"I can do that."

***

Three hours later, after Sam and Kurt had showed Ace around Bridgeport and then took him out for pizza in a hole-in-the-wall restaurant off the bike trail, he and Ace were sitting on the back deck. Sam had taken off to see one of the new buddies that he'd made.

"All right, spill," Kurt said. "What's going on with you?"

Ace shifted uncomfortably. "Why do you think something is going on?"

"Probably because you are never secretive."

He scowled. "I can keep a secret."

"Yeah, but you never do."

Looking a little sheepish, Ace propped up one of his feet on the base of the chair next to him. "True that."

"So, what's going on? Is it Finn?" he asked.

"Yeah."

Ace could hardly look at him. Ace, who used to always act as if he didn't have a care in the world. Who'd played his position on the defensive line like no one was ever going to stop him. "What happened?"

"His mother found somebody new." He paused. Swallowed. "Again."

Liz was Ace's ex. If he wasn't so close to Ace, he'd be more vocal about how she was every man's cautionary tale. Liz had been a bar hookup that had turned into a two-week relationship, based essentially on compatibility in bed. She also was flighty, spoiled, and temperamental. Kurt had always figured any two of those traits was a red flag. All three? Well, it had been a recipe for a nightmare relationship.

"Why do you care about who Liz is hooking up with?"

"Because the guy is stupid as all get out." His lips pursed. "He's also wanting her to move to Reno."

"Liz can't go anywhere. Finn is a freshman."

"She doesn't care about that." His expression tightened. "And neither does her man. Shoot, I don't think they even stop their lovefest long enough to give Finn the time of day. Every time I see him, he looks a little more lost."

Finn was a big kid. He took after his father in build and temperament. Because of that, a lot of people made the mistake of thinking that he was older or more mature than he was. But the fact was Finn was the product of a brief affair between two very different people. And while Ace had always done his best to have a relationship with him, Finn had always lived with his mother and been subjected to her schemes, various relationships, and whims.

"He still playing football?"

"What? Oh, yeah. He's started on JV, and Coach said before the end of the season they're going to put him on the field of varsity."

"That's good."

"That's good, but it ain't enough."

"Hell, she's not thinking of pulling him now, is she?"

"Sure she is. And she's not only thinking about it either. Liz is already looking at condos or something out there."

"What are you going to do?"

Ace's expression tightened. It was obvious he was trying hard to hold on to the last of his emotions "Last night Finn came over and I laid it out. Gave him a choice."

"Between ..."

"Staying with his mom and going to Reno, or moving in with me." He paused, then looked directly at Kurt. "Or, maybe even coming here."

"What? What about your job?"

Ace shrugged. "I'm a mechanic, Kurt. I can get in a garage anywhere."

"What did Finn say?"

"He wants to go with me." Ace shook his head slightly. "Kurt, he didn't even think twice about it. He just sat there and listened to me give my spiel, then told me he wanted to be wherever I was," Ace's voice was thick with emotion. "It surprised the hell out of me, if you want to know the truth. But I have to tell you, it made me real glad, too."

"Of course he wanted to be with you. Your life has always been about Finn."

"I've tried for it to be. Some days don't go as well as others."

Kurt now had a better idea of what Ace had been going through since his boy's birth. "That's all you can do, buddy."

Ace sighed. "That's when we really started talking. I told him to tell me what has been going on with his mom. Really."

"Did he share?"

"Yeah." Looking pained, Ace said, "He's been having a time of it for the last couple of years, and I haven't even been aware of it."

Hearing that, a lot of things went through Kurt's mind. He was surprised to hear that Finn was having a hard time. The last time he'd seen the kid, he'd seemed as happy as ever. But more than that, he was surprised by Ace's statement. He'd always assumed that Ace was more involved with his son than that.

But he didn't want to be critical. After all, he didn't have a kid and had no idea what was involved. Not really.

That was why he simply sipped his beer.

Ace raised an eyebrow. "That's it?"

"You know I don't know what to say."

"How about what you're really thinking?"

"I don't know jack about raising kids, Ace."

Ace stared at him long and hard before nodding. "You're right. You don't. It's hard, man." When Kurt stayed silent, he continued, throwing out each word as if it was a barb that had been embedded in his skin. "Liz has never been easy, but I always thought she was a decent mom. Finn's a great kid."

"He is. She must have had something to do with that."

"I think so. She looked after him and at least did the right stuff. I mean, it wasn't like she abused him or didn't make him go to school or anything." He sighed, rolling his bottle of Bud between his palms before eyeing Kurt again. "But the older he got, the more I took up the slack."

Kurt couldn't get a handle on what point Ace was trying to make. "Did you resent that?"

"No. Hell, no. But, Finn knew that I was doing more."

"Nothing wrong with that."

"He also knew why I was." He shook his head. "But this last move? Liz has really gone off the deep end. And then Finn started telling me about the things she's been pulling. She's been leaving him alone at night a couple of times a month."

Kurt's stomach sank. "He's only fifteen, right?"

"Yeah. And here's what makes me so pissed off. I would have been happy to have him on those nights. I'm always home. I could have picked him up. But she just took off."

"Why didn't he call you?" Thinking of something, he said, "Wait a minute, did she not let him?"

"From what I can tell, she never actually told him to not call me. But it was pretty freaking obvious that she didn't want him to."

"What did she do?"

"She told him only wussies would do stuff like that." Ace's voice turned even more strained. "She made him feel stupid for being scared, Kurt."

Kurt was feeling so pissed off, he was half ready to get in Ace's truck and drive all the way to Spartan that night and get the kid himself.

Which brought up a good point. "Where is he now? He's not sitting home alone, is he?"

"No. He's with a buddy of his. After tonight's game, Jackson's dad is taking the two of them on a fishing trip. Believe me, if I had thought that he'd be home alone with Liz, or by himself, I would have brought him here."

So there it was. Ace was moving his kid who he'd never actually lived with for longer than a week at a time out to Ohio. All so he could give him a stable life and something to hold on to.

It was commendable. But more importantly, it was the right thing to do. Ace was stepping up. "So we have a ton to do this weekend while you're here."

"That's it? You're not going to ask me a dozen questions or caution me to think about what I'm doing?"

"Why would I? You've obviously thought it through." Realizing how excited he was about the possibility, he continued. "Then, of course, there's the fact that I'm getting something out of this, too."

"Another teenager to help raise?"

Kurt knew Ace was expecting him to make light of that and make a joke right back. And maybe he should do it. But he couldn't, because right at that moment he was too relieved to have his best friend in the world living in the same town as him. "I'll have you around again," he said lightly. "And after the way things have been? I'll take it."

Ace's expression tightened. "Yeah. All right."

That was high praise from Ace.

CHAPTER 12

"You get your chips your way, I'll get my chips mine."
—PHIL IVEY

With a wave of her hand and a few clicks on her computer, Emily at last reached the end of the day's lesson. "So, that, everyone, is why you can't take a good theme for granted. The theme of friendship and honesty that flows through *Cannery Row*'s pages is as relatable today as it was when Mr. Steinbeck wrote the story."

Looking around at her honors English freshmen, she smiled, hoping to see some answering looks of awareness. Maybe even a couple of eager, outstretched hands.

Sadly, they seemed more than a little underwhelmed. Or maybe they were just bored.

Even her three usual brownnosing girls didn't look particularly interested. One of them was currently doodling flower designs around the edges of her paper.

"Really, kids?" Emily said, one hand on her hip. "That's all you've got to say?"

Anna quirked up an eyebrow. "Nobody said anything, Miss Springer."

"Which is my point. What's going on that has your minds elsewhere?"

Those three girls in the front row looked at each other but said nothing. Neither did Anna. Nor Anna's best friend, John. Not even the cheerleaders in the back, who usually had a lot to say about everything.

Just when she was about to start walking the aisles, Edison, the backup quarterback, spoke. "There's a game tonight, Miss Springer."

"There was one last Friday night, too, Edison. And while I can understand why you aren't all that interested in my lesson, I can't say the same thing about the rest of the class."

Anna spoke up again. "I think everyone's thinking about Homecoming."

"Come now. I know all about Homecoming Week. But that isn't happening for almost another month."

"People are getting asked this week," Marissa, one of her three brownnosers said. "It's kind of a big deal."

"Ah."

John looked her over. "Was Homecoming a big deal when you were in high school?"

He might as well have added, "in the Dark Ages."

She nodded. "Yes. It was a big deal, even back then."

Anna perked up. "Did you get asked your freshman year?"

Feeling twenty-four pairs of eyes firmly fixated on her for the first time all hour, Emily nodded. "I did."

Now even the cheerleaders were looking at her with new interest. "Who took you?" one of them asked.

She caught herself before saying Philip's name. "That was a long time ago. It's nothing you need to worry about. Now—"

"Do you have a boyfriend now, Miss Springer?"

"Now? No." After all Kurt Holland wasn't her boyfriend. Not officially. Was he?

"Do you date?"

"That's none of y'all's business." But just then, her gaze wandered over to Sam's. He was half slumped down in his chair, but his blue eyes were fastened on her face. She was probably imagining it, but she felt like he was waiting for her to lie to him, to the whole class.

Edison perked up. "So does that mean you are?"

"It means I date. Yes, Edison."

Anna looked around at the rest of the class and grinned. "Who are you dating?"

"Oh, look. The bell is about to ring. We better wrap up the class." Pointing to the assignment she'd displayed earlier, she said, "Y'all might have distracted me but I'm not going to forget assigning this. We'll go over these discussion questions on Monday."

And ... at last the bell rang.

With a whoosh, the entire class got up. Most rushed out the door like they were afraid she was going to pull them in. Several other kids paused on their way out to say goodbye or wish her a good weekend.

It had been a frustrating hour, but it had been a pretty amusing one, too.

Actually, moments like that were why she liked teaching at Bridgeport High so much. The kids still acted like kids. They said hi to her in the hallway, they asked about her dating, they got excited about homecoming and football games. In short, they made her believe that her job was worthwhile and, more importantly, that it might help their future.

"Hey, Miss Springer?"

Seeing Sam pause in front of her, she smiled. "Yes?"

He seemed to gather himself, then blurted, "Do you think you'll see my brother again?"

She would have thought talking to Sam about Kurt would've been awkward. And maybe it should have been. At the end of the day, she was still a teacher and Sam was still a student.

But it didn't feel that way. "I hope so." She would if he called. It was on the tip of her tongue to ask if Sam thought Kurt was going to call her. At least she had the presence of mind to keep that question to herself.

Sam didn't need that burden on his shoulders and she didn't actually want to know right then if he did or not. It seemed that she got older but inside she was still the same awkward teenaged girl she'd once been.

"I guess we'll see what happens," she murmured, hoping she sounded more lighthearted than she felt.

Sam shifted his weight. "Kurt has a buddy in town this weekend. His name is Ace."

"You know what? He'd told me about that, but I'd forgotten. Ace is here for the poker game, right?"

"Yeah. I think he would've come up no matter what, but Kurt got him here for that." Sam grinned. "It's going to be great."

"Will you be playing poker, too?"

"Yep."

Sam's expression reminded Emily of a little boy who was looking forward to playing in the woods all day. It was beyond cute. "I feel like I should be the responsible adult and say something about the dangers of underage gambling, but I think I'll leave it alone."

Sam looked affronted. "We're not doing anything bad, Miss Springer. It's just a poker game in our garage."

"I hope you have a good time. I know my brother's looking forward to it."

Sam smiled again, then edged toward the door. "I gotta go."

"Have a good weekend."

After gifting her with another quick smile, he left the room. Emily stayed at her door, watching as the kids darted out, chatting with a few, and joking with a couple of her teacher friends.

Then, when the hallways had finally cleared a bit, she unlocked her purse from her desk's drawer and checked her phone.

She had four text messages, one from her brother and three from Kurt.

Three from Kurt! He had been thinking of her, too.

Feeling once again like her sixteen-year-old self, Emily clicked on Kurt's messages first.

Was thinking about you.
How was your day?

It was certainly better now.

Feeling a little dreamy—which she would never admit to anyone— she clicked on the next text. It had been sent two hours after the first.

Hoping you can't get to your phone
and aren't just creeped out by my
messaging you.

Then, fifteen minutes ago.

Okay. I'm not great at this, but looks
like I need to leave you alone. No
worries.

No worries? Well, now she was worried.

Quickly she texted him back.

No! I like your texts. This
is the first time I've had a
chance to look at my phone
since lunch.

Almost immediately, he typed a reply.

Sure?

Smiling, she nodded. Then typed,

> Very sure.

Listen, my buddy came into town. He's
got a situation going with his son. I had
hoped to see you again, but I don't
think that's going to happen. I'm going
to need to be with him until Sunday.

Feeling disappointed, she tamped it down because she could totally understand that he had other commitments.

> I understand.

She paused, then wrote,

> Thanks for letting me know.

While she was staring at her screen, waiting for his response, her phone rang.

She smiled when she saw Kurt's name. "Hey."

"I can only text so much," he said by way of greeting. "Can you talk now?"

"I can," she said as she shut her door. "I mean, I'm still at school but the kids are gone. I'm in my classroom." The second she said that, she wished she could hang up and have her far more cool-and-collected self replay the last minute. Kurt did not need to know her life story.

"Good. Listen, do you understand about tonight? If you don't,

I get it. But I hope you do. I didn't want to treat you like this, but I'm kind of in a tough spot."

Taking a seat on one of the desks, she allowed herself to smile. That sweet explanation, combined with that faint West Virginia drawl was a killer combination. "Of course I do," she said with a smile. "Um, is poker still going on? I know it's none of my business, but if it isn't, then I need to call my brother and let him know so he doesn't show up in your garage with a pack of beer."

"Heck, yeah, it's still going on." She could practically feel his grin. "Tell Brenden to come over around six thirty, if he still wants to play. I'll be looking for him."

"He left two messages on my phone. I bet they're about tonight. I know he's looking forward to it."

"Forward them to me if you want and I'll talk to him about the game." Sounding sheepish, he added, "You've got enough to do without worrying about that."

She smiled as she walked around her classroom, picking up pens, books, and someone's forgotten sweatshirt. "You know, I think I will do that. I feel kind of foolish, passing on information about boys' night like I'm Brenden's mother."

"I sure don't think about you like that," he teased. "Now, about Sunday night, what time can I pick you up?"

She sat back down in her chair. "Wait a minute. I thought our date was canceled. I mean, didn't you just apologize for that? I thought you were going to be busy with your friend?"

"Ace will be heading back to Spartan on Sunday. He's got to see his kid and head to work on Monday morning. I know it'll have to be an early night, but I'd still like to take you out then, Emily."

In the safety of the empty classroom, she allowed her grin to grow even wider. "In that case, how does six or seven sound?"

"That sounds good. I'll be at your house at six on Sunday. Thanks, Em."

"You're welcome. Have a good time with your buddy."

"Yeah, I will. I'm kind of worried about him, if you want to know the truth. He came out here to check on me, but I'm thinking now that it's me who's gonna have to do the checking-up-on."

"That's how it goes sometimes. We all have to check on each other."

"Maybe so." He paused. "Crap. I gotta go now. See you soon."

He hung up before she could tell him goodbye.

Shaking her head, she skimmed her brother's texts and saw that they were all about poker. He was wanting to bring their brother-in-law, Chris, and maybe even another neighbor. What did she think about that?

Not wanting to get more involved in a boy's night than she already was, she forwarded them to Kurt.

Then she leaned back in her chair, smiling at her phone. She had a date. Dreamy Kurt Holland was taking her out on a real date. It was the first one in forever that she'd said yes to and was actually excited about. What was it about this guy that made her melt a little every time she thought about him?

She wished she knew.

Her door swung open and Campbell popped her head in, a look of concern in her eyes. "You okay?"

"Of course. Why?"

"Your door was shut and you're sitting by yourself at your desk, staring at your cell phone," she pointed out as she wandered in. "That's never a good sign. Did something happen?"

"Yes, but not in the way that you're thinking."

The worry drifted out of her eyes. "And you're speaking in riddles because ..."

"Kurt Holland just called and asked me out on Sunday night."

Campbell trotted to the door and closed it firmly. "And you're okay with that?"

"I am."

"Even though he's one of your kiddo's brothers. And he's running a poker game in his garage."

"Even though all of that is correct." Unable to help herself, she smiled. "I know he's nothing like me on the outside, but I think that's what I'm finding attractive. I like that he's different." Before Campbell could voice another objection, she said, "I told him about Danny, Campbell."

Campbell strode to her side. "What did he say?"

"I think if Danny had been standing on the other side of the door Kurt would've gone out there and confronted him."

"Sounds like his brother!"

She chuckled. "That same thought actually did enter my mind. And even though it might not be all that politically correct to say so, I kind of liked that he wanted to go out and hurt Danny."

"You should. Heck, I want to go hurt Danny." Campbell studied her for a long moment, then she smiled wider. "What are you going to wear?"

"For my date on Sunday? I don't know."

"What?"

"Campbell, he just asked me. Not everyone thinks of her outfit first thing. And it's not going to be anything fancy."

"I don't know why not." She shook her head in dismay. "Well, I know what we're doing tonight. We're going to T.J. Maxx."

"Not shopping. And not there." She had nothing against that store. Especially not for everyone else. But for a girl who didn't like to shop, sorting through a bunch of clothes was torture.

"Emily, girl, you need date clothes."

"I have a lot of clothes. Besides, I'm sure I'll just wear a pair of jeans and a top."

"You can't go out with Kurt Holland dressed like that."

She looked down at her dark jeans, Bridgeport polo, and Top-Siders. "I'm dressed for school. Of course I'm not going to wear a Bridgeport T."

"What did you wear yesterday?"

She had to think about it. "Khakis, a button-down, and blue flats."

"And the day before?"

"A long skirt and flats." With a sudden start, she realized that she only had one flattering skirt and that was the one she'd been wearing when Sam had gotten into trouble. And that her jeans were suitable for school ... but not for catching Kurt Holland's eye. "You're right. I need to go shopping."

"Great. So, if we're not going to T.J. Maxx, are we headed to the mall?"

"Yep." Warming up to the idea of both getting something just for Sunday night and to have Campbell's eye for it, she hopped off the desk. "Want to have dinner, too?"

Campbell smiled. "Of course. I'll pick you up at your house at five."

"You're a good friend. Thanks."

"No reason to thank me. If I don't have a hot date planned, then at least I can make sure you're ready for one."

Emily smiled. She didn't know if Kurt was the type of guy to take women on hot dates or not. But she was starting to think that all he would have to do was talk to her and anything they did would be amazing.

CHAPTER 13

FROM LES LARKE'S
TIPS FOR BEGINNING POKER PLAYERS:

Pay attention to the small things.
They can make or break a good game.

Ace looked around the garage with a critical eye. "It ain't much, but it will do, yeah?"

Kurt studied his garage. It now had a large poker table from a discount store smack in the middle of it, a makeshift bar made out of the former owner's tool bench, extra chairs, a large cooler filled with beer, and a box filled with new decks of cards and chips off to one side.

Yeah, it wasn't much, but considering how it had looked two weeks ago, he privately thought it was pretty damn impressive. "For hosting the first game, it's all right," he said.

"I can't believe we got so lucky at Goodwill." Looking like he'd fallen in love, Ace ran a hand over the top of the "genuine fabricated wood" poker table.

"It is a good one," Kurt agreed. They'd found the table in a back corner of the resale store. He'd been planning to run to Sam's Club and pick up a plastic round table there, but Ace had told him to pull over when they'd passed the resale shop. Made of cheap stained wood and covered in ugly green felt, it was both ugly as sin and kind of the best thing he'd ever seen in his life. He couldn't fork out thirty dollars for it fast enough.

After that, it had been fairly simple to go out and buy eight chairs—which had been another story. He'd been planning on six chairs at the most, but Ace had been the one who had pulled out another pair of twenties and gotten two more, saying that Kurt needed to be prepared.

He hadn't had the nerve to confess that he had no idea what to prepare for. He was just the new guy in town. It wasn't like he had people dropping by his house day and night asking to hang out with him.

Ace folded his arms across his chest and eyed the garage carefully. "When you get more guys, we'll get some round tables. You can start posting the winners on that wall, too."

The winners? "Ace, I think you're getting ahead of yourself. This thing might not happen again."

"Sure it will. Guys like having a place where they can hang out. And they like poker. It's all good. But you've got to post the winners, because everyone needs bragging rights."

It was only because Ace was in a bad spot that Kurt didn't start giving him grief about his poker dreams. Instead, he simply nodded. "You can take care of tonight's posting, buddy."

"Will do." Looking around, he said, "I'll write down some rules for you, too."

"Rules, as in poker rules?" This time, he didn't bother trying to hide the incredulousness in his voice.

"Hell, yeah. Otherwise guys will complain." Ace grinned. "And you know what rule number one is going to be?"

"I've no idea."

"Rule number one is there ain't no rules."

Kurt laughed. "I'm going to tell everyone who shows up—all six of us—that you came up with the rules."

"Go for it."

Ace sat down, pulled out a cigarette, and took a deep drag. If his best friend had a flaw, it was that he smoked. It used to be just a couple a day. He'd gone through a whole pack today though. He was really stressed out about Liz and Finn.

They'd talked some about it, but since Kurt had never been married, or really even had a serious girlfriend since Becky in high school, he didn't know what to say. He'd decided it would be better to let Ace talk about what was bothering him when he was ready.

"When is that guy coming over? Brenden, you said his name was?"

"Six thirty."

"You think he's any good?"

"I don't have any idea. Like I said, I barely know the guy."

"Because he's Emily's brother."

"Yeah." Glancing at his phone, he said, "We've got an hour. Do you want anything to eat?"

"We ate enough wings to keep us going for hours."

"I'm good, too. But Sam won't be. He'll say he's starving."

Ace grunted. "The kid's seventeen. Of course he's going to be hungry again."

"There's plenty of food for him. I hope so, anyway." Why was he even acting like Sam's stomach was his chief concern?

Because he was acting like a wuss and not saying what was really on his mind. "I know you already told me about Finn and Liz, but do you want to talk about it some more?"

Ace sighed. "Not really."

"Okay. I mean, if you're sure ..."

Ace lit up another Marlboro. "Do you think I'm crazy for wanting to move out here? Maybe I'm being just as selfish."

"If Finn is okay with the move, then I don't think you're making a mistake at all. I'm not going to say the move is going to be easy, but I think a fresh start is going to be good for both of you."

"Even though I'm just a mechanic?"

"Everyone needs mechanics, so don't knock it. And don't start talking like you're 'just a mechanic' either. I've seen you restore vehicles that other guys would've written off. Every shop in town is going to want you." Kurt also knew that Ace's good ole boy act covered up the fact that he not only made a lot of money in his shop but he had a great financial mind. He probably had more money in his savings account than half the people in Bridgeport.

Ace extinguished his cigarette. "Then there's Finn fitting in."

"Why wouldn't he fit in?"

"What if he doesn't make the team for next year?" Ace's brown eyes filled with even more worry. "He'd be crushed."

"Bridgeport High will want him. They'll be thrilled he's here. Hell, the coach will probably search him out the first hour he's on campus."

That picture brought the first hint of a smile. "That just might happen. Finn's got good hands, Kurt. And he's huge. He could play offense or defense."

"He'll get noticed here, too. Coaches from big universities will be scouting him out. You'll get him taken care of," he added, knowing how much it would mean to Ace if Finn attended college.

Ace shook his head. "That's the carrot, ain't it? Finn getting a free ride to college." He whistled low. "He'd be set for the rest of his life."

"Let's make it happen soon, then. Why don't you plan on coming out here in January?"

Ace took another long pull. "You think this place is worth me uprooting our lives?"

"I do," he replied after giving it some thought. "It's taken me some time to get adjusted, and it's not perfect, but I'm liking it. And if I like it, you will, too."

Ace raised his eyebrows. "Maybe. I mean, we ain't that much alike."

"We're more alike than different. And we want the same things, too." Clasping his best friend's arm, Kurt looked him in the eye. "I wouldn't steer you wrong on this. Start making plans to move here in January. It's going to be good for both of you. Shoot, it'll be good for me, too."

"You sure you're don't want me here just to play poker?"

Kurt grinned. "Of course I want you here for poker. But it ain't the only reason. Not by a long shot."

CHAPTER 14

FROM LES LARKE'S
TIPS FOR BEGINNING POKER PLAYERS:

Suited cards aren't all that great. This is the ultimate beginner's mistake ... they get all caught up thinking about what they want instead of what's right in front of their face.

Emily was starting to think she needed to talk to her students more about dating. Because, with the way she was feeling right now, she was in way over her head.

Which was pretty embarrassing. It wasn't like she hadn't had experience dating. She certainly did. So much so, she could probably write a book about dating dos and don'ts. She was familiar with the awkward silences, the searching for topics to talk about, and the hesitant statements. Feeling like she might as well have been standing in front of the guy in her underwear, she felt so exposed.

So, why she was having a hard time dealing with the fact that none of that was happening, she didn't know. She shouldn't be worried about why things felt too right with Kurt Holland. She should be celebrating the fact that she might have actually found the One.

Unless she was the only person who felt that way.

That statement settled in and brought forth a steady stream of good old-fashioned panic. Shoot! What if she really was the only one who felt that way?

She knew what would happen! After only one "real" date, she had set herself up to be disappointed and embarrassed. And she was going to have to see his little brother for the rest of the school year.

What was wrong with her? She needed to get a grip on herself before—

Just then Kurt pulled into her drive.

Quickly, she rushed into her bedroom. Threw open her closet door and eyed herself in the full-length mirror. Against her better judgment, she was wearing a sundress.

Campbell had picked it out.

Looking at herself this way and that, she couldn't deny that the pale blue broadcloth fabric was pretty. The starched cotton gave the dress a bit of an old-fashioned quality. But the low back, thin straps, and the way it fit her like a glove before softly flaring out into a flirty skirt was as sexy as anything she'd tried on in a long time.

It was absolutely not something she would wear to church or teach school in. Or hang out on the couch by herself in.

And that was why Campbell had declared it to be the perfect thing to wear.

Emily had been so pleased by the way she looked, by the thought of Kurt gazing at her in appreciation, she'd forked out too much money for that dress. Then, like a woman possessed, she'd spent even more money at the outlet mall. She'd bought some adorable patent leather slides with a two-inch heel because they helped make her legs look more shapely. She'd bought a cute designer purse she had no need for.

And yes, she'd bought herself a whole new Victoria's Secret wardrobe all while pretending she wasn't thinking about Kurt one day appreciating all that satin and lace, too.

Now, here she was—all dressed up from top to bottom, and seriously having second thoughts about everything.

Just as she was about to go stand in her closet again, the doorbell rang.

Shoot! What if she was too dressed up?

There was only one way to find out, she realized as she headed to the door. Pinning a smile on her face, she prepared herself to be ready for anything.

Gym shorts. Another stained and muddy T-shirt. Maybe him sucked into an old Abercrombie button-down leftover from high school.

But when she turned the handle, she realized she had been ready for anything . . . except the splendor that was Kurt Holland on a date. He had on dark jeans that fit him like a glove. Dark brown cowboy boots that looked like they'd been polished during the last month or so. And a crisp white button-down that obviously came from the cleaners and definitely had not been purchased back when he was in high school.

If Campbell was here, Emily thought she'd call him dreamy.

Emily would know that she would be right.

"Hey," he drawled, his blue eyes lighting with unconcealed admiration. "Don't you look like a picture."

"Hey," she said right back. Because, you know, when you're an English teacher you have a wealth of vocabulary options at your disposal. Shaking her head, she smiled. "I mean, it's good to see you. And thank you." She stepped back. "Won't you come in?" Lord, she sounded like she was seventy-four! "I mean, do you want to come in for a drink before we go out?"

He shook his head. "Can't. We have reservations to keep."

Her pulse jumped a little bit. "Let me grab my purse," she murmured as she trotted to the couch.

Kurt stood at the door and watched her, pure appreciation shining in his eyes the whole while. When she got back to his side, he held out his hand for her keys to help her lock the door.

After that was taken care of and the keys were tucked back in her purse, he took hold of her hand and walked her down to his truck. After he'd given her a hand into the passenger seat, he paused.

"Sorry. I was going to wait until later to do this."

She gazed up at him in confusion. "Hmm?"

Then there was no time to talk because Kurt was kissing her like he couldn't wait another second. Before she knew what she was doing, Emily had wrapped her hands around his neck and was kissing him back like she didn't want him to stop.

Like, ever.

When Kurt pulled away a few glorious minutes later, he smiled. "You good?"

"Uh huh." Oh, Lord. Really, that was all she could say?

"Good." He smiled at her for a second, looking really pleased and maybe a little bit smug, too.

But since she was having trouble catching her breath and couldn't seem to form coherent words, Emily figured he might feel justified.

It was a heck of a kiss and their date had been going on a total of ten minutes. At this rate? Why, there was a chance she was going to be showing off her Victoria's Secret a whole lot sooner than anticipated. Why that idea didn't bother her at all, she had no idea.

CHAPTER 15

*"Baseball is like a poker game. Nobody
wants to quit when he's losing; nobody
wants you to quit when you're ahead."*
—JACKIE ROBINSON

Kurt was no expert, but he was sure this date was going real well. Emily had liked his choice of restaurant, had smiled at him often, and had even shared some stories about her family with him.

She'd also been doing everything to let him know that his attraction wasn't one-sided. She'd smiled and leaned into him and had taken a couple of opportunities to touch his hand. Sure, all those things might have been right out of his middle-school mind, but he was feeling like God was rewarding him for doing something right.

He'd left his home, his friends, and his security to start something new for himself and his brother. He'd taken a chance to give Sam something that he deserved, even though Kurt didn't know quite how to go about doing that.

Emily's acceptance of a dumb ex–football player who had barely made it out of high school chemistry made him think that he was worth more than his parents or his teachers had led him to believe.

Now he just had to make sure that he didn't mess it up.

"Kurt, you okay?"

"Hmm? Oh, yeah. Sorry." He took a sip of his beer. "I was just thinking about my parents."

She sat up straighter. "I know your mom is gone. Is your dad going to come into town soon?"

"I kind of doubt it. He's old school. It's my job to go see him, not the other way around." Of course, there was more to their separation than that. Dad had accepted Sam's decision to go with him to Bridgeport. But that acceptance didn't necessarily mean he'd embraced it. Kurt had a feeling that his father was secretly waiting for him to call home and admit that he'd made a terrible mistake.

"There's a holiday in October. Maybe you and Sam can go see him then. I mean, if you want to."

"Yeah. I might do that." He hesitated, then added, "I need to look out for Sam, you know?"

Her brown eyes full of sympathy, she shook her head. "I'm afraid I don't. But you don't have to tell me. I know it's hard to talk about family."

She'd given him a reprieve. Part of him wanted to take it. Keep his insecurities close to the chest. But something told him that if he wanted this relationship between them to grow stronger, he was going to have to do something more than just flirt and give her a burger.

He leaned forward. "My brother is finally settling in. I know he's been having a hard time adjusting to a new school and is missing all his friends."

"That's to be expected, don't you think?"

"Yeah. But I'm afraid that if we see our father too soon, he could sabotage everything we've accomplished. Dad's not in a real good place right now. There's a good chance he could needle Sam with doubts."

"Do you think he would really do that?"

"I think he would say what was on his mind and not realize the damage he was doing." He fingered the edge of his Budweiser. "And if he does, I think there's a real good chance I'd tell him exactly what I thought about that." Just imagining the conversation made him grimace. "So, even though I'm a grown man and Sam's already lost his mother, I'm attempting to keep up the distance. Do you think that makes me a bad person?"

She reached out and covered her hand with his. "I think it makes you human, Kurt. You want the best for Sam."

"Even if it means limiting his time with our dad?"

She sipped her wine. "Let me ask you this. If your father got in the car and told you he was on his way, would you ask him to turn around?"

"Of course not."

"If Sam came to you and said that he wanted to go see him would you refuse to let him leave?"

"I couldn't do that even if I wanted to. And I don't want to."

She squeezed his hand before she released it with a smile. "There's your answer, then. You're doing what you think best—and your brother and father are doing the same. If they really wanted to do something different they would."

"I never thought about it that way. Thanks."

"I'm glad I could help."

He was charmed. Completely charmed. "You this good with your students?"

"What? Speaking my mind?"

"Asking questions and getting me to speak my mind."

She smiled. "I wish getting my students to listen to me was as easy."

"It's not?"

"You're forgetting that my students are in high school. They know everything right about now," she said, humor bright in her voice.

"It's their loss, then."

Their server had long since picked up their plates. "Do you want another glass of wine?"

She shook her head. "I'm good. What about you?"

"I'm good, too. How about we get on out of here?"

"I think that sounds like a fine idea."

Remembering how she'd felt in his arms, remembering the way she'd kissed him in his truck, he was anxious to get her alone again. He held up a hand and signaled the server over and asked for the check.

He figured he would let her decide what to do next. He could take her home and drop her off at the door … or maybe she would want to invite him in.

And once she did that, he could finally pull her close and show her what he thought about her.

When she shifted, staring right behind him, he reached for his old wallet in the back pocket of his Levi's. Turned to look for their server.

And came up short by the way the couple was glaring at Emily.

"Now I understand a whole lot better why you sided with Sam Holland and against Garrett," a man said.

It took a sec, but Kurt remembered that the couple were Garrett's parents. He'd seen them scuttle out of the principal's office the day he and Sam had gotten in that fight.

The couple looked much the same as they had in the office. Buttoned-up and button-downed tight. Khakis, cotton oxford, conservative navy knit dress paired with flats. Far different than his jeans, boots, and white oxford.

But what mattered the most was the way they were acting as if they'd run into some loser. Like he didn't belong in Bridgeport and never would.

As far as he was concerned, he didn't have a thing to talk to them about. This was Sam's battle and he'd handled it and had faced the consequences too.

But by the way Emily had jumped to her feet, she was of a different mind-set. "Mr. Condon. Julie," she said nervously. "Hello."

Garrett's dad sidled in front of his wife and eyed Emily with disdain. "You know I wasn't going to say a word right now, but since both of you are here, I might as well have my say."

"We should discuss this at school."

"No, I don't think so. I'm never stepping foot inside that building again if I can help it. You've ruined Garrett's reputation. He almost got kicked off the football team because of you."

Emily stiffened. "I think we both know that isn't fair."

Kurt didn't care for the way they were speaking to her, what they were saying, or how they'd chosen to attack her in the middle of Paxton's.

He got to his feet and walked to her side.

"This isn't the time or the place to do this," he said quietly. "Y'all need to get on your way."

"You think so? You think we should move on so that the two *y'all* can finish your meal—or whatever you're up to?"

Kurt didn't like anything the guy was saying. He was also inclined not to start fighting Emily's fights until she would welcome his interference.

But he really had a problem with people making fun of his accent like he had a character flaw.

He stepped forward and didn't hesitate to use either his taller height or his greater weight to his advantage. "If you've got a problem with me, you probably ought to come right out and say it. Seeing as I'm not real skilled on social niceties."

Emily pressed a hand to his bare forearm. "Kurt, it's okay."

Well, there was his answer. He wasn't going to win any points with her by making a scene in the restaurant. Or more of a scene, anyway.

He didn't like it, but he liked her enough to abide by her wishes. "All right, babe," he murmured. He turned to her, intending to help her back to her seat when the guy grabbed his arm.

"No wonder that kid of yours got off with barely a hand slap. Now I know how it works. Kids whose parents are sleeping with their teacher get special treatment."

That was that.

Not caring that the restaurant was filled, that it wasn't what Emily wanted, or that it wasn't even a fair fight, Kurt allowed generations of habits to roll into his body.

Next thing he knew, he'd slammed his fist into the guy's jaw and was standing over him.

The man's wife gasped. Two women at another table squealed.

Emily was probably pissed as hell, too.

But as he was standing over the guy, none of that registered. All that did was clearing this creep's misunderstanding. "She's not that kind of woman. You'd best start treating her with respect. And while you're at it, you should get one thing clear: Sam Holland ain't my son, he's my little brother."

The guy was dazed but awake and coherent.

"Now I see how your brother acted the way he did. He simply didn't know any better."

Most of the time he would've let a comment like that roll off his shoulders. He didn't have anything to prove to anyone and he'd long since stopped trying.

But everything that the man was saying hit a nerve. "He knows how to get along just fine. Including the fact that it's not okay to talk crap about decent women."

Emily pulled on his arm. "Kurt. Let's go."

Her voice was urgent and it brought him up short. Pulling himself together, he stepped back. Emily's needs had to come first. She worked with these kids. Had made a life here in Bridgeport. She didn't need him interfering with her life. Nodding, he threw down a trio of twenties on the table and reached for her hand.

Looking relieved, Emily placed it in his. Even from that small touch, he could feel the tension emanating from her.

He ran his thumb along the back of her hand.

Diners and waitstaff eyed him as he led them through the maze of tables.

"Sir!" the manager called out. "I need to speak to you about what just happened."

He stopped and pivoted to face him. The manager's face looked set, like he was gearing himself up to do something distasteful.

Realizing that he was most likely going to get thrown out of the restaurant in front of Emily, Kurt stood straight, intending to simply take it.

With a deep breath, the manager started talking. "We're going to need your contact information in case there's a further problem."

"There won't be. I'm leaving right now."

"I'm afraid I'm still going to need it. If I may have your cell phone number …"

"Why? No damage was done." Well, beyond the fact that Garrett's parents had just ruined his date. And no way was he going to be responsible for something that happened in the restaurant that he hadn't even been aware of.

"Even so …"

"Ken, don't be too hard on Kurt here," Emily interjected. "He was defending me. Mr. Condon was saying a lot of really bad things about me. Both Kurt and I tried to turn the other cheek, but sometimes you don't have a choice, you know?"

Ken's whole demeanor changed. Whereas before he looked ready to call the police, now he was acting like Emily was relaying an amusing antidote. "Is that right?"

Emily nodded. Smiling slightly, she added, "I would have hit him myself if I thought I could."

Everything about this situation was rubbing him wrong. "You don't need to fight my battles, Em."

She looked up at him and smiled. "I think maybe I do. I mean, you're fighting mine."

Kurt felt something shift inside of him. He couldn't remember the last time that he thought someone actually did have his back, no matter what.

Fearing that he was about to embarrass Em again by leaning down to kiss her, he said, "I think we should probably be taking off now, Ken." Holding out his hand, he decided to compromise. "My name is Kurt Holland. Let me know if you need me to pay for any problems I caused tonight."

"That'll do." Ken shook his hand. "You're new here, aren't you?"

"I am."

"Well, just so you know, Bridgeport isn't perfect but it's all right. Welcome."

"Thanks."

Grinning, he reached out for Emily's hand again. "You ready?"

Raising her chin, she cast him a soft look that made him feel like he'd finally done something to be proud of. "Yeah," she said softly.

Funny how that one word combined with her sweet smile told him everything he needed to know.

CHAPTER 16

FROM LES LARKE'S
TIPS FOR BEGINNING POKER PLAYERS:

*Don't show if you don't have to. Having a bit of
mystery about your game is always a good thing.*

Emily kept sneaking glances at Kurt as he drove. She couldn't help
it. So much about their date had felt momentous, starting with
his kiss.

Oh, that kiss! It had certainly taken her off guard. Not because
it had been so perfect but more because of her reaction to it. Ever
since Danny, she'd kept her guard up. She didn't act impulsively,
and she really didn't trust men easily.

But instead of making sure to keep up some kind of reserve in
order to guard her heart, she'd reacted to that kiss with complete
enthusiasm. She also hadn't regretted it.

She'd also been just as drawn to Kurt because of the way he'd
shared so much about his father. She'd known he didn't usually lay
his emotions or his worries out easily, but he'd trusted her enough
to do that. It had felt really special.

Then after dinner, when the only thing on her mind had been
to enjoy his attentions again, Garrett Condon's father had lashed
out at them.

Kurt hadn't missed a beat. He'd come to both his brother's and her defense. It hadn't been overbearing, though. He'd stood back at first, allowing her to stand up for herself. She'd appreciated that so much.

So much so that she'd been actually kind of gratified when he'd hit Ryan Condon. She knew she shouldn't have been glad that the man had gotten his comeuppance, but she actually kind of was. He was a bully, just like his son.

Emily realized then that she might as well face the truth. She was smitten. Flat-out gone.

She'd always imagined she'd end up with a man who was a whole lot more like her. Maybe a teacher or a principal. Someone from the suburbs like herself. Who shared a lot of the same experiences she did growing up.

But Kurt Holland, with his sexy West Virginia accent, form-fitting jeans, T-shirts, and boots and drop-dead good looks? She kind of hadn't stood a chance.

Now, as he drove with one hand laid on top of the steering wheel while he lazily guided his truck down the dark winding streets of Bridgeport, it was all she could do to not stare at him.

Or worse, say something revealing that he might find uncomfortable.

She settled for relaxing against the tan leather and reliving their night together.

When he pulled onto her street, he coughed. "Have I ruined everything?"

She sat up. "What? You mean with our date? No."

"You sure?" With his free hand, he raked his fingers through his hair. "Tell you the truth, I'm currently at a loss as to how to make things right. I know I'm supposed to tell you I'm sorry, but I'm really not."

She was thankful that all her years teaching school had given her some practice keeping her expression neutral. Otherwise she'd be grinning like a little girl on Christmas morning. He sounded that dejected. "Kurt, I'm not mad at you."

As if she hadn't spoken a word, he continued on. "Here's the thing. I couldn't really get mad at Sam for when he hit that kid because I would've done the same thing. Shoot. My dad would've done it, too." His voice thickened. "We don't hold with men shooting remarks like that toward our women."

Our women. She couldn't help it. She started smiling. "Is that what I am?"

"Damn. I messed up again, didn't I?"

As he parked on her driveway and turned off his engine, Emily looked at him in the dim light made by the sconces by the front door. "Kurt, it's okay. Ryan Condon is a jerk. He's had that reputation for a while. And I've been teaching for several years now. I don't expect everyone to always see eye to eye with me."

"He was being out of line."

"He was."

"I don't know how you women here in Bridgeport settle things either. You pissed I didn't continue to stand back and let you handle it?"

Though she was pretty sure she already knew the answer, she wanted to hear what he would say. "Would you have been able to do that?"

"Hell, no."

Unable to help herself, she started laughing. "Well, there's my answer."

Peeking at her, he smiled sheepishly. "Sam hadn't been kidding when he said that I wouldn't have sat by and let some kid talk trash about my girl. If I had been in Sam's situation, I would've done the same exact thing."

"I've kind of figured that out, Kurt." Hoping to inject some humor into the conversation, she said, "Seems you do have a better right hook than your little brother, though. Sam didn't draw blood."

"Sam is way better behaved than I've ever been." He stopped himself with a groan. "Well, I've now officially dug myself into a very deep hole."

She held up her thumb and index finger a few inches apart. "Maybe. Or maybe not."

"I don't know what else to say now."

"How about you just answer this, then. Do you want to come in?"

His head snapped around. When his gaze met hers, there wasn't a shred of remorse lingering there. In its place was something a whole lot more heated. "Yeah."

She felt chill bumps raise on her skin. One word and bam. She was toast. She reached for her car door.

"Hold on, babe."

"What?"

Looking at her steadily, the expression in his eyes illuminated by the street light a block away. "I do want to come inside, but I don't think I'd better."

"Why? Was I being too forward?"

"Not at all. It has more to do with the way you make me feel."

There went those chill bumps again. "I don't understand how that could be a bad thing then."

Like he couldn't help himself, he ran a finger down her forearm. "Let me put it this way. If I went inside, I'm not real sure I could keep things to just a couple of kisses."

She leaned closer and whispered, "Maybe I'm not just asking you for a couple of kisses, Kurt."

He closed his eyes like he was trying to gather his composure. "See, darlin', that's the problem. I'm trying to do this right. And that means we ought to take things a little slow."

She almost groaned in frustration. "I'm not seventeen."

"I'm so glad about that. And, baby, we both know that I'm not either. And that is why I've got no problem waiting a little longer. I don't want you waking up tomorrow and wondering if we made a

121

mistake. And, well, I don't want to wake up tomorrow and feel like I have to explain myself to my little brother."

That reminder jarred her away. "I guess I can understand that."

He brought his hand to her cheek. Cupped it lightly. "Are you sure? You okay with that?"

Her nerves calmed down a little, reminding her that she hadn't just been anticipating his kisses and his touch, she'd also been a little apprehensive about where things would go next.

"Yes, I think I am."

He unbuckled his seatbelt, then leaned over and unbuckled hers. "Good to know. Come over here, then."

"Because ..."

"Because I may not be ready to get into your bed but I sure am ready to feel you against me. Will you let me do that, Em?" he whispered.

What could she say to that?

Then, it turned out that nothing needed to be said because she felt two warm hands curve around her waist and pull her into his arms. Not caring that the skirt of her dress was edging up her legs, she settled her body against his, instinctively curving herself against the harder planes of his.

To her surprise, the position was more comfortable than it had been back when she was seventeen. She would have thought the opposite.

Looping her arms around his neck, she pressed her lips to his throat. "Are we going to make out in your truck, Kurt?"

"Nah. Just share a couple of kisses." His lips brushed her cheek then trailed down her jaw and into her neck. Each one felt like a mark on her skin. Light, sweet touches that would be imprinted into her memory and tease her, making her ache for him again.

After he raised his chin and their lips met, she ran her fingers through his hair as the kiss turned deeper.

Minutes later, when he pulled away, she felt a little breathless.

How could three or four kisses bring back those goosebumps? "We're too old to be necking in the driveway."

"Baby, I know you're real smart and all, but it's becoming real obvious that you don't know everything," he said before brushing his lips against hers again.

Another kiss led to more, which led to a moan when he pulled her close once more. When they finally broke apart and he came around to help her out of his vehicle, she felt flushed and languid and deliciously kissed.

"I had a good time tonight, Emily," he said as he took her keys from her and unlocked the door. "Thank you."

"Thank you, Kurt," she whispered as he leaned down and gently kissed her one last time.

Then he stood and watched while she walked inside. "Lock up, all right? I'll call you soon."

"'Kay," she replied, probably far too dreamily. After she watched him walk back to his truck and start the ignition, she turned and closed the door.

When she was alone at last, she sighed. Kurt Holland was like no man she'd ever dated. He was handsome and caring. Forceful and yet considerate of her needs. He had a drawl, could kiss like a dream, and had a whole lot more patience than she did.

And he wanted to take things slow because he wanted what was happening between them to last—and he wasn't afraid to admit it.

It had been a heck of a first date. She could hardly wait for the next.

CHAPTER 17

FROM LES LARKE'S
TIPS FOR BEGINNING POKER PLAYERS:

*It's better to make cheap mistakes than expensive ones.
If you're a novice, don't go in too big or too fast. There
will be plenty of opportunities to go further later.*

The call came at 6:05 the next morning.

With a groan, Emily rolled over and attempted to ignore it. When her mother's shrill ringtone sounded again, she glanced at the clock and put a pillow over her head.

When it sounded a third time, followed by a text, Emily knew she had no choice but to answer it. "Hi, Mom. Guess you couldn't wait until this afternoon to get on the phone?" Over the last few years, she'd instituted a "do not call before work" rule with her parents.

They often forgot just how early her days began during the week, not realizing that if her students reported to school at ten after seven, she was usually running around like crazy before that.

"You know I've been waiting all morning, just sitting around and watching the clock, Em. You aren't going to make me wait all day, are you?"

"Of course not." Though she kind of wanted to.

Stifling a yawn, she sat up in bed, thankful she'd put on her cute light blue cotton shorts and matching top to sleep in last night. She needed to feel like she was properly dressed to tackle the upcoming conversation.

"So, it sounds as if you had quite a night, dear."

Her mother's voice was laced with amusement. That was a good thing. The bad? That she'd called already armed with information. Now Emily was going to have to answer questions instead of being the one to dole out information. "I did," she replied.

"Come now. You've got to tell me more about all the commotion than that."

She sighed. "What have you heard? And more importantly, who told you?"

"Well …"

"Come on, Mom. Wait. Was it Brenden?" Because if it was, she couldn't wait to give her brother a call and remind him about the time she'd hid the letter from college that said he'd been put on probation for disorderly conduct.

"As a matter of fact, I did hear from Brenden, but he wasn't the only person to let me know they saw you and your date out at Paxton's last night."

"Do I even want to know who else called you?" For heaven's sakes! She got home after 11:00 and it was just now 6:00 a.m.

"Probably not." For the first time her mother's voice sounded contrite.

Emily didn't press further. All the drama was getting to be exhausting.

Leaning her head back against her headboard, Emily closed her eyes. Her female students always complained about the high school rumor mill. She'd never had the nerve to let them know that women's penchant for gossip didn't disappear with age.

Or that it wasn't a strictly female trait, given that Brenden had already been on the phone.

She cleared her throat. "Obviously you heard about Kurt and Mr. Condon."

"Well, I heard that Kurt Holland dramatically defended your honor. And that you defended his, too."

"The experience wasn't quite that noteworthy," Emily replied, though it actually kind of was. "One of my students' parents was being difficult and Kurt reminded him not to take out his disappointments on me."

"He sounds like a keeper, honey. When are you going to bring him by so we can meet him?"

"Not any time soon." She wanted Kurt to want to go out with her again, not get scared and run away.

"Really? That's hardly fair. Brenden met him already."

"Brenden was interested in poker. And he and Samantha showed up at my place when Kurt was here."

"Oh." Just as Emily released the breath she'd been holding, her mother perked up. "You know what? I think your father likes playing poker, too."

"Is that right? I never knew that," she said as she slipped out of the covers and headed toward the kitchen. It turned out that it wasn't enough that she was properly covered. She needed a strong caffeine injection, too.

"When is the next game scheduled? Do you know?"

"Nope." She poured fresh water into the carafe, added fresh coffee into the filter, then pressed start.

"Oh."

Though she knew better than to encourage her parents, Emily said, "Dad should probably ask Brenden about the next game. He'll know."

"I'll have him do that, honey. Of course, that means once Daddy meets Kurt only your sister and I won't have met your boyfriend."

"I'll see what I can do about that, Mom. Maybe I'll bring Kurt over for lunch one Sunday."

"He could join us for church," she said, sounding much more hopeful. "Does he go to church?"

"I'm not sure." She stared at the coffee pot, practically willing it to brew quicker.

"You haven't talked about your faith yet?"

"Not yet, Mom." Just as she was preparing herself to fend off another barrage of questions, her phone dinged, signaling an incoming text. "Oops. I've got to go."

"Okay. Let me know about next Sunday." "Will do. Love you, Mom," she said before reaching for her coffee cup. After taking two fortifying sips, she looked to see who'd texted. Maybe it was Kurt?

Want to go for a run tonight

It was Campbell. Not Kurt. She swallowed her disappointment.

idk

Come on. I heard about last night.

Yep, that rumor mill was running like clockwork for women of all ages. Reaching for the carafe, she filled her cup again, then typed her response.

Fine. I'll meet you at the
parking lot.

She definitely did not want to go for a run or talk to Campbell about last night's events. But a three-mile run equaled ice cream.

And even though it was only a quarter past six in the morning, she knew it was going to be an ice cream kind of day.

CHAPTER 18

"Trust everyone, but always cut the cards."
—BENNY BINION

Sam had been at Bridgeport High for five weeks and he felt like he was drowning. He had too much work and had too many teachers assuming that his previous school had already covered most of what they were covering.

It hadn't.

Within the first six or seven days at Bridgeport High, Sam had discovered that the curriculum back in Spartan hadn't been as extensive. Actually, it was filled with enough gaps to make the gorge out by the New River feel like the Grand Canyon.

The worst part of it was that he couldn't tell Kurt. His brother had moved his whole life so he could get a full scholarship into a fancy college. More than once, Kurt's eyes had gleamed with pride whenever he talked of Sam attending Stanford or Vanderbilt. In the past, it had always made Sam feel good, like he was worth something.

But now? It made him feel like crap.

What was Kurt going to say if he found out that Sam might even be making Bs in some of his classes? Making a slew of Bs on his report card wasn't going to get him into one of those colleges.

"Sam?" Miss Springer called out at the end of class. "Give me a minute, please."

That was Miss Springer's way. She didn't go out of her way to embarrass anyone in class. If she wanted something or had a concern, she'd ask the kid to stay late. And "ask" wasn't really what she did either. She was as good at telling kids what to do as any other teacher in the school.

While a couple of guys cast apologetic glances his way, Sam walked up to Miss Springer when the room had just about cleared out. She was sitting primly behind her desk.

"Yes, ma'am?" he asked before remembering that no one pulled out the ma'ams here and that the female teachers didn't even like hearing it all that much. Most just kept saying that it made them feel old.

Feeling his cheeks heat, he looked down at her desk. "Sorry," he muttered.

She shook her head like it wasn't even a thing. "Listen, I ... well, I wanted to talk to you about that last vocabulary test."

"Yes?"

She shuffled the papers around on her desk until she pulled out his. "Well, you made an eighty-eight."

"That's a B."

"You're right. It is." Staring down at his paper, she ran a finger along his mistakes. "For a lot of kids, an eighty-eight would be something to be happy about."

He couldn't take his eyes off those slashes of red. "But not me?"

After pushing the paper away, she looked him in the eye. "I know. You're not perfect. It's just that, well, even some of your right answers surprised me. The definitions of the words were correct, but they looked like they were memorized."

Now Sam was getting antsy and feeling more than a little defensive, too. What was wrong with getting the right answer? "I did memorize them. And if I got them correct, I don't understand why that's a bad thing."

The sides of her lips turned down. Almost like Miss Springer was disappointed that he wasn't easily grasping what she was saying. "It's just that I would've thought you would've had a better handle on the implied meaning of the words." She paused. "Is it just me? Or am I right in getting the feeling that you are struggling with these vocabulary words?"

The worry in her eyes made him take a deep breath and take his time answering. She wasn't getting on his case. She wasn't mad.

She was just trying to figure it out.

Kind of like what he'd been doing.

"It's not just you," he said, feeling like a load had just fallen off his shoulders. "I feel like I'm playing a part in a school play and I don't even understand how I got it in the first place."

"You have the highest standardized test scores in the class. Maybe even in the school, Sam. Then, there were your grades back in Spartan ..."

"I know. I made all As."

"That's why this eighty-eight concerns me." She studied him with her deep brown eyes that always made him think of the does in spring. "Is it me? Maybe you're used to a different way of teaching?"

She was giving him an out. She was that nice. No wonder Kurt was so interested in her. Leaning against one of the desks across from her, he knew he had to tell her the God's honest truth. "It isn't you. I don't know why I scored so high on those tests, Miss Springer. I'm a good test-taker, I guess. But a lot of those words on your quizzes, I've never seen before."

"Have you been studying for them?"

"Yeah. A lot."

She glanced at the phone on her desk. "I know you're ready to get out of here, so I'll let you go. But, um, regardless of what is going on with your brother and me, I wanted you to remember that

I was your teacher first before I was your brother's …"

"Girlfriend."

She smiled. "Yes. Before I was Kurt's girlfriend."

Ugh. He so did not want to be thinking about Miss Springer and his brother—not any more than he already had to.

He backed up a step. "Well, okay."

"If you want, I could tutor you a little bit. Help you with some of that vocabulary. It will help you the rest of the year."

"Thanks. I'll think about it." As in he wasn't going to do that.

Her brown eyes flickered with something that looked a lot like disappointment. "All right, then. Thank you, Sam."

After giving her a head nod, he exited the room, hoping Kayla was still around. Remembering that she probably had cheer practice, he decided to walk to where they practiced, just in case she had a minute. Then he could see if she needed a ride home.

Thinking about Kayla in those cheer shorts of hers. Looking forward to having her all to himself while he drove her home had its advantages, too. Already he felt better.

"What's the grin for, Holland?"

He turned and felt his insides twist up. Garrett Condon was standing in front of him, acting like he had a new picture on his phone. "What's it to you?"

"Nothing."

"So …"

Garrett glanced at his buddy Luke, who had just walked up but didn't look like he wanted to be there at all. "Just wondered what else you were cooking up with Miss Springer. Or do you call her Emily?"

"What the hell are you talking about?"

"I'm just hoping you get along with her since she's so tight with your brother now—and that she'll likely be out of a job soon."

Sam knew he should walk away. But there was no way he could, not when Garrett was bringing up his brother. "Why's that?"

131

"It's against the rules for her to be dating students' relatives. Plus my dad's gonna file charges against your brother. And when that happens, the principal's probably going to tell Miss Springer that she has to go, too."

Sam was feeling blindsided. "I don't know what you're talking about."

Garrett's expression was all innocence. "You don't know that your brother slugged my father at Paxton's in front of everyone on Sunday night?"

"No." Though it was opening him up, he couldn't resist getting more information. Looking over at Luke, he said, "What happened?"

But before Luke could answer, Garrett spoke again. "You really don't know? That wasn't why you were in Emily's room all cozy?"

The kid's voice was loud now. It sailed down the hallway, no doubt into the rooms of the faculty still at school.

"I don't know what your problem is with me but I think you're acting like an asshole."

Garrett scowled. "Oh, yeah?"

"Yeah."

Luke started looking uncomfortable. "We should drop it, Garrett."

"Why? So he can beat me up again?"

"I didn't beat you up," Sam retorted. "Don't make it into something it wasn't. And it ain't my fault that neither you or your father can get over the facts. You messed with my girlfriend and got what was coming to you. But instead of dealing with it, neither you nor your parents will let it go."

"I'll let it go when I'm sure that you're not getting special treatment because your brother is screwing your advisor."

Only the knowledge that another fight would ruin everything that his dad and Kurt planned stopped Sam from giving him a bloody nose.

He turned around and started walking.

"You walking away, Holland?" Garrett taunted. When Sam ignored him, his voice rose. "So I'm right? You are getting special treatment?"

Just as he was about to throw his future away, a teacher walked out in the hall and started chewing on Garrett.

Sam grinned when he realized it was Mrs. Filmore, who was as old as the school and mean, too. When he heard her say "detention," it was all he could do not to start laughing.

He continued to smile as he walked out the back of the school to where the cheerleaders were. He heard them before he saw them. They were all in a line and following one of the seniors through some complicated dance routine.

He watched for ten minutes. Long enough to admire Kayla in those shorts and long enough for her to catch sight of him and smile. But after another five minutes, it was obvious that she wasn't going to be getting done anytime soon. After making sure she had a way home, he walked back to the parking lot.

Only when he got into his truck did he allow his problems to resurface. Both his grades, the vocabulary, and the fact that Kurt hadn't seen the need to tell him about hitting Garrett's father.

That's when all the stress in his life rolled back into his chest and threatened to suffocate him.

There were some days when he wasn't sure if he was ever going to make it through the week, let alone the school year and getting into college with a scholarship.

Then there were days like today, when he would give just about anything if he could get on the highway and start driving back home.

CHAPTER 19

FROM LES LARKE'S
TIPS FOR BEGINNING POKER PLAYERS:

*Play against opponents worse than you. If you only
play against tournament winners, you'll always be the
loser. That won't help your game!*

There were twelve checkout lines at Walmart. Clerks were only at two of them. Looking at his cart, which was full to overbrimming, Kurt shifted and looked restlessly around him. He was sore, covered in sweat and grime, and he was pretty sure he'd gotten a blister on one of his heels from his new work boots.

And then there was the new mower he'd put a bid on. The seller was supposed to have given him an answer that morning, but here it was four o'clock, and he'd still not responded.

It was frustrating.

He really needed that mower. If he could get it, then he could hire another two guys and pick up some jobs.

Which meant that he'd have an even better cushion in the bank account to get through the winter.

As the customer three people in front of him finally swiped a credit card and went on her way, Kurt rolled his cart forward another couple of inches. He half prayed that the next person in line would simply pay for his items and not feel like chatting to the clerk about the weather.

His phone ringing was a welcome relief.

"Hey, Dad," he said. "What's up?"

"Hello, Kurt," his father said quietly, his voice sounding thicker than usual. "I didn't think I'd catch you on the phone. Thought you'd still be working since it wasn't near five o'clock yet."

Kurt heard the criticism in father's tone but tried to ignore it. "I've told you I usually stop this time of day. I'm at the building by seven or seven thirty most mornings." He stopped himself from saying what was really on his mind, which was if his dad hadn't expected him to pick up, why did he call in the first place?

"What are you doing now, Son?"

Worry started traipsing up his spine. "I'm standing in line at Walmart. Why? Do you need something?" He looked around, tempted to pull out of line so he could concentrate on his dad's words. Maybe he was sick or something?

"Since it ain't too convenient for you to bring me home some TV dinners, I'll say no."

His father had just made a joke. He sort of felt like trotting out one of the doors of the supercenter to see if the sky was still intact.

His father hadn't called to chew on him. No, he'd simply called to say hello. "How are you, Dad?"

"Pretty good. Ace stopped by to see me last night. He said y'all had a real good time together over there in Cincinnati."

"Yessir, we did."

"I heard y'all played some poker, too."

"We did. There ended up being six of us. We played Texas Hold'em in the garage."

"You found yourself that many men?"

"Yessir. It wasn't a crowd, but it was good enough."

"You win anything?"

"Nah. We kept a limit on the betting so nobody lost more than twenty bucks. We had a good time though. That's what mattered."

"Sounds like a real good time. Sorry I missed it."

He was? Impulsively, he said, "I was thinking about hosting another game in two weeks. You should come up for it."

"Is Ace coming back then?"

No way was Kurt going to share what Ace had told him about Liz and Finn. "I don't think so, but I'm not sure," he hedged. "But even if he stays back, you could come. If you wanted to, that is. You know we'd love to see you."

As his dad waited to answer, the line moved up again. The woman in front of him was setting her things on the conveyor like she worked on the line. He was going to get on out of there in no time.

Finally his dad spoke again. "You got room in your place for your old man?"

"You know I do."

"I'll think about it, then."

Kurt knew he wasn't going to get any more of an assurance than that. "All right. Good enough."

"How's Sam doing at his fancy new school?"

"Well enough, I reckon."

"That boy, you really think he's going to make something of himself, don't you?"

For the first time he could remember Kurt heard hope in his father's voice. "Yeah, Dad. I really do. I can't help but think that God gave him that brain for a reason."

"Maybe He did at that." He coughed. "I better get on my way and let you get to your grocery shopping."

"Yessir." Kurt opened his mouth to tell him something more—he wasn't sure what—but his father ended the call.

"You about ready?" the checkout girl asked.

"Huh? Oh, yeah." Reaching over, he started laying the items on the conveyor belt, feeling both melancholy and hopeful about the future.

***

He would have given anything to feel half as hopeful an hour later. Sam was in a snit and was bound and determined to make sure Kurt got that way, too.

The kid had been laying on the couch when he got home and acted like it had been an inconvenience to help unload all the groceries. His attitude hadn't gotten any better when Kurt had told him to finish putting everything away while he showered.

And now Sam was eating a can of soup and a roast beef sandwich with a big frown on his face. Honestly, the kid was acting like the simple supper was a huge disappointment, like he was used to someone cooking up meat with two sides.

"Wanna tell me what's going on with you?" Kurt asked after he rinsed his dish and set in on the counter to dry.

"Nothing."

That one word had been spit out like a curse word—and grated on him something fierce. "How about you try that again?"

Sam scraped his chair back. "Why do you even care?"

Where did that come from? Confusion and irritation matched with a real good dose of exhaustion and worry caused Kurt's tone to harden. "It might have slipped your mind but I'm real new at this parenting stuff so I don't know how I'm supposed to answer that. Except to remind you that I'm your brother. That's why I care."

"I didn't ask you to try to be my parent."

"Well, someone had to be since our father decided to take an early retirement." He leaned forward. "And don't start acting like this arrangement is a surprise or that we didn't talk about it either. 'Cause we did before we moved and since we got here, too."

"I didn't say it was a surprise."

"I know you didn't, 'cause you haven't said anything worth-while since I walked in the door." Just as he was about to tell his little brother exactly what he thought about that, he got a good look at Sam's eyes.

Shoot. The kid looked like he was about to start crying.

He stood up, thought about a beer, then decided on a glass of cold water. After drinking about half, he sat down on one of the other kitchen chairs. "Sam, when I was your age, I had Mom. She made chicken-fried steak, she did the grocery shopping, and she always acted like doing laundry and looking after us was something special."

He sighed, hating to bring up the memories but knowing that it was important. "Dad worked at the mine. He was a lot younger so I don't remember him complaining about his back so much. I do remember that he worked with Ace's dad and they went fishing every chance they could get."

Sam didn't say anything, but everything in his body language showed that he was listening intently.

So Kurt continued. "And me? Well, I went to school. I wasn't all that good at it. But I was pretty good at football. Not like Troy or even Ace, but good enough to be on varsity for three years. That was high school for me. I knew I wasn't going to go to college."

"'Cause we didn't have the money."

"You're right. We didn't. But it wouldn't have mattered if we had. I didn't want to go. I had just always planned on making money outside instead of in the middle of the earth." He paused, then continued. "What I'm trying to say is that I had a different life than you do. I'm trying to understand what you're going through, but I don't always know. You've got to talk to me."

Something in Sam's posture changed. "Do you ever wish you weren't here?"

"Hell, yeah."

His eyes widened. "Really?"

"Of course, really. Life is different here. The people are different." He thought about that, then corrected himself. "Or maybe it's just that they like different things."

"Some of 'em are spoiled."

"Yeah. Maybe that's it ... or maybe not." He shrugged.

"Maybe it's just that I miss my friends. I miss hanging out with people I've known all my life, just like I know you do."

"The guys back at home are all playing ball and having field parties."

"I know you miss playing football. I know you miss Coleman and the rest of your crew. But, things here are also real good, Sam."

"You mean that, don't you?"

Kurt nodded. "Just because it hasn't been easy doesn't mean I hate it. But some days are hard. I mean, I know jack about running my own business. If I didn't have Troy helping me out I probably would be having a heck of a time already working on my loan."

"I could help you out more."

He shook his head. "You already work twelve hours a week for me. If I need you more, I'll let you know. Look, I didn't say all that because I thought you needed to be reminded about Mom and Dad. I said it all because I'm trying to get you to remember that I don't have a clue about any of what you are going through. My life was real different. I had both parents and my goals were smaller. But that doesn't mean I don't care or want to help you if I can."

"Kurt, I'm okay."

"I know you aren't. But this doesn't work if you don't talk to me."

Sam leaned back his head. Then, like he was about to divulge a terrible secret, he sighed. "Fine. First off, I'm making a B in English. Miss Springer called me back after the bell and talked to me about my grades."

"Is a B bad? I always thought Bs were pretty good." They'd been really good in his world.

"Bs are all right for most people. Not me, though. I need to get into college."

"You will." Thinking of all the letters and brochures Sam received every day in the mail, he said, "Colleges have already started scouting you out."

"Kurt, I need to get a full scholarship to college and I'm not playing sports so it needs to be academic. And Bs don't cut it. I need to get straight As."

"What does Emily say you need to do?"

"Miss Springer volunteered to start tutoring me. She thinks my vocabulary is low."

"Then you better let her tutor you, Sam."

His brother hung his head.

"What else is going on?"

"School is a lot harder than I thought it was going to be," Sam said hesitantly. "I'm doing okay in everything else, but I've got to study, like, all the time. It's like I've got gaps that need to be filled in."

"Nothing wrong with studying."

"You don't understand. I'm having to teach myself stuff everyone else around here already learned. And it's only October. If I don't get better, I'm going to be making Bs in everything and I won't get into college at all."

Kurt's head was spinning. Never had he imagined that the school year would be anything but a walk in the park for his little brother. "Want me to talk to the principal about it? Or Emily?"

"No. Miss Springer is my advisor and I'm seventeen. I can talk to her on my own. I ... well, I just haven't known how to tell you." Looking like he was afraid Kurt was going to start storming around the room, Sam said, "Are you mad?"

"What? Hell, no."

"Promise?" His voice was tentative.

"I promise, Sam," he said, hoping he sounded even more positive. "Now, is there anything else on your mind?"

"Yeah." Sam stood up and carried his dishes to the counter. "Then I got in an argument with Garrett."

"Another one? Sam, I told you to give him space."

"That was kind of hard to do since he was bound and

determined to tell me that his dad was going to raise hell with the school about you."

"Me?"

"It seems that Garrett's dad is real sure I got special treatment because you're screwing Miss Springer."

Seeing red, Kurt rose to his feet. "You better apologize right now, Sam. That ain't no way to talk about your teachers or the woman I'm dating."

Sam rolled his eyes. "I didn't say those words, Garrett did. I was too busy staring at him like an idiot because you didn't tell me that you hit his father on Sunday night."

And just like that, the tables were neatly turned, and he was the one on the defensive. "I was hoping you wouldn't find out about that."

"If you didn't think word would get around then you're smoking crack. Of course everyone's going to be talking about it. This town is small, and everybody gossips like they get paid to do it."

Kurt couldn't disagree with that. "Don't worry about Garrett's father or the rumors. I'll fix it."

"I don't know how. The damage's been done."

Kurt realized then what he was going to have to do. He was going to have to cool things off with Emily for a while. It wasn't fair to make his brother deal with that crap.

It was going to hurt but they'd done too much in order for Sam to have these opportunities.

"Yeah," he said lightly. "You're probably right." He picked up the pot and started rinsing it out.

Sam stared at him. "Are you mad I told you?"

"Mad? No. Not at all. I should've told you about that argument with Mr. Condon. I didn't because I was embarrassed. And, if you want to know the truth, I wasn't all that sorry about it either. You and me ain't all that different when it comes to handling bad situations."

Sam stared at him for a moment. Then, to Kurt's surprise, he started grinning. "Guess you can take the Hollands out of West Virginia, but we're still just two hicks at the end of the day."

Kurt laughed. "Maybe you're right, kid. So, is there anything else we need to talk about? Might as well get it all out now."

"Besides struggling in school for the first time in my life, feeling guilty because I may not do what you moved your whole life here for me to do, and feeling squidgy because asshole kids are talking about my brother screwing my teacher? I'm good."

"Not that it is any of your business, but Emily and I have not been screwing around."

Sam groaned. "TMI!"

Feeling his cheeks heat, Kurt forced himself to continue. "What I'm trying to say is that I respect her. I respect Emily enough to take things slow. All I've done is kiss her." Of course some of that kissing had been on the heated side …

Sam wrinkled his nose. "I really don't want updates on this. Like, ever."

"Understood. I don't intend to tell you any more. I just, well, I started thinking about you and Kayla." And he was remembering that "respect" wasn't always the main thing on his mind when he'd been dating in high school.

Sam groaned. "Kayla and I are taking things slow, too. Real slow. Like, glacially slow."

"If you ever need to talk or …"

"I don't. Believe it or not, Dad already had that talk with me."

"No way." Kurt hadn't thought their father would've taken the time to discuss girls with his brother. All of a sudden, memories from that long-ago conversation hit him hard. He couldn't resist grinning. "Did he bring up vegetables?"

"Oh, yeah. I couldn't look at an ear of corn for two months."

Kurt started laughing. Then laughed so hard he couldn't even sit up. When he finally caught his breath enough to look at Sam, his little brother was grinning like he used to do when he'd won a slew of tickets at the county fair.

For a while there, after their mother's cancer diagnosis, their father's descent into depression, and with the stress of the move, Kurt had been afraid that his brother wasn't going to be able to ever laugh like that again.

A sense of peace filled him. No matter what the future held for them, this moment was real good. Worth a lot of grief just to have it.

CHAPTER 20

FROM LES LARKE'S
TIPS FOR BEGINNING POKER PLAYERS:

*Don't play when you're mad, sad, or in a generally
bad mood. Other players will notice this and take
advantage of your weaknesses. Plus, playing poker
this way won't lift your spirits.*

"You babysitting on Saturday night?" Sam asked Kayla as they
walked through the front lobby of Bridgeport High.

Kayla smiled at him, then felt a burst of satisfaction fill her as
she noticed more than one girl looked their way with an envious
expression. She actually couldn't blame them, since everyone
considered them a real couple now. One of her girlfriends said they
even looked like they were meant to be together.

She wasn't sure if they looked like a match or not. Today, she
was in her cheer uniform because it was game day. Sam was in his
usual jeans, tight T-shirt, and brown cowboy boots. He'd just gotten
another haircut, so his brown hair was cut real short, almost like
a military cut. It suited him though. So did his tan. He looked as
gorgeous as ever.

He was also carrying her laptop and chemistry book.

It was sweet. She'd never seen another boy carry her girlfriends' books. The first time he'd tried to do it, she'd tried to stop
him, explaining that no one did that here at Bridgeport. Sam had

looked real surprised, then shrugged and took her things anyway. She'd learned right then and there that Sam Holland didn't put a whole lot of stock in what everybody else did. He did what he wanted. End of story.

She was starting to imagine that he must have been a heart-breaker back at his old school. He was smart, crazy handsome, he'd played on his old school's football team, and did things like carry his girlfriend's books.

She didn't know how she'd gotten so lucky.

His pace slowed. "Kay, do you know your schedule for Saturday yet?"

"Hmm? Oh, sorry. No. I'm not babysitting." She smiled at him. Waiting.

But instead of smiling like he was pleased, he looked worried. "All right, then."

"Why?"

"You know why. I want to see you."

"Then why are you looking like something's wrong?"

He swallowed. "It's just that I wanted to take you to the movies."

A dark theater next to Sam? She couldn't resist smiling. "That sounds good. I like movies."

If anything, her response seemed to make him more uncom-fortable. "I've been so busy with school I haven't been able to work as much as usual. I don't have a lot of extra money."

He'd also taken her out to eat twice last week. "Would you like to come over and watch movies in our family room?"

"You'd be okay with that?"

"I'm fine with it. I don't want you spending all your money on me, Sam."

He still didn't look convinced. "Your parents won't mind if I'm over for a couple of hours?"

"Sam, you know my mother loves you. She's told me twice that you're the most polite boy she's ever met in her life. She'll be glad

145

we're at my house." Lowering her voice, she added, "She's probably going to be happy that she can check on us every twenty minutes." Which would be better than her annoying sister joining them.

He stopped in front of her class. Lowering his voice, he leaned close. "It will be hard to keep my hands off you, but I'll try."

She laughed. So far they hadn't done anything but kiss a few times. She knew he'd never try anything at her house anyway. "Let's plan on it then. I'll let my parents know." Glancing into her classroom, she realized almost everyone was already sitting down. "I better go in."

"Here's your books. I better get on, too."

"See you after school? I don't have to be back here until 5:30." Even when Sam didn't drive her home, he still met her at her locker.

"Oh." A shadow slipped in his expression again. "I've got to meet with Miss Springer."

"Will you be meeting with her long? If not, I could wait and you could take me home." She smiled. "I'll even treat you to some fries if you want."

"That sounds great, but, um, I don't know how long I'm gonna be. I'll call you later. Or I'll see you at the game, okay?"

"Oh. All right." He was acting weird. If he hadn't just asked her about Saturday night, she would've thought he was mad at her.

"I better get to class. See you, Kay." He turned away before she could kiss his cheek, something she'd recently started doing that he thought was kind of cute.

"Yeah, see you," she murmured as she watched him walk away. Something was wrong. Something was really wrong with him.

***

It was just as well that Sam hadn't been able to give her a ride home because her coach had ended up calling an emergency practice because Missy was sick and so all of their formations had to be changed.

Luckily, they'd done stuff like this before and were done within forty-five minutes. And, thank goodness, Megan offered to give her a ride home.

"Thanks for the ride," she said as they climbed into her sporty little VW Bug.

"It's no problem, though where is Sam? I thought he was your permanent ride now."

"He said he had to meet with a teacher. I guess it took a while."

Megan gripped her steering wheel tighter. "I bet they wanted to talk to him about how smart he is or something."

"What are you talking about?" She knew Sam scored real high on his SATs and a couple of other standardized tests—he'd shared that with her during one of their first conversations—but she didn't think his big brain was common knowledge.

"Caroline sat next to him in physics. She said he finished most of the work first but tried not to make a big deal about it."

"How did she know what he was doing? Was she watching him or something?" A sharp pang of jealousy hit her hard. Caroline was everything she wasn't. Confident and model-in-a-magazine pretty. Plus she had money so she wasn't always scrambling around to make ends meet—or letting her boyfriend pay for all her meals.

Was that what was wrong? Was Sam thinking she was taking advantage of him?

Megan laughed. "You are so whipped."

"Maybe." She smiled with a shrug. "I guess I am."

"I knew it. You are in love with your brainiac boyfriend."

There it was again. "Megan, what exactly happened in physics? I need to know, 'cause if it was bad, Sam will never tell me."

"Fine. Mr. Wexler started making a big deal about it. Caro said he made such a fuss that the whole class was embarrassed for Sam."

"Ugh. Mr. Wexler is creepy. Poor Sam."

"Yeah. Even the regular brownnosers felt bad for him. But Caroline said that your boyfriend just shrugged it off like it was no big deal."

A burst of happiness filled her again. That was Sam, she was discovering. He took everything in stride. "He's so great."

Megan grinned. "You are so into him."

"I can't help it."

"You are so lucky," she gushed. "He seems like the best boyfriend."

"He is. He's coming over on Saturday night to watch movies."

"I would say that was boring, but it sounds perfect."

"Yeah. It does." She just hoped she wasn't imagining that they were closer than they really were. Or that she hadn't done something that he didn't like.

All the sudden, every little insecurity she had came out sharp and painful. What if he wasn't thinking she was as perfect for him? What if he was starting to wish she was in a bunch of AP classes, too?

As Megan pulled down her street, she looked worried. "Hey, I didn't say anything wrong, did I? I mean, you don't think I want him or anything?"

"Of course not."

"So we're good?"

"Of course." She pasted a smile on her face. It was one her mother would know was fake in a heartbeat but maybe Megan wouldn't think anything about.

When Megan started talking about their cheer routine and the latest schedule, Kayla pretended she cared about all that.

But as she walked to her door, all she could think about was Sam. Something was bothering him. Something pretty big. Somehow, someway, she was going to have to figure out how to get him to tell her what it was.

CHAPTER 21

By the time Sam walked out of Miss Springer's classroom at four thirty, he was thinking he should call up Anton and apologize to him. Back home, Anton had always been teased because he couldn't read as well as everyone else.

When they were small, Anton used to break out in a cold sweat when their teacher made him read out loud. Later, he was always in the remedial classes and had been called all kinds of names.

Course, that had all changed when they'd gotten into eighth grade. Anton had gotten huge and was a starter on both the basketball and football teams. Then, nobody was going to tease him about anything.

Sam had almost forgotten about Anton's problems in school. In his circle of friends, nobody went around discussing grades or report cards anyway. Other stuff mattered, like the fact that Anton had been the first in his group to letter in a sport. When he'd shown up in his new jacket, Sam had been as jealous as all get out.

But now, after sitting and struggling and feeling like half the school knew he was having to get extra help, Sam felt like calling up his buddy and apologizing for never offering to help the guy.

***

"How did it go?" Kurt asked as he walked in the door at six that night.

Sam had just pulled up directions on his phone for how to mash potatoes. He was going to learn how to cook something decent if it killed him.

"All right." Thinking about how easygoing Miss Springer had been, Sam added, "Miss Springer said my only problem was my familiarity with the words. So every week she's going to give me a list of words that I gotta learn, then when we're together we have to have a conversation where we use them."

"Sounds easy enough."

"Yeah. There's a heck of a lot of words she wants me to learn, though. I don't know how we're going to talk about anything that makes sense."

"You'll figure it out."

Sam nodded. "Yeah."

"So, what are you doing now?"

Sam held up his phone, showing off the screen. "I'm trying to figure out how to fix potatoes."

Kurt opened a drawer, pulled out two potatoes, and set them on the counter. "All you do is wash them, poke a couple of holes in them, and put them in the oven for an hour."

"I want them mashed."

"Then you boil the heck out of 'em and add a bunch of milk and butter."

"The last time we tried that they turned into paste."

Kurt frowned. "Yeah. I guess they were pretty bad." When his gaze drifted to the package of chicken breasts, he smiled. "You cooking tonight?"

"Trying to."

"What are you going to do to the chicken?"

"I'm grilling that."

"What's the occasion?"

"Nothing. Just figured I'd start helping out more. Plus, I'm starving. I want something before I go to the game."

"Huh." His brother watched him for a moment before walking over to the kitchen sink and scrubbing his hands. "What are your plans for Saturday?"

"I'm seeing Kayla."

"What are y'all gonna do?"

Hating how lame it sounded, Sam mumbled, "We're going to watch movies at her house."

Grabbing a paper towel, Kurt looked at him curiously. "Kayla doesn't want to go to the movies?"

"I can't afford it."

"You need money?" Kurt pulled his wallet out of his back pocket. "I think I've got an extra fifty bucks."

"I don't need it."

"You sure?" He walked closer. "You know, I just now realized that you haven't been working much this week because of all your homework. Plus, you paid Miss Springer, right?"

"Yeah. It wasn't much."

"What did she charge? Only twenty bucks, right?"

Sam nodded. Kurt told him that he and Miss Springer had argued about her getting paid to tutor Sam. They'd compromised on twenty dollars.

Kurt rubbed his head like Sam was giving him a headache. "I should've given you some money. Like an allowance or something."

That made Sam feel like even more of a disappointment. "Because you got all kinds of money from Dad."

Kurt pulled his chin up. "You know Dad wasn't giving me money."

"I don't need any either. I'll be fine."

151

"Sam, I'm gonna keep saying this until you get it, okay? Your life is supposed to be different than mine. I want it to be."

"I don't want to mooch off you."

"Here in Bridgeport, I'm not just your brother, I'm your guardian."

"So?"

"So that means you've got to listen to me some," he said with exaggerated patience. "I'm supposed to be taking care of you."

He was seventeen, not seven. "I'll let you know if I need any cash, okay?"

Kurt threw up his hands. "Fine. While you try not to burn the house down, I'm gonna go take a shower. I smell like crap."

When Sam was alone in the kitchen again, he leaned against the counter and tried to figure out what to do next. He needed to get better grades. He needed to figure out vocabulary. He needed to get some money so he wouldn't lose Kayla.

And he needed to do it all fast and without losing his brother's respect.

Too bad he didn't have an idea about how to do any of that.

CHAPTER 22

FROM LES LARKE'S
TIPS FOR BEGINNING POKER PLAYERS:

Take the time to understand your position in the game. This will save you lots of costly mistakes.

Emily knew something was wrong the moment she saw Kurt on her doorstep. She now knew him well enough to know that he was always respectful of her space and her time. He didn't show up places without warning or do things on the spur of the moment.

At least, she hadn't thought so.

But as she spied his haggard expression, Emily knew whatever he had come over to say wasn't good. Feeling dread pool in the pit of her stomach, she opened the door to let him in.

"I'd like to tell myself that you couldn't wait to see me, but I don't think that's why you're here," she teased.

"Hey, Emily." He fussed with his ball cap then stuck it back on his head, now with the rim facing backward. "You're not wrong. I have been wanting to see you …"

"But …"

He stuffed his hands in the back of his cargo shorts. "But yeah, you're right, too. I'm sorry to show up out of the blue like this, but do you have a few minutes free? I think we need to talk."

"I have as many minutes as you need." She waved a hand at her old college T-shirt and nylon shorts. "I was just looking for a reason to stop cleaning my shower." When he didn't smile at her artless comment, Emily ushered him in. "Want to come sit down in the living room?"

She started walking, dread filling her with every step. Was he here to break things off with her? She didn't know why he'd want to do that, but she couldn't think of another reason he would have shown up at her door looking as agitated as he did.

Kurt followed. His footsteps were slow. It was almost like he was trying to put off whatever he'd come over to talk about.

"Have a seat. Would you like a glass of water or something?"

"Nah, I'm good."

When he perched on the edge of the couch, every bit of his body looking tense, she said, "My mom always told me that it was better to get the hard stuff over with. So, um, whatever you have to say? Just spit it out." She sat down across from him and braced herself.

He took a deep breath and fisted his hands on his knees, then, right before her eyes, seemed to center himself. When he finally spoke, his drawl was coating his words like a thick slab of peanut butter. "I really like you, Emily."

Emily was so surprised, she almost laughed. "I like you, too." She smiled at him as she leaned back in her chair. "Boy, you had me going there for a minute. I thought you'd come over here to tell me you found someone new to date."

"No, that ain't it at all," he blurted, his accent thick. He frowned. Rubbed the scruff on his cheek. "Actually, I can't think of another woman I would ever want to spend so much time with. I think about you all the time."

His words were sweet and artless. So frank and bare, she was half ready to go tackle him on the couch. But what wasn't sweet was his expression. He was looking like his dog had just died. "Thinking about me is good, right?"

"Yeah. But not really."

"Maybe you could explain that a little bit?"

"I'm trying, but this sucks. Here's the deal, Emily. I do like you. I do think about you a lot. One day soon, I'd like us to see each other exclusively."

"One day soon?" Her stomach was now in knots. Kurt's words and emotions were all over the place and she was having a heck of a time keeping up. "What's wrong with now?"

"I started realizing that we've got ourselves a conflict of interest. On account of the fact that you are Sam's English teacher."

"So we're breaking up because of Sam?" She thought back to yesterday's tutoring session with Sam. She'd thought it went all right. At first he'd acted embarrassed to be there, but after she'd shared her plan, he'd perked right up.

At least, she thought he had. "Did Sam say something to you about yesterday's tutoring? Did I upset him somehow?"

"No, it ain't that at all. It's the fact that the lines between us all are getting crossed."

"Kurt, um, you may have forgotten this, but even if me teaching him was a problem—which it isn't—I won't be his teacher next semester."

Some of the lines in his cheeks eased. "Shoot, you know I had forgotten that. So we won't have to wait that long. We can start up again in January."

She remembered Campbell once telling her about a guy her sister dated who never kept a girlfriend around the holidays because he didn't want to buy a Christmas gift or take her to office parties. If she didn't know better, she would wonder if something like that was going on.

Except he seemed so sincere about it.

Making a decision, she stepped around her coffee table and took a seat next to him on the couch. "Kurt, talk to me. I don't understand why you suddenly think this is a problem. What's changed?"

"Sam had a … well, an altercation with Garrett Condon a couple of days ago. Garrett mentioned that I slugged his dad."

"And let me guess, Sam wasn't real happy about that."

"No. He actually had some choice words for me, threw quite a few of them back in my face."

"I think teenagers are pros at saying hurtful things from time to time, Kurt. Sam is smart, but he's still only seventeen."

"Yeah, I know. But, well, there's something else he brought up that got me thinking. Sam mentioned that Garrett and his parents have started telling people that Sam's been getting special treatment because I'm, ah, seeing you."

"It's sweet you care about my reputation, but it doesn't really matter what Garrett or his father thinks. We know what's true." When his expression didn't ease, she added, "Believe it or not, I've already mentioned our dating to Terry Hendrix."

Looking alarmed, Kurt straightened. "You talked about us to your principal?"

She nodded. "He didn't act like the news was fantastic, but he agreed with me, that me dating a student's older brother wasn't anything to be concerned about. Especially since it's our private business."

"But see, that's the thing. Bridgeport is small enough that anything we do isn't going to be all that private. People are going to see us together."

"I appreciate you looking out for me and my reputation, but I'm fine."

"For now. But you know how rumors are spread."

Emily studied him. Looked at his rigid posture. The hard set of his jaw. The resolution in his eyes. He'd come over to break things off, not discuss their future.

He didn't want to hear her arguments or try to make things work. It seemed he had an answer for everything. He didn't come over to talk things through with her. He came over to inform her about his decision.

Which really kind of ticked her off and made her sad at the same time.

She stood up. "I think I understand now. Thank you for coming over to tell me in person."

He scowled. "It wasn't like I was going to text you or something. I don't want to not see you, but I'm trying to do the right thing here."

"I understand." Though she actually didn't.

He got to his feet. "Emily, this isn't easy for me."

Maybe it wasn't. But she sure knew what was happening wasn't easy for her to hear. "Goodbye, Kurt."

His dark blue eyes looked stormy, almost silver as he got to his feet. But that was surely her imagination. "I'll give you a call in January."

"You'd better not. I'm not going to be available."

He paused, then kept walking.

She stood there, her back to him as he opened and then shut her door behind him.

When she was finally alone she sank back down in her favorite comfy chair. Then she curved her hand in as tight of a fist as she could and hit the cushion.

Why did everything have to be so hard? She'd finally found a guy who was everything she'd ever hoped he would be. He was handsome and hardworking. Had a job. He treated her with kindness. He'd moved his whole life to another state so his little brother could have a future he'd never had.

He'd befriended her brother and her brother-in-law. She'd thought he was darn near perfect.

And then, what did he go and do? He broke up with her the moment things got difficult.

He broke her heart and walked away.

Huh. Turned out he wasn't perfect after all.

CHAPTER 23

FROM LES LARKE'S
TIPS FOR BEGINNING POKER PLAYERS:

Don't stay in a hand just because you're already in it. Sometimes it's better to cut your losses and walk away ... even though it might hurt at the time.

Driving down Broadway, Kurt barely noticed anything but his pain.

He'd known cutting things off with Emily was going to hurt but he hadn't counted on it hurting so bad. He felt like crap. Like he was that guy in the news who had cut off his own arm in order to free himself.

Okay, maybe that wasn't the right analogy. That guy had desperately wanted to live. Him? Well, maybe he was just running scared.

He felt like he had been thrown headfirst into the deep end of the pool and he was trying to tread water while keeping his little brother afloat.

Realizing he had once again compared his situation to some life or death scenario, he cursed. He needed to man up and stop feeling sorry for himself. Sooner or later he was going to have to call Ace and tell him to drive up to Bridgeport to kick his ass.

Parking in the drive outside his garage, he eyed the front door. He knew what he needed to do. That was go sit in front of his computer for the next two hours and work on statements and entering in the day's jobs.

But given his current mood, he knew he'd likely make mistakes that he'd have to spend twice as much time fixing tomorrow or he would get so stressed out about the business all his doubts would set in again.

He couldn't do it.

That left only one other idea.

Pushing the remote on his garage door, he walked inside and turned on the light. The room was pretty much the same way he'd left it after the last poker game. Neatly swept, though now covered with a fine layer of dust.

A large table with six chairs was in the middle. To one side of the garage, an old table he'd found discarded on a neighbor's driveway held piles of poker chips. Two decks of cards lay next to them, one unopened. Underneath the table was what used to be his pride and joy—a Yeti cooler that a couple of his cousins had gone in on together to buy him for high school graduation. They'd given it to him with big smiles, grinning even wider when he'd opened it to find a layer of Dr. Pepper, and underneath that a twelve-pack of Corona.

His father had looked at that cooler and shaken his head, saying it was a giant waste of money. But to Kurt it had symbolized freedom and more than one dream—that one day he was going to have a couple of things that meant a lot to him. The chance to be his own boss. A house. A good truck. Friends to count on.

What he'd hated to admit even back then was that he'd wanted more than what his father had ever been able to get— years of back-breaking work underground, followed by an early retirement alone.

The thought made him feel ashamed that he couldn't feel more pride in his father's choices. He'd done the best he could. He'd surely done his best for him.

Just like he was now trying to do his best for his little brother.
It was just a crying shame that he was struggling so much with it.

When his phone buzzed, signaling an incoming text, he almost
thanked God. He needed to get out of this funk, and fast. It was his
friend Troy.

Hey. What you doing?

Kurt shook his head. Troy was his one of his oldest friends.
He was the reason Kurt had chosen Bridgeport instead of some
other town to move Sam to. The guy had played ball with him
and Ace in Spartan, but had been so talented that he'd earned
himself a scholarship. He'd gone to college at Ohio University over
in Athens, playing ball for them and studying accounting. Now
he'd made a life for himself in Bridgeport and had a successful
accounting firm.

But even though he'd done all that, he still texted like a
twelve-year-old.

Taking a seat on one of the chairs, he texted back.

Sitting in the garage. You?

U playing poker?

Nope. Sitting alone.

He didn't bother adding that it was eleven on a Saturday
morning. Not too many guys were up for an early morning poker
game. Reading his text again, Kurt hesitated before pressing SEND.
His text sounded lame, but what did you do? It wasn't like he had
anything to prove to Troy.

Want company?

Sure. You alone?

Nope. Jim and me just did 9. We'd B
up for a game if U R

Come over. I'll see if I can
find two more guys. But
poker later @ 6

K. We could eat first

Shaking his head, Kurt's thumb scanned his contacts and reached out to Brian, one of his new workers who was an all-around decent guy.

Thinking about playing
tonight. 6. You free?

Ten minutes later Brian and one of his buddies said they'd be over around 5:30.

Kurt smiled. He had a poker game. Walking in the house to change clothes, he passed Sam who was doing some texting of his own while eating what looked like the contents of half his refrigerator.

He looked over at him. "What's going on?"

"I've got some guys coming over to play poker. You still going over to Kayla's?"

"Yeah."

"Great. Want to have dinner with Troy and me before you head over?"

"Yeah. Sure."

When Kurt walked back to the garage, he thought about Emily's brother Brenden and her brother-in-law, Chris. Though he figured that cooling things off with Em meant cooling things off with them, too, he wondered if the guys would feel the same. Maybe not. Poker was poker, right?

Taking a chance, he went ahead and texted them about the game, too. It would be up to them to decide whether they wanted to come over again.

CHAPTER 24

FROM LES LARKE'S
TIPS FOR BEGINNING POKER PLAYERS:

You can't bluff someone who's not paying attention.

Campbell wiped away a line of sweat from her forehead with one of her light pink towels. Then she frowned at Emily. "You know, most women like to go out after a breakup. They get dressed up, put on cute dresses and high heels, and flirt with men who buy them drinks. They don't go to extra classes of hot yoga."

They'd just finished another hot yoga class and were standing in the back of the room trying to recover. It was their third class in five days and Emily didn't blame her girlfriend one bit for complaining.

Especially since she wasn't sure if the extra workouts were helping her mood much.

As she stuffed her own damp towel in her gym bag, she said, "Think about how much healthier this is. It's cheaper, too."

"All I'm doing is thinking about how many extra showers I'm having to take a day. It's getting pretty old."

"Maybe we're losing weight?"

"I doubt I am. I've been in so much pain, I've been single-handedly eating a pint of Graeter's chocolate–chocolate chip ice cream every night when I get home." Looking at Emily's figure, she frowned. "Besides, you don't need to lose anything. You never did. Actually, you're looking kind of peaked, if you want to know the truth."

"Thanks for that."

"Only keeping it real, Em."

Since she was feeling kind of piqued, Emily didn't bother arguing too much. The truth was that she *had* lost weight. Not a lot, but probably six or seven pounds. Enough to make her jeans feel loose.

After draining her water bottle and gathering the last of her things, she asked, "You ready to get out of here?"

"Yep." Picking up her Vera Bradley tote, Campbell led the way, once again looking far too pretty for a girl who had just sweat out half her body weight.

When they got outside, Campbell gestured to the mother and daughter who'd been working out next to them. They were gulping water and staring longingly at the door to El Fenix. "They've got the right idea. Want to grab some tacos?"

Unlike Campbell, Emily both looked and smelled like a wet rat. "I can't go inside like this."

Looking her over with a critical eye, Campbell grinned. "I think you are right about that. I know—I'll go in, order, and when it's ready, we'll escape to your place and pig out."

"I'm not really hungry." As much as she liked the idea of indulging in a Mexican feast, she just wanted to shower and watch mindless hours of TV until she could fall asleep.

"Do you have wine at home?"

"Of course."

"Then you're set. We'll drink some wine and eat tacos."

"While we're all gross and sweaty."

"No, silly. You can let me use your shower." She patted her tote. I have an extra pair of leggings and a T-shirt in here."

"Why am I getting the feeling that you planned for this?"

"Because one of us needs to make plans. So what do you want? Your usual burrito?"

Emily shook her head. She felt like trying something different this time. "No, get me some tacos. And some guacamole. And maybe some chips and salsa, too."

Campbell smiled. "I'm on it." She disappeared into the restaurant, bold as brass.

Emily wished she had even half the confidence that her cousin did at that moment.

Two minutes later, she was wishing she had even that little bit back, because that would mean that she didn't feel like sinking into the ground when Kurt Holland's truck pulled up.

She was staring at the back fender and wondering why she hadn't run into the gym's locker room and freshened up when both of the truck's doors opened.

"Miss Springer?" Sam called out.

He sounded puzzled, like he wasn't really sure it was her. She wasn't surprised. She was pretty sure she looked like something out of *The Walking Dead*. "Hey, Sam." Then, because she was an adult, she forced herself to lift her chin and meet Kurt's eyes. "Hi, Kurt," she said, just as she realized that her embarrassment wasn't complete. He had another man with him, too. "Hi."

At least he looked as uncomfortable as she was. "Hey, Emily. Looks like you went to hot yoga again?"

"Obviously." After another tight smile she turned to Sam. "Going out for Mexican?"

Sam looked from her to his brother. "Uh-huh. What are you doing?"

"My girlfriend went inside to order. She'll be out soon." Please, God, let her be out soon.

The other guy, who was tan, built like a quarterback, and had light blond—almost white—hair, stepped forward with his hand outstretched. "Hi. I'm Troy Gordon."

"Hi," she said, shaking his hand. "I'm Emily Springer. Nice to meet you."

Troy looked from her to Kurt to Sam. "So, how do y'all know each other?"

Kurt stepped forward. "Emily and I—"

No way did she want Kurt talking about their nonexistent dating life. "I'm Sam's English teacher."

Something new entered his eyes. "Good to know."

Kurt narrowed his eyes ... just as Campbell flew out the door, somehow looking like she'd been out shopping instead of sweating. Even her fairy-princess hair was down and perfectly curled. "They said five minutes, Em. This was a great idea. Oh!"

Immediately all three guys turned to her. Emily could practically see the appreciation in their eyes. "Campbell, this is Kurt, his brother, Sam, and their friend Troy. Guys, this is my best friend, Campbell."

"Hi." She smiled at Sam. "You should probably call me Miss Weiss. I teach freshman math."

"Were you doing hot yoga, too?" Sam asked.

She smiled. "I was."

"Campbell might be my best friend, but I often hate her," Emily joked. "She has a freakish way of always looking good, even after exercising. It's annoying."

Campbell looked down at herself and frowned. "Emily tends to exaggerate. I need to get cleaned up, and fast."

"I think you look fine," Troy said. "More than fine."

Sam grinned down at his feet.

Feeling Kurt's gaze zeroed in on her, Emily said to Campbell, "You know what? I bet those five minutes are already up. I'll go in and pay with you."

"There's no need to do that. I've already paid."

"Camp ..."

"Don't worry about it. It wasn't a big deal. Besides you're nursing a broken …" Her expression fell. "You know what? I'm going to go back in. I think our food's done by now."

"I'll go in with you," Troy said. "Sam, want to cool off inside?"

"Sure." After a kind of half wave her way, Sam followed Troy and Campbell into the restaurant. Leaving her alone with Kurt.

He leaned against his truck and folded his arms. "Nursing a broken what?"

No, no, no. She was definitely not going there. "I don't think we have anything to say to each other."

"You know I didn't want things to be like this."

"Like what?" she pushed, just because she was irritated with him enough to push it.

"Awkward," he explained, just like that was something meaningful. He shifted, pulling the black ball cap lower on his forehead.

She wondered if he did that so she wouldn't be able to see his eyes, or so he couldn't see hers.

But did it even matter? "I think things are going to be awkward between us no matter what."

"It doesn't have to be, though. I bet if we tried, the two of us could be friends."

Oh, hell no. He was not going to start throwing that friendship line her way. "Um, I don't think so."

He flinched. After glancing around them, as if to make sure their conversation was completely private, he pulled up the brim of his hat. "You know I didn't mean to hurt you," he said, sincerity shining in his deep blue eyes.

"But you did. And you knew what was going to happen, too."

Looking affronted, he stood up straighter. "Emily, you know I didn't intend for this to happen."

"I know that. But I'm not sure if that even matters. You knew I trusted you, and you knew I didn't trust easily. So that's where you're wrong, Kurt Holland. You definitely did want things to be like this. I wanted to work things out. I wanted to try to help you."

"You couldn't have."

"You wouldn't let me," she countered, hating that her voice was quivering with emotion. "Instead of trusting me back, you broke things off. And that's why I'm so upset."

He gazed at her a moment longer, then nodded. "You're right. that's exactly what I did. I didn't know it was going to be so hard though." Looking almost like he was talking to himself, he added, "I think I made a mistake."

She was torn between shock that he'd admit it and irritation that he was being so honest. What had ever happened to good old evasion tactics? "I don't know how you expect me to respond to that."

"I know. But maybe you would have an easier time to respond to this: I already miss you."

He already missed her.

If they were standing in the parking lot out in the open she would have started crying. Or maybe started yelling at him, really loud. He was playing games with her. Oh, maybe not intentionally, but it was close enough for her to feel a little used. She turned away. "If you see Campbell, tell her I'm in the car."

"Emily—"

Still afraid to look at him, she kept her back to him. "I'm really sorry, Kurt, but I don't think we have anything more to say to each other."

"I'm thinking you're wrong," he said quietly. "I'm going to fix all this."

She didn't say a word about that. After all, hadn't they already said everything they could?

She turned on the car, blasted the air conditioner, and closed her eyes. She prayed for strength and patience, and maybe, if He was so inclined, to stop meeting hot guys right after hot yoga.

Her door opened and Campbell slid in, holding a large white shopping bag filled with delicious-smelling food. "Guess what?"

"I can't even imagine."

"Troy asked me for my number! Isn't that something?"

It was familiar, that's what it was. Smiling tightly, she put her car into reverse and pulled out of the parking lot. "It sure is," she said with what she hoped was a good dose of enthusiasm. "Well, don't hold back. Tell me what he said."

"First of all, Troy said he knew it wasn't what girls wanted to hear anymore, but he thought I was pretty. Can you believe that?"

"Ah, yes, I can. You are pretty."

Campbell shrugged. "I'm all right. And, look. I've been around enough to know when guys feed me a line. So I know that was what he was probably doing. But then he said something that got my attention."

In spite of her bad mood and heartache, Emily was sucked in. "And what was that?"

"He said he was hoping he could have my number and we could text each other for the next week because he was busy all weekend with something that he couldn't get out of."

Emily inwardly winced. After debating for a moment, she said, "Campbell, not to be mean, but he probably already has a date lined up."

"Oh, that's what I said! But he told me no and that he'd volunteered to help at the youth fair at Nesbit Park next Saturday." Her voice softened. "Troy's going to be helping with the football camp for little guys. That's when I said I was going to be working at the fair, too."

"You are? I didn't know that. What are you going to do?"

"I'm helping out in the reading tent. We plan to give every child and teen who stops by a free book. All kinds of publishers and authors have donated books."

"That's great."

"Uh-huh. Would you like to sign up to volunteer?"

"It's not too late?"

"Not at all. As a matter of fact, we're going to need at least one more volunteer because Troy asked me out for ice cream at the end of the day. Isn't that something? So fun!"

"That's great. I'm happy for you," she said, and really hoped that she sounded happy, too.

Because her insides were as jealous as could be. Here her best friend had just fallen in insta-love with the buddy of a guy who Emily had assumed would one day be her boyfriend.

Now it looked like their spots had been exchanged. It seemed she was destined to always be the third wheel.

As she pulled into the parking lot, she was fairly sure her heart felt like it was breaking all over again.

"Aren't you so glad we worked out and stopped to get dinner? This is turning out to be one of our best nights ever."

She wasn't hungry. She wasn't happy.

But she'd learned to fake it with the best of them. "I'm so happy for you."

"You sure? You don't sound happy."

"I'm just in real need of a shower. Do you mind if I go first?"

Campbell's expression cleared. "Nope. I'll dig in while it's hot." She held up her phone. "And check my phone. I think Troy already texted me."

Emily couldn't get to the shower fast enough.

CHAPTER 25

FROM LES LARKE'S
TIPS FOR BEGINNING POKER PLAYERS:

*Try to be patient and disciplined. Bad things happen
when you let emotion take over.*

"Emily'll come around. All she needs is time," Troy said after they
ate too much Mexican food and then said goodbye to Sam, who was
heading over to see his girl.

"Maybe she will, but I don't know. She's not happy with me."
He didn't blame her, either.

"Women change their minds. Haven't you heard that's their
prerogative?"

Kurt barely refrained from rolling his eyes. Comments like that
were vintage Troy. Words like *prerogative* were part of his regular
vocabulary. Every time Troy said stuff like that, it reminded Kurt
of Sam, and how he was really hoping and praying he was doing
everything all right by him.

Sitting down at the table, Troy grabbed a handful of poker chips
and started sorting the colors. "Her gal Campbell is sure a sweetheart. When I texted her, she texted me right back."

"Don't suppose you want me to mention how you sound like
you're sixteen with a hard-on."

But instead of being offended, Troy threw back his head and laughed. "Yeah, I guess I do. I'm owning it, though. It's been a while since I've been so taken by a woman."

"You only talked to her for ten minutes. What happened?"

Maybe he needed some dating moves or something?

"I don't know. There was something about her that I wanted to know. Something genuine." He paused, then added, "She didn't look like she cared that I played ball in college or that I've got my own business now. What mattered was that I was volunteering at Saturday's Kid Fest over at Nesbit Park."

"I haven't heard about that. What is it?"

"A bunch of organizations around Bridgeport set up booths and activities. I'm helping out at the football clinic. She's working the literacy fair."

"Sounds like a fun event for a good cause."

Troy nodded as he leaned back in his chair, one arm over the back of it. "It is. I go every year. Most of the folks you meet here in Bridgeport like helping to make the community better. Not everyone is all about golf clubs and gated communities, you know."

Since he knew for a fact that Troy belonged to a golf club and lived in a gated community, he kept his mouth shut. But it did give him something to think about. Had he been stereotyping the town and acting like he didn't have much in common with the other men in the area because he didn't wear polo shirts or hadn't gone to college?

"You ought to join me," Troy said, pulling him out of his musings.

"Where? At Kid Fest?"

"Yeah. In the football clinic. I could use the help and you were a great receiver." He waggled his eyebrows. "Plus, there's a good chance I'll be taking off early with Campbell. Get this. I'm taking her out on an ice cream date."

Kurt knew he was grinning from ear to ear. "You going out for ice cream, Troy?"

Troy laughed. "Maybe. And yes, I know it's going to be a new experience for me. I don't recall doing something so innocent with a girl since I was about eleven or twelve."

"I'm thinking that age was probably closer to eight. Even before you discovered girls you weren't that good."

"You got that right." Troy shrugged as he stared at him intently. "Anyway, how about it? Why don't you put on some cleats and help me out, for old times' sake?"

"You sure anyone's gonna want to listen to me? I didn't play college ball."

"First, no one expects us to be pros, just competent. Secondly, you could've played in college if the time had been right."

Kurt wasn't sure that was true. He hadn't had the grades or the money. But then he reminded himself that volunteering wasn't about him anyway. And to be honest, doing something with Troy and a bunch of kids sounded better than working on his computer or moping around the house and thinking of all the ways he had let Emily down or had possibly sabotaged Sam's chances. "I'll be happy to help you out. Just let me know what time."

"Will do." His eyes were shining. Kurt was tempted to ask what was on his mind but decided to let it go. Honestly, he couldn't handle any more of his buddy's good humor. "So are we going to play cards or what?"

"I told them six." Looking at his phone, he added, "Everyone should start showing up in about fifteen or twenty minutes."

"Great. I'll text Jim and a couple of other guys to tell them to get on over here."

"Wait a minute. Have you had guys waiting for you to let them know about the game?"

"Heck yeah." Looking as confident as ever, Troy grinned. "One of the guys even gave these poker nights a name: the Bridgeport Poker Club."

Kurt laughed. "It's got a nice ring to it, but it doesn't sound classy enough for this place. And, you know, I don't *just* like to play poker."

Troy nodded, like their conversation was about something important. "You know what? You're right. I like doing other stuff around town, too. Kayaking. Fishing. Golf. Tennis."

"I'm sensing a pattern here and it involves a lot of sports."

Troy shrugged. "For me, yeah. But not everyone." He snapped his fingers. "I've got it. It's the Bridgeport Social Club. What do you think?"

"I think ... I think it sounds real good." Kurt grinned. "Perfect." He paused. "'Course, having a name for a group of guys getting together ain't necessary. I mean, most times, it's just poker."

"Haven't you figured it out yet, Holland? Poker is bigger than all of us. Hell, some guys even say it's all they've got."

Since he didn't have Emily at the moment, Kurt reckoned they might be right.

***

Sam had been there almost an hour, but as Kayla kept sneaking glances at him, she was getting the feeling that he still hadn't relaxed.

He was sitting on the sectional with her but not real close. Actually, she was almost certain that he'd made sure one whole couch cushion was in between them. So far, he hadn't been too interested in any of the shows they'd flipped on either. He kept texting or staring at his phone.

With every minute that passed by, Kayla was becoming more and more certain that asking him over had been a really bad idea. So was wearing the new shorts and top she'd bought at the mall. And the brownies she'd made that morning but he hadn't touched. And the Cokes she'd asked her mom to run out and get at the end of her shift at the hospital but he'd refused.

No doubt, Sam Holland would have rather been at some field party with a lot of other kids, a cooler of beer, and a lot more freedom.

"Do you like *Arctic Freeze*?" she asked, naming the reality show about a bunch of fishermen that they'd had on almost the whole time. "If not, we can watch something else."

His head popped up. "No. It's fine." Then he went back to his phone.

Now she was beginning to wish he hadn't come over at all. Feeling even more frustrated, she sighed.

He heard. "What's up?"

"It's pretty obvious that you don't want to be here. You don't have to stay, Sam."

The phone dropped to his side. "What are you talking about?"

"You're sitting over there and staring at your phone. I may not have your big brain but even I can tell that means you're bored." Sam looked shocked. Really shocked.

His expression might've been kind of funny if she felt like laughing.

"Kayla, your mother is home. She could come down here any minute and see us together."

"I know that. But she knows we're seeing each other, Sam. I'm not saying I want to make out or anything, but you could move a little closer."

He scooted her way. Not close enough to touch her or anything but at least now she didn't have to raise her voice to talk to him. She leaned back and tried to watch the show again.

She made real certain that she didn't sigh again when he pulled his phone back out, but she definitely did start thinking of ways to end the night early.

As if he finally was reading her mind, he grabbed hold of the remote and put it on mute. "Kayla, I'm sorry. I know I've been acting like a jerk."

"Why? Did I do something you're mad about?"

"No. Of course not. I've just got something on my mind. Actually, I've got a lot of things and I don't know what to do."

"Can you talk about it?"

"Yeah, but it's not anything good. You might not want to hear about it."

"Sam, don't you get it yet? I don't need you to act like everything's always great."

He stared at her a little longer, his blue eyes studying her face like he wasn't sure if he believed her. Seeing him act like that made her kind of sad. Obviously he'd been burned before. Maybe a lot of times. "All right. Here goes," he said at last. "I might make a B in English."

With anyone else she would have rolled her eyes. Maybe thrown a pillow at them. But she knew him well enough by now that this wasn't good. "Are you upset because you're not used to making Bs or upset about college?"

"College. And maybe a little bit of both." He closed his eyes. "I hate talking about this because it makes me sound like a jerk. But school here, well, it's caught me off guard. It's been a lot harder than I expected."

She knew that admitting those things had been hard for him. "What are you going to do?"

"Miss Springer is tutoring me on vocabulary. That's what I was doing on Friday afternoon."

"What does your brother say about everything?"

"Kurt acted like it was no big deal, but I think he's pretty bummed. I let him down, you know?"

"No," she told him with complete honesty. "You're just as human as the rest of us, Sam. You can't expect to be perfect all the time."

"We moved here because I was so smart. But maybe I'm not that smart after all," he said slowly, worry and doubt shining in his eyes. "Maybe I was just smart for my crappy little town, but now that I'm here, I'm just average."

"I don't think you're that, Sam. You're a whole lot smarter than me."

He hung his head. "This is why I didn't want to talk about it. I sound needy."

Unable to handle the space between them anymore, she crawled onto his lap. Sam froze for a second before wrapping his arms around her and holding her tight. "If I ask you something, will you promise not to get mad?"

For the first time since he arrived, his lips curved up. "Will you promise to stay on my lap and let me hold you?"

She kissed his cheek. "Um-hmm."

"Then shoot."

"Okay." Bracing herself for his response, she said, "Have you ever thought about what would happen if you don't get your fancy scholarship to a real good school?"

His entire body tightened. She knew he was trying hard not to lash out his frustration.

So she started talking quickly. "I'm not trying to be mean, Sam. I really want to know if you've thought about what would happen."

"I'm going to disappoint everyone, Kay."

"Not everyone. Not me." Reaching out, she pressed a hand on his chest, right over his heart. "What about Coleman and the rest of your buddies at home? Are they going to be upset?"

"Cole?" He looked surprised that she asked. "Well, no. He doesn't care about Ivy League schools."

Taking a chance, she murmured, "What about your dad?"

"No one in my family's ever gone to college before. He doesn't care what the name of the institution is."

"So all you're really worried about is Kurt?"

"Yeah." He closed his eyes then opened them. "I mean, no. Kurt's already said he wasn't upset about that B."

Feeling like she'd at last made some progress, she kissed his cheek again. "I could be wrong, but I think maybe everything's going to be okay if all those dreams don't come true."

He stared at her for a long moment, his expression turbulent before it cleared. Then, to her surprise, he pulled her toward him and kissed her hard. "Thank you."

She giggled. "You're welcome."

Footsteps, sounding like they belonged to a giant, started on the steps. "Kayla, I'm coming down to check on you," her mother called out.

She scurried off his lap just as her mother poked her head in the room. "You two behaving yourselves?"

"Yes, ma'am," Sam replied, sounding almost innocent.

Kayla couldn't help but smile when her mother eyed her closely. "We're just watching TV, Mom. That's it."

After her mother nodded and walked back upstairs, Kayla dissolved into laughter. "Oh, Sam. I swear she thought we'd been doing nothing down here but making out."

He smirked as he slipped his arm around her. "It'd be a real shame if you got a talkin'-to later when all we did was chat about my future. Come here, Kayla."

When he kissed her again, it was long and sweet. Almost as perfect as their talk had been.

CHAPTER 26

FROM LES LARKE'S
TIPS FOR BEGINNING POKER PLAYERS:

Take frequent breaks.

It was amazing how many people Emily knew in the coffee shop line. After teasing a couple of her juniors and sidestepping an impromptu conference with the parent of one of her seniors who was taking an independent study, she spied Sam Holland with Kayla.

They were sitting at a back table and sharing some kind of frozen concoction that no doubt had about a thousand calories. After longingly eyeing the drink for a moment, she allowed herself to watch them. Oh, but they were cute together! It honestly looked like a bomb could have gone off in the place and neither of them would notice.

They were so young and had any number of challenges ahead of them, but a part of her hoped that they would be one of those couples who stayed together no matter what. The kind who would be fifty or sixty years old one day and tell people about how they'd been high school sweethearts.

"Here's your skinny vanilla latte, Miss Springer."

Realizing that Jeremy had been trying to get her attention for a couple of seconds already, Emily took her drink from him. "Thanks."

"Anytime," he said with a smirk.

She was just about to walk out when she saw that Sam must've gone to the bathroom, because he was no longer sitting at the table and Kayla was looking straight at her. Emily walked over, hoping the girl hadn't noticed her watching them. "Hi, Kayla. How are you this afternoon?"

She smiled. "Good. Sam and I are about to go to the movies. My mom gave me some money to take him out for a change."

"That was nice of her."

"I told Mom she didn't have to, but Mom said that I should accept and not worry about paying her back, 'cause you never know what the future will bring."

"That sounds like something a mom would say," Emily teased. "But good advice, too."

Turning her head, Kayla watched for Sam. When she was satisfied he wasn't around, she nodded. "I thought so, too. Sam seems so perfect, I sometimes forget that he's got problems, too. Mom reminded me that his problems might not be mine but are still important."

Feeling like Kayla's mom might as well have been talking directly to her, Emily felt her composure slip. She'd been so focused on her pain, she'd forgotten that Kurt's worries about his involvement with her had been very real. He hadn't been playing a game with her, he'd been needing her support. Then, later, when he'd apologized and tried to make amends, she hadn't let him, minimizing his words and actions again.

Darn it, she knew better!

Kayla was looking at her with a worried expression. "Miss Springer, did I say something wrong?"

"Not at all." She shook her head. "I just remembered that there was something I needed to do." Seeing that Sam was on his way back, Emily stepped toward the door. "I better go do it. Have fun at the movies."

Still looking puzzled, Kayla nodded. "Okay."

Emily hurried out the door before she had to say anything to Sam. As she got to her car, she realized that she hadn't lied. She absolutely did have something she needed to do—forgive Kurt Holland and move forward.

***

"This here is Kurt Holland," Troy said. "He just moved here from West Virginia. We grew up together. He's good people."

The fifth—or maybe the fifteenth—guy Troy had introduced him to stuck out his hand. "Good to meet you. I'm Cal. Welcome to Bridgeport."

"Thanks," Kurt said. "Glad to be here."

"What do you do?" Cal asked.

And so it began again. Kurt briefly shared about his lawn business, pulled out a business card, and listened to Cal talk about his job, wife, and kids. Troy added to the conversation from time to time, easily illustrating that he was just as good at working a room as he was running the football down the field.

A couple minutes later, Cal shook his hand again. After promising to give Kurt a call soon about hiring his company to do some snow removal in the winter, he walked to his wife's side.

When it was just the two of them again, Troy looked pleased. "I'm real glad we ran into Cal, Kurt. He's got a lot of connections around Bridgeport. Shoot, all around Cincinnati, too. He's going to be a good guy to know."

"Sounds like it. Thanks again for introducing me to everyone."

"No need for thanks. They're going to be glad to know you." Just as he looked about ready to take Kurt over to some more people, his phone buzzed. Scanning it quickly, he frowned. "Sorry, Bud. I've got to go. That's my sister Jennifer. I told Nick I'd take her home when she got tired."

Kurt knew Jennifer was in the middle of her second trimester with her first baby. Her husband, Nick, had gone to college with Troy. After they'd married, they'd decided to join Troy in Bridgeport since Troy and Jennifer's parents had moved to Florida when they retired.

"Tell her hey," Kurt said.

Troy smiled. "Will do. I'll introduce you to Nick one day soon. He wants to join the club. You're gonna like him. He's a good guy."

As Kurt watched Troy walk away, he was reminded how different his life would be if he hadn't played ball with him back in high school. Troy had been a good friend back when they were teenagers, and he'd gone above and beyond simple friendship with everything he'd done for Kurt and Sam since. Kurt hoped he'd be able to repay him one day.

After Troy disappeared in the crowd, Kurt scanned the rest of the park. It looked like Kid Fest was a roaring success. There had to be almost a thousand people milling around the area. Fifteen to twenty booths were set up along the perimeters. Some were fancy with professionally designed signs, programs, and swag items to give away. Other booths were obviously made by children. Their posters were hand drawn and the kids and moms manning the booths had homemade snacks.

But it all fit together. The enthusiasm, the way everyone was working together. The obvious pride that everyone had in their community.

And it hit him then that he was a part of it. He'd spent three hours with Troy at the football clinic. Over and over, he'd shown little guys how to grasp the ball and throw a pass. It had been obvious that a couple of the boys had simply wanted to be around some men who were paying attention to them.

No matter what happened with Sam or his father or his business, Kurt felt that he'd already accomplished something pretty incredible. He'd begun to make a place for himself in Bridgeport. In spite of all his doubts, he was putting down roots.

Feeling better about himself and what he'd done, he started for his truck. Sam was going to be at the fair either with Kayla or with his friends, so he was going to take advantage of the time to be by himself for a while.

Mentally running a grocery list in his head, he decided to make himself a couple of cheeseburgers on the grill. Maybe buy a bag of french fries and have those, too.

Then he saw the literacy tent. About a dozen preschoolers were surrounding Emily Springer, who was sitting on a fold-out chair and reading a picture book to them.

Her long brown hair was pulled back in a ponytail and she had on a soft-looking ivory colored sweater, faded jeans, and a pair of fuzzy Uggs. She looked so sweet. So cute in the midst of all those little kids … and so happy.

Unable to stop himself, he walked over to join the group. Crossing his hands over his chest, he stood to the side, grinning when Emily made each of the characters sound unique … and full-out laughing when she pointed to the rhinoceros on the page and let out a loud roar.

Obviously distracted by his laugh, she paused and scanned the crowd. She smiled more brightly when she spotted him.

Kurt breathed a sigh of relief, pleased that things were better between them. When the book was finished, all the kids scrambled to their feet and crowded around her.

"Kurt, do you feel like helping?" she called out.

Suddenly sitting by himself had no appeal whatsoever. "Absolutely." He smiled down at the sea of tiny faces staring back at him. "What do you need me to do?"

"It's time to do my favorite activity … pass out books!"

The kids cheered. He couldn't stop himself from grinning at the little four- or five-year-old girl standing by his side. He leaned down. "Do you like books?"

"Uh-huh."

"Me, too," he said. "Let's go see what Miss Emily has for you."

In reply, the little girl held out her hand. After a moment, he realized that she was waiting for him to hold her hand. Touched by how trusting she was, Kurt gently clasped it and let her lead him to where Emily and her girlfriend Campbell were now pulling books out of cardboard boxes and giving one to each child.

"Hey, Kurt!" Campbell called out.

"Hey. What do you need me to do?"

"Open boxes."

"I'm on it." He opened the box she pointed to, carefully set it on top of the plastic fold-out table, then turned to the women again. "Anything else?"

The women exchanged amused glances. "Uh, yeah."

"What? Oh," he said as soon as he saw another eight boxes tucked over to the side. "All these, too?"

"If you don't mind," Emily said as she walked to his side. All the children she'd been reading to had already taken their books and walked to their parents' sides. "I've got another four groups coming and Campbell is about to head out."

"I really am sorry about this," Campbell said. "If I hadn't promised my sister I'd watch her game, I'd stay."

Emily waved off a hand. "Don't worry about it. Go!"

As Campbell trotted off, Kurt stepped closer. "Who's coming to help you?"

Emily smiled. "You, if you don't mind."

"I don't. So, help with the boxes?"

"And, maybe read out loud a little bit too? The little ones would love to hear a big guy like you read one of their favorites."

She wasn't asking for much, though for a second, it sure felt like she was. He didn't have experience with kids. Hell, he'd practically ignored his brother when Sam was that small.

"You're going to do fine, Kurt. Don't worry so much."

Her sweet tone, combined with her belief in him, settled his nerves—and made him realize that he actually had been worried about being good enough. Where had that come from?

He held out a hand. "Bring it on. I'm ready."

"Have you read Dr. Seuss before?"

"What? Like *The Cat in the Hat*?"

"Exactly like *The Cat in the Hat*," she said, handing him a blue hardcover book that brought back long-forgotten memories of sitting in a circle in kindergarten and listening with wide eyes while Miss Jefferson read the story with a thick West Virginian accent.

Feeling almost like he was in a daze, he sat down in the chair and smiled at the group of five little boys and girls sitting in front of him. "Y'all like Dr. Seuss?" he asked.

Two of them nodded. One little boy with a crew cut, bandage on his elbow, and a Star Wars action figure in his hand stared at him skeptically. "I've never heard of 'em."

"Then you're in for a treat," he replied as he opened the cover. He cleared his throat and spoke the words that were so familiar they fit almost like a good pair of comfortable socks. "The sun did not shine. It was too wet to play. So we sat in the house all that cold, cold, wet day."

One of the little girls in a blue knit dress giggled and leaned closer. He looked at her and winked, and flipped the page. Three more little guys came over to join them.

And standing off to the side with a group of parents, Emily gazed at him like he'd done something brilliant.

He hadn't. But he was starting to hope that she would think he had.

CHAPTER 27

FROM LES LARKE'S
TIPS FOR BEGINNING POKER PLAYERS:

Don't wear sunglasses while playing.
You look like an idiot and it doesn't help anyway.

"Your boyfriend seems like a good guy, Miss Springer," Nancy Moore, one of her high school student's mothers, said. "I didn't know you were dating anyone seriously."

"This relationship is pretty new." She figured that was a safer statement than relaying the fact that her dating life really wasn't any of her students' parents' business.

"If he's visiting you here and reading to a group of preschoolers, I'm guessing he's serious. Men don't do those things unless they are."

"You think so?" she asked before thinking the better of it.

"I know so." Nancy tilted her head to one side. "I know it's none of my business, but you sound skeptical. Are you?"

"No. Not at all. Well, maybe." Thinking of Danny, she said, "Sometimes, no matter how much I want to forget a past relationship, the problems that I had with him keep haunting me."

"I can see that," Nancy said, her expression concerned. "Well, for what it's worth, I'll tell you something that's always helped me."

"What is that?"

"It's something my grandmother always said." Looking a bit dreamy, she continued. "New shoes are for people who go out walking."

Emily thought that was both obvious and a bit condescending. "Ah."

Nancy laughed. "I know. It's not that great of a saying—unless it's from your grandmother. That said, I've always liked it. I've taken it to mean that it's better to take a walk and experience something new than to sit still and keep everything nice and neat."

She smiled again as she patted Emily's arm. "You don't need to say a thing, dear. Like I said, it might not mean a thing to you. And if it doesn't? Well, that's quite all right. Looks like your man is finishing up. I'll go see if I can help match up preschoolers and parents. I tell you, sometimes I think their parents need a little guidance, too!"

Before she realized she was doing it, Emily glanced down at her shoes. Darn. They were awfully neat. Not a scratch or a mark on them.

And that was how she'd been living her life. Safe and sure. Tentative. Predictable. So afraid of making mistakes. So afraid of getting hurt again.

Looking at Kurt, who was tentatively hugging a preschooler with one hand and still clutching that book with the other, she felt a new surge of warmth pass through her. Kurt Holland really was her new pair of shoes. Yes, they were currently giving her a couple of blisters and weren't entirely comfortable. But they were nicer than anything she'd had before. And that said a lot.

"Did I do okay?" Kurt asked as he strode up.

"You did great," she said as she wrapped a hand around his arm. "Thank you again. I know this isn't your wheelhouse."

"It was fun." His voice lowered. "When I first sat down, one of the little boys blurted that he would rather be playing his Xbox. But by the time Thing One and Thing Two appeared, he was laughing along with everyone else."

"I used to call that a magic moment when I was a student teacher."

As he usually did, Kurt was looking at her directly, like what she had to say actually mattered to him. "What do you call it now?"

She felt a little shiver run through her. "Rare. High school kids don't get too excited about books all that much. Even though I'm trying my best to make it so."

"Sam seems to think otherwise."

"Sam is an anomaly."

"Would you make fun of me if I admitted I have no idea what that means?"

Trying not to smile, she shook her head. "I just meant he's unusual. A little different than the average high school senior. Sam's pretty special, Kurt."

His expression softened. "I know now isn't the time, but I want to talk to you about everything, Em."

"Everything?" She raised an eyebrow.

"Yeah. Sam. Your tutoring. Me and my idiot ways. You and how you're feeling." He lowered his voice. "Can we do that?"

Thinking of those shoes again, Emily nodded. "I'll be done here in about two hours. I could stop by your house then …"

"How about I stay here with you and then we'll head back to my house together?"

"Hey, I could even get a tour of the infamous poker garage."

He laughed. "Get ready, it's going to knock your socks off."

Chuckling, too, she couldn't resist teasing him a little bit more. "My brother seems to think it's like a boys' clubhouse. Are you even going to let me in?"

"I'll make an exception for you."

There went those little shivers again. Boy, where Kurt was concerned, it seemed as if her body had no control. Honestly, if they continued the conversation much longer she was going to need to put on a sweater.

"Miss Emily!" a little boy called out as he ran to her side. Placing one sticky hand on her leg, he looked up at her and smiled. "Hi!"

"Hey, Jackson," she replied, kneeling down so that they were at the same level. "Looks like you've been eating ice cream."

"Uh-huh. Chocolate."

"My favorite." She smiled at him as she stood back up. "Looks like we better get back to work. Do you feel like reading another book?"

"Can I read *Green Eggs and Ham*?"

If she hadn't already started to fall in love with him, she would have right then and there. "Absolutely. I'd love to hear you read all about Sam-I-Am."

***

Three hours later, Emily parked on the street outside his house and carefully pulled herself out of her car. She'd knelt down, hugged kids, and loaded enough books and boxes that she felt like her arms and back were on fire.

She sure didn't remember her back hurting so badly after a day spent with little kids. When had she gotten so old?

Kurt was waiting in his driveway next to his truck. "You okay?"

"I don't know," she said honestly. "I'm exhausted."

"I can't tell you how glad I am to hear that."

"Why?"

"I do landscaping all day and I'm worn out. Those kids are cute as all get-out but a handful." Taking her hand, he walked her to a panel by the garage door, punched in a code, and waited while the garage door slowly slid up.

She grinned, appreciating his joke. "There's a reason I'm a high school teacher." She was about to tell him a story about once substituting in a kindergarten class when she got an eyeful of the garage.

Kurt had painted the walls with a thick coat of white paint and hung up a couple of sports posters. It looked like someone had cut up a poster board and written down the day of the latest poker game and the standings on it.

Cards and chips were stacked on a table on one side, and in the center was a really ugly poker table. Black folding chairs surrounded it. A couple more rested against the back wall. Under the table was a large Yeti cooler.

The whole thing smelled faintly of beer, stale cigarettes, cigars, and maybe … old socks? Unable to help herself, she wrinkled her nose.

"I know. It's not real fancy in here."

Walking forward, she rested her hand on the table. "Or real clean."

He laughed. "I guess I won't have to worry about you showing up at the next game, huh?"

"Not yet. But never say never."

He grinned again as he took her hand and pulled her into the main house. Inside, it was well-organized and clean. The white countertops in the kitchen were wiped down, the furniture looked new and well made.

"I know, it's not much," Kurt said from behind her.

"That's not what I was thinking at all. I like it."

He looked relieved. "Thanks, Em. Have a seat. Do you want a beer or something?" He walked to the refrigerator and opened it up. "We've got some Cokes."

"Water sounds good, if you don't mind."

"I can do that." After he got them two glasses, he sat down next to her on the couch.

Emily sipped from hers as she saw him do the same then visibly prepare himself to say something. Just when she was about to tell him that they didn't have to talk about anything important, he spoke.

"When I came over and told you that I thought we should wait to see each other, I really thought it was for the best."

"I know."

"I was also wrong." He hung his head. "Honestly, I don't really know why I let Garrett and his parents get to me so much. It's not

190

like me to give a damn about what jerks like that think. I've sure never let them tell me what to do."

"I didn't like you making that decision, but I understood it, Kurt. You're trying to do your best with Sam."

"I am. But I started realizing that I can't control everything. I can't make sure Sam gets all As. Or gets a scholarship. Or even gets into the school of his dreams. All I can do is my best." He turned to face her. "And my best is seeing you. You make me happy, Emily."

A lump formed in her throat. "You make me happy, too."

"I finally remembered, these next couple of months? Well, they're going to pass. Shoot, a year from now, Sam will be in the middle of his freshman year somewhere and will probably be calling me saying he needs more money."

"He's going to go to college, Kurt. And he's going to earn some scholarships. Maybe not to Ivy League schools but he'll get to achieve his dream. I'm going to help him."

"What I'm trying to say is that's Sam's life, and Sam's dream. Me? I've wanted my own company, to live in a house that I can call my own ... and one day have a wife and a family of my own." He swallowed. "Don't be scared. I get that we're new. I get that maybe we aren't made for each other. But I don't want to lose that chance. I don't want to lose you before I've even gotten the opportunity to see, Emily." He closed his eyes in frustration. "Damn. Sometimes I just really wish I was smarter. Then I could explain myself right."

Not even caring that there were tears in her eyes and that she was as grubby as all those kids' little hands, she wrapped her hands around his neck and hugged him tight. "It was perfect," she murmured, kissing his jaw. "I don't want you smarter, better, different, or anything. I think you're amazing just how you are."

And then, so he wouldn't protest again, she kissed him.

When he held her close and deepened the kiss, Emily knew that he felt the same way.

CHAPTER 28

FROM LES LARKE'S
TIPS FOR BEGINNING POKER PLAYERS:

Don't accidentally expose your cards to other players.
New players often keep too many cards in their hands.

"Hey, Holland!" Chris Miller called out as he made his way down the bleacher to his side. "You save me a place?"

Sam glanced at Jackson and grinned before replying. "Yep. I told you we would."

"Just checking!" Chris replied before climbing up to the third row and moving down the metal bench.

As expected, pretty much everyone he was displacing was groaning or muttering as they either stood up or shifted so Chris didn't step on their feet. All the while, Chris kept up a steady patter of apologies and warnings as he navigated his way down. "Excuse me. Sorry. Watch out, nachos coming through."

"I need to remember that nacho comment," Jackson said. "It works like a charm."

"Yeah, it does." Sam laughed as a girl two seats down lifted up her knees so Chris could pass.

When his buddy finally reached their side, he sat down with a pleased smile on his face. "Finally. You wouldn't believe how long the lines were over at the concession stand. And they were already out of chili dogs."

"The fourth quarter is about to start. All the good food is usually gone by the end of the first half."

Chris shrugged. "Here," he said, handing Jackson his nachos. "Next time, you're getting your own."

"No prob. Thanks," Jackson replied. Popping a chip in his mouth, Jackson eyed Sam. "How come you aren't eating? Out of money?"

"I don't have a lot to spend here, but that ain't it."

"He's taking Kayla out after the game," Chris supplied.

Jackson looked at the fence. Right on the other side stood the varsity cheerleaders. They'd been taking a break but had just gotten back on their feet.

Bridgeport had nine varsity cheerleaders and another ten JV. The cheer coach allowed some of the girls to "cheer up" for a couple of games a season. But that wasn't Kayla. She was on varsity full time.

Looking at her, Sam had to remind himself to not continually stare at her. She was so shy, she'd probably get embarrassed by his attention. But it was hard to take his eyes off of her. She was talented, looked awesome in the black-and-gold cheer uniform, and looked real cute with her hair in a high ponytail with a black bow.

But it was her smile that kept his eyes on her. She looked happy, and whenever she glanced his way, she smiled happily at him. He loved that.

"You two are official now, aren't you?" Chris asked.

"Yeah. I guess we are."

"Did you ask her?" Jackson asked.

"Like did I ask her to go steady with me?" Sam teased. "Like they did in the fifties or something?"

Jackson flushed. "Never mind."

Belatedly Sam remembered that Jackson had confessed to him the other day when they were grabbing dinner that he'd never had a girlfriend but liked Melissa Young a lot. "Hey. I'm sorry. All I did the other day was ask if she'd be mine."

Chris gaped. "Whoa. That's pretty intense."

Remembering the way Kayla had blushed as she'd nodded, Sam smiled. "It was. But good."

"Don't get mad, but I think she's really pretty," Jackson said. "You're lucky."

"I'm not mad. And I am lucky. She's real pretty." As far as he was concerned, she was the prettiest girl in school. "She's a sweetheart, too."

"You're lucky that she gives you the time of day."

"I know it."

As if she sensed they were talking about her, Kayla looked his way after the cheerleaders finished their routine. He smiled back, already anxious to be alone with her after the game.

When the Lions were at the ten-yard line, he focused on the game again. To his surprise, he hardly felt more than a small tinge of disappointment that he wasn't playing. Actually, given how much time he'd had to put into his studies during the past two weeks, it was probably for the best. He didn't know if he'd have been able to buckle down on all that vocabulary so well if he'd been running to practice every night.

When the team scored, he stood up with everyone else and clapped with the fight song.

Beside him, Chris was singing off-key but louder than probably anyone else in the stadium.

That made him and Jackson crack up. "You're an idiot, Chris."

"I know. But all the girls love me."

"I don't!" Regan said from behind them.

Chris turned around and grabbed her hand. "Come on, Regan. Don't break my heart."

"In your dreams, Chris."

When other kids started giving Chris grief, Sam took a sip of the Coke he'd been working on and watched Kayla some more.

When everyone sat back down, Jackson said, "It's hard to believe that you've only been in Bridgeport since August. It feels like we've known you for years."

"I feel the same way."

"Do you still miss your old school?"

"Sometimes. But not as much as I thought I would." He thought about it some more. "I miss my old friends and playing football. And my dad, of course. But coming here was the right decision."

"You'll get a scholarship. I'm sure you will."

"You're only saying that 'cause you got yourself a good one to NKU."

Jackson shrugged. "My parents are relieved. We don't have a lot of money for college, you know?"

Since they'd been talking about that for a while, Sam nodded. When he realized Chris was listening, he said, "Not everyone drives a new tricked-out Malibu and has parents who don't mind sending him across the country to study engineering."

"Hey, I am pretty smart. And that Malibu is where it's at," Chris joshed.

"It's an awesome car," Sam agreed.

"Hey, my dad heard about your brother's poker game," Jackson said. "Does he let anyone in?"

"Pretty much."

"When's the next one?"

"He's got a poker game tonight. You should text your dad and tell him to stop by. If he can't get in, there's usually a cash game or he could at least meet Kurt."

"You don't think he'd mind?"

"Nope. Just have him tell Kurt that he's your dad."

"Okay. But will you text him, too?"

"Sure."

He pulled out his phone. When he looked at the screen, he was taken by surprise, Kurt had already texted him three times.

Quickly, he responded.

> Game's almost over.
> Everything okay?

Almost immediately, Kurt shot off another text, which was weird.

I don't know.

Feeling like something wasn't right, Sam texted back.

> Do you want me to come
> home?

Do you have plans?

> I was going to take Kayla
> out.

After five minutes, Kurt texted again.

Go spend time with her but come
home by eleven. Can you do that?

Usually his brother didn't care when he got home on the weekends. He typed his response quickly.

> I can do that. BTW Jackson's
> dad was wanting to stop by.
> Is that okay?

Yeah.

Chris nudged him. "Hey, stand up. Game's over and Kayla is looking at you."

"What? Oh, sure." He stood up and yelled and cheered while the announcer called out the score. "Jackson, my brother said to tell your dad it's fine for him to stop by."

"I'll tell him."

They started walking down the metal bleachers, following the rest of the student body as they began to exit. After telling his buddies goodbye, he made his way to the fence where Kayla was putting all her stuff together on the other side.

"Hey, Kay."

She lifted her head and smiled at him. "Hi."

"You did a good job tonight. You looked real good."

Her smiled turned wider. "Thanks. I kind of messed up one of the routines but Miss Becky said she didn't think anyone noticed."

"I didn't." 'Course, he wouldn't have said a thing even if he had noticed a mistake. "How long is it going to take you to get out of here?"

"Not long." She bit her lip. "Ten minutes? I need to sign out and run to the bathroom."

"I'll wait for you outside by the field house."

"Thanks, Sam."

When he turned away, he was surprised to see that the stadium already looked half empty. Glad that nobody but a couple of parents were heading to the field house, he checked his phone again. The screen was empty, but something didn't feel right. He hoped nothing had happened with Kurt and Miss Springer again.

When he got to the field house, Ms. Everett came over. "Hey, Sam. How are you?"

"Hi Ms. Everett. I'm good, thanks. It was good game."

She smiled. "It was. So, what are you and Kayla doing tonight?"

"I haven't had a chance to ask her yet, but I was thinking of getting her something to eat and then going for a walk around the lake again. I can't stay out too late tonight. My brother wants me home."

"Want to come over on Monday for dinner?"

"Yes, ma'am. Thanks."

"Great. Oh, here she comes. I'll grab her bag and then you can get on with your plans."

Sam stuffed his hands in his pockets as he watched her mother give her a hug, gesture over at him, and then grab her bag.

After they headed toward the parking lot, she joined him. "Sam, half the time I think my mother likes you as much as me." She paused. "Not in a creepy way or anything."

"Yeah. I figured that. I like her, too."

She lifted her chin. "And me?"

Unable to resist, he lowered his head and gently kissed her lips. "I like you a whole lot."

He wrapped his arm around her as he walked her to his car. Drove her to McDonald's so she could eat. Then, he drove her to the lake.

But unlike the first time they went there, they didn't do a whole lot of walking. She let him kiss her and hold her close when he'd guided her to one of the benches.

All too soon, he took her home, with promises to call and text her later.

He was still thinking about how good she'd felt in his arms when he drove back home.

Grinning when he saw the number of cars parked on the street, Sam knew that the night's poker game was a success. And, from the noise coming out of the garage, it was obvious that a lot of the men had decided to get a little rowdy.

Figuring that Kurt just didn't want to worry about him, too, he wandered in. Only one table was still going.

Some other men were watching the rerun of a game on the TV in the back of the room.

"Hey, Sam," a voice said.

Sam turned on his heel. "Dad?"

"Yeah. I decided to surprise you both."

Looking over his father's shoulder, Sam met Kurt's gaze.

As he expected, his brother looked pensive and ill at ease. "How is Kayla?"

"Good." Feeling awkward, he added, "Ms. Everett asked me over for supper Monday night."

"You want to go?"

Feeling their father's gaze on him, Sam nodded.

"That works for me, then," Kurt said quietly.

Feeling like something important had just passed between them, Sam exhaled. Whatever was going on with their dad wasn't going to affect how things were with him and Kurt.

"Sam, come on over and give your old man a hug," his dad called out in an overly loud voice. "Or have you already forgotten me?"

Sam hugged his father tight. "Of course not."

And it was true. He hadn't forgotten his dad. But things did feel different.

He felt older and more distant.

But the look in his father's eyes he remembered clear as day, as it was now obvious that Kurt had, too.

His father was up to something. Hopefully they'd discover what it was real soon.

CHAPTER 29

FROM LES LARKE'S
TIPS FOR BEGINNING POKER PLAYERS:

*Don't be afraid to fail. Every successful poker player
will tell you that they've learned more from losing
than from winning.*

On Monday night, after a particularly stressful day which had
included a conference with the parents of a student who was failing
her junior honors class, breaking up a fight near the parking lot, and
an interminable English department meeting, Emily just wanted to
collapse in front of the TV.

Even Campbell's guilt-inducing phone call about having to go
to hot yoga alone hadn't changed her mind. She literally couldn't
wait to put on one of her brother's old college T-shirts and some
flannel pajama bottoms and eat a grilled cheese sandwich.

And maybe follow it with half a pint of ice cream.

That was why she almost didn't answer her doorbell. But when
it rang again and was followed by a text from Kurt announcing that
he was standing outside her door, she suddenly felt that maybe her
awful day had just gotten a whole lot better.

"Hi, Kurt," she said with what was probably the biggest stupid
smile on her face. "I didn't expect to see you today." She leaned
forward, sure he was going to kiss her hello.

Instead he shoved his hands into his jeans pockets. "Hey, Em. Sorry I came over without calling first. Is this a bad time?"

She shook her head. "Is everything okay?" Of course the moment she asked, she wished she could take the question back. Because of course it wasn't.

"Yeah, well, I wanted to talk to you about something and didn't want to do it over the phone."

All of the newfound confidence she'd been feeling about their relationship faded. Stepping back, she kind of waved a hand toward her entryway. "My place is a mess, but do you want to come in?"

"Thanks. I won't stay long."

She turned and led the way to the small deck she had outside the kitchen door. Suddenly, she decided if they were about to break up she knew she didn't want it to happen on the couch, where she'd have to walk by it every day and be reminded about it. "You know what? Today's weather is so perfect. Do you mind if we sit out here?" she blathered in a rush. "After being in my building all day, I can hardly sit inside, especially since there's hardly a drop of humidity. Oh! I've got iced tea. Would you like some iced tea?"

He studied her face for a moment before nodding. "Sure, honey. Wherever you want to be is fine."

He'd called her honey. Some guys dropped endearments like crumbs on the floor but not Kurt.

She exhaled, hating that it sounded as ragged as she suddenly felt. After pasting a smile on her face, she said, "Go on out and I'll get our drinks."

He reached for her hand and tugged her toward him. "Wait a sec." Still staring at her intently, he said, "You thought I came over here to break up with you again, didn't you?"

She shrugged.

He winced. "I'm sorry. I didn't even think that might occur to you."

"No need to apologize."

He brushed away a lock of hair from her forehead. "Yeah, there is. It's going to take me a while to regain your trust, isn't it?"

She smiled, liking how he again inadvertently gave her a hint that he was serious about her. "I hope not."

"I'm rusty at this relationship thing, but I swear I'll do better. 'Kay?"

She nodded. "Listen, it's not just you. Remember, I've been burned before so I'm afraid I immediately think of the worst scenario right away."

"We need to change that, don't we?"

Embarrassed that she'd gone all emotional on him when he'd obviously come over for support, she squeezed his hand once before pulling her hand from his. "Go sit down, Kurt. I'll be right out."

When he walked out to the patio without another word, Emily gripped the edge of the countertop and breathed a sigh. She meant what she'd said. Sure, he'd hurt her, but she was also responsible for the way she often prepared herself for bad news.

She needed to stop doing that. It wasn't a good habit for either of them to fall into.

Feeling better, she quickly filled up two glasses with iced tea then stirred a little bit of sugar into each glass. When she got outside, Kurt was sitting at her small table, his elbows resting on his knees. His eyes were closed. She wondered if he'd been praying or merely resting his eyes. He did look tired.

Without a word, she handed him his glass then sat down across from him. With Campbell, she would have eased into the conversation, maybe chatting about how she'd attempted to grow strawberries, but a bunny kept eating all of them and she didn't have the heart to ruin his snack.

But with Kurt? Being direct was best.

"What's going on?"

Holding the glass between both of his hands, he said, "Last night, just two hours before some guys were expected to come over to play poker, my dad showed up."

He sounded really uptight about this. So much so, she was confused. "I thought you got along with him."

"I thought I did, too." He frowned. "No, what I thought was that he was okay with me moving to Bridgeport and taking Sam with me. But it turns out I was wrong."

He sounded so down. "You came to Bridgeport for Sam, Kurt. I knew practically from the first moment I met you that you wouldn't have come here without him." She paused. "Or would you? Had you been planning to come to Bridgeport for a while and just used Sam as an excuse?"

"No. Not at all." He set his glass on top of a magazine on her table. "Emily, as soon as we got those scores and the counselor gave us a call, I went to the school. After the counselor talked me through everything, I knew I had to do something."

"Wait a second," she interrupted. "I'm kind of confused about why you were the one to decide to move here. Can you walk me through it all?"

"Walk you through what?"

He still didn't seem to get it. "Kurt, you're Sam's brother, not his father. Why were you the one meeting with the guidance counselor and not your dad?"

He blinked, like he thought it was obvious. "Because my father wasn't going to do anything."

"He didn't care that the school called? Or he didn't know what to do when he heard about Sam's scores?"

Kurt's blue eyes clouded before she shrugged. "I don't know, to tell you the truth. Last spring, Dad was still having a hard time with my mother's death and then getting laid off. Shoot, we all were." Looking like he was trying to keep his emotions in check, he paused, then leaned back. "You know what? I think if Sam had pushed Dad to go to school, he would've. But I'm also fairly sure it wouldn't have gone real well."

She couldn't help but notice that his accent had become thicker, something that happened when he was emotional. "All right then. So, instead of your dad, you went up to the high school and met with the counselor."

"Yep. Mrs. Neely."

"Did Sam go, too?"

Kurt looked a little exasperated, like he wasn't sure why she was questioning him so much. But Emily was starting to feel like she needed the whole picture. Even more importantly, she was feeling like maybe Kurt needed that whole picture, too.

"Yeah," he said. "Sam went." He took a long sip of tea then leaned back. "Almost the minute we sat down, Mrs. Neely shoved his score sheet across the table at us. She was smiling big time, like she'd just found out that the Easter Bunny was real."

Emily laughed. "I bet she was excited. Sam's scores are excellent. In the top two percentile."

"Maybe real good describes those scores here in Bridgeport. Back in Spartan though? They ... well, they were incredible. Mrs. Neely said she'd never seen a student score so high and she'd been the guidance counselor at the high school for fifteen years."

"It must have been so exciting. What did Sam think?"

He waved a hand. "Shoot. Well, you know Sam. I think he was both embarrassed that she was making such a fuss and trying to figure out why he and I had to come in to talk to her about it."

She smiled. "I can see him acting like that."

Looking a little chagrined, Kurt said, "To be real honest, I was feeling kind of the same way. I mean, in my world, you don't get asked to come to the high school's office for good reasons."

Emily laughed. "I get that a lot, which is kind of a shame. So, I'm guessing that she told you how good those scores were and that Sam had a bright future?"

"Yeah. But she also said that he was going to need more than their school could give him. She said something like if we didn't do something to ensure his future it would be a travesty." Kurt drained his tea. "When we left her office, I was holding a folder filled with boarding school applications."

Emily blinked. "Wow. She wanted Sam to go away to school?"

"Yeah. Mrs. Neely had done a lot of work, to tell you the truth. She'd called up two boarding schools, talked to the financial folks, and pretty much got a verbal promise from both of them that Sam could get a full scholarship to go. Books, room and board, uniforms, you name it."

"That's incredible."

"Yeah. I didn't know what to do. I mean, I had never heard of anything like that happening before."

Emily hadn't ever heard of it either. "She must have really thought Sam deserved that opportunity."

Kurt grunted. "He didn't see it that way. He was pissed, if you can believe that."

"I actually can. He didn't want to leave his home and his friends to go to some strange school and wear a uniform."

He chuckled. "You've got it. Out of everything she said, after all the fanciness she told us about, that was what he was fixated on."

"That's normal. Teens like fitting in."

"Well, Sam was acting like a teenager, all right," he said dryly. "I didn't know what to tell him. But when we did get home, I sat him down and made him help me relay all of it to our father."

"And let me guess—your father wasn't too excited about the scholarship to the fancy school either."

"Not even a little bit. Matter of fact, he was offended. Said that just because he lost his job and his wife it didn't mean that the school had to start making a charity case out of Sam."

Emily waved her hand. "Ouch."

"Yeah, the whole thing absolutely sucked. By the time we were done talking—which was really arguing—Sam had taken off, my father had opened a third beer, and I was wondering why in the heck I cared so much about a bunch of test scores."

"Let me go get you more tea," she said, needing a moment to figure out a way to help him. Walking back to the kitchen, she thought about all her experience with both high-performing students and what she knew about standardized tests.

But as she walked back she realized she might know a lot about school but not a lot about raising a brother. Kurt didn't need her advice, he needed her to listen to him.

"Here you go." After she put the glass back on the table, she said. "Now that I have a better understanding of what happened, why did you decide to leave Spartan?"

"For my mother." Impatiently, he corrected himself. "Sorry. I mean for our mother. See, Mom was smart. Not Sam-smart but pretty bright. I knew if she'd been the one who'd been sitting in Mrs. Neely's office, she would've been tickled pink."

"Would she have sent him away to boarding school?"

"She probably would've if that was what Sam wanted. But it would've killed her. She liked being around us. Liked being involved at school. Liked knowing our friends."

Emily leaned back. Some of what he was saying she'd heard before. Some of it was new. But she knew he wasn't simply restating everything again. There was a purpose to the topic. She knew enough to know that it was best to let him talk and get to his point at his own time. Rushing him wouldn't help anything.

He sighed. "So, I guess you're wondering why I'm bringing this up."

"It doesn't matter to me. I'm glad you wanted to share."

Something new and special flashed in his eyes before he leaned back as well, crossing one foot over an opposite knee. "All right. I came here for a reason. I need your help, Em."

She stopped herself just in time from saying "anything." "What happened, Kurt?"

"Since Dad arrived, he's been hinting about a couple of things. He says he's here just to check on us, but there's a light in his eyes that's new. I'm pretty sure there's another reason."

"Are you going to ask him or are you going to wait for him to bring it up?"

"Last night, I was all about waiting for him to get to his point. But now? Well, I'm starting to think if I don't press the issue he's going to end up hurting Sam."

"How could your dad hurt him?"

"I don't know." Pain entered his eyes. "Am I letting my own fears get the worst of me? My father loves Sam. Of course he's not going to hurt him."

Making a sudden decision, she reached out and took hold of his hand. "Here's what I think. You need to hope for the best but prepare yourself for the worst. And with that in mind, you need to call him out and ask him."

"So, be blunt with him."

"I'd probably call it being direct. You know, when I advise my high school students about initiating tough conversations, I give them some advice. It might not sound like it pertains to you, but I think it might be helpful. Would you like to hear it?" she asked hesitantly.

He was staring at her intently. "Absolutely."

"All right. Here it is: it's always better to know."

Still staring at her with those dark blue eyes, a line formed in between his brows. "You're right. It sounds like bullshit but it's not."

"I promise, you'll be happier when you know what he wants."

With a groan, he stood up then looked down at her. "So, I guess I'm going to go ahead …"

"And leave," she finished with a smile. She got up a little more slowly. Stretched her hands toward him. "Good luck."

He curved his fingers around hers. "Was this a bad idea?"

Boy, she hoped not. "I guess you'll have to tell me after you talk to your father."

"No. I mean, was this a bad idea between you and me?" He

stepped forward, close enough for her to feel the warmth from his body. Close enough to notice that he'd showered recently but hadn't shaved.

Close enough for her to have to drop his hands and curve her own around his waist.

"Did I overstep myself? Was this too much, too soon? Was me coming over totally selfish?"

Her mouth was a little dry. She told herself that it was only because it was late in the day, she was tired, and he'd caught her off guard.

But the rest of her was shouting loud and clear that her reaction to him was because it was Kurt. It was because he was everything she'd ever wanted in a man. He was caring. He was decent. He was willing to sacrifice his happiness and his wants and needs for someone he cared about. Then, there was the fact that he was handsome as all get-out.

And had a dreamy accent.

"You haven't overstepped yourself," she said lightly. "I'm happy that you came over to talk."

"Happy?"

"All right. How about this? I'm glad. It means you value my opinion and that means a lot to me."

He blinked. "You are starting to mean a lot to me. Maybe you've been meaning a lot to me for a while now."

He'd come over. He'd allowed himself to become vulnerable in front of her. It was time for her to try to allow herself to show what she was thinking too.

"Maybe I know you mean a lot to me, Kurt Holland."

The hand that he'd rested on the middle of her lower back curved around her hip. The gesture somehow felt both intimate and far too distant.

His voice thickened. "Maybe next time I come over we can talk about something else besides my problems with my father and brother."

"Maybe we can," she said softly.

He bent toward her and kissed her sweetly. A sweet, chaste kiss. It was far from the passionate kisses that they'd shared on his couch after the fair.

But in some ways, it seemed to promise something enduring in their future … if they were willing to take that chance, to gamble on it.

When he released her, he pressed his lips to her brow. "I'm sorry. I've got to go."

"I know. Call me later. Let me know how it goes."

"Yeah. I will. Thanks, Emily."

"Anytime," she said as she walked him back to the door.

Minutes later, after she'd closed the door after him and sighed, she realized that things between them had changed again.

There was the promise of a future between them, now. A promise of something sweeter to come.

CHAPTER 30

FROM LES LARKE'S
TIPS FOR BEGINNING POKER PLAYERS:

Have fun. If you're not, what's the point?

"Where did you run off to?" his dad asked when Kurt entered the kitchen. "I walked out here twenty minutes ago and the kitchen was dead. At first I thought you were taking a nap, but I saw your truck was out of the garage."

It was all Kurt could do not to let his temper rise. "You thought I took naps at five in the afternoon?"

"I have no idea how you run your house. Hell, after hardly saying more than hello to me, Sam went upstairs and fell asleep."

"He's in high school. He'd sleep all day if you let him." Kurt also knew that he'd been up the night before studying for two exams and writing a paper. "Anyway, sorry I was gone. I thought you were watching TV in your room. I ran out to get some milk and eggs and bread."

"You get some decent milk?"

Luckily, he had. "Yeah. Whole milk. Just the way you like it."

"You didn't have to go out special for me." But still he sounded pleased.

"You're my dad. It's never trouble."

That honesty seemed to take him aback. Or maybe it was the fact that his father never responded in kind. He bent his head and took a sip of the coffee he must have just brewed. "Hope you or Sam still likes whole milk, seeing as how I'm leaving in the morning."

"You sure you're ready to go?"

"Yeah. This ain't my home." Looking around the kitchen his voice lowered. "Sometimes I can't figure out why it's yours. It doesn't seem right, both my sons living away from me."

Though he'd just gone over everything with Emily, Kurt's conscience still pinched. "Dad, you know Sam and I are glad to see you. But I've had the feeling that there is another reason why you came out here. Do you think you're ready to tell me yet?"

"Actually, there is something I wanted to tell you in person. I wanted to tell Sam at the same time, too, but maybe it's just as well that it's just the two of us."

"Well, don't make me wait any longer. What is it?"

Suddenly looking pleased as punch, his father grinned. "Here it is. We got some good news back in Spartan. Word's out that they're going to reopen the mine."

"Really?" he asked, floored. "I never thought that would happen. I thought with all the new regulations, most of the mines were closing."

"I guess the president is making good on his campaign promises."

Kurt was struggling. Part of him wanted to state the obvious, that the days of men making a good living in the mines was a thing of the past. That his father should be thankful that he'd gotten out with his health and any type of retirement package. That he should be looking forward, not behind.

But Kurt's heart was thinking another story. For the first time in months his father looked hopeful. He was excited about working again. Excited to have his pride back.

Who was he to try to squash that?

"What are you going to do?" he asked at last. Keeping his voice even, he added, "You going to try to go back to work?"

"You bet I am. I headed up a crew for eight years. I could do it again. There's a lot I can show to some of the young pups."

"That's great, Dad." Well, it was great for his dad, if the rumors were even true.

It wasn't great for his health or for Kurt and Sam, though. They'd worry about him, just like Kurt had for most of his life. It wasn't that the mines weren't safe, it was that there was a large propensity for accidents and for unsafe things to happen—especially for a man in his fifties. Fifty wasn't that old, but mining was a young person's job. "If they offer you a job and you want to go back, I'm happy for you."

A touch of the light that had been shining in his father's eyes dimmed before he visibly straightened. "This is a good thing, Son. A great thing for our town."

"It is." There was no denying that.

He took another sip of coffee. "That's why I wanted to drive here and tell you and Sam in person. It was too big of news to tell you over the phone."

"Yeah." He turned away. Poured himself more coffee. Tried not to focus on the fact that his dad hadn't come to see him or Bridgeport. Or, the hardest news to swallow. That he hadn't been so worried about Sam that he'd come to see him.

"So, what do you think?"

Kurt turned around again. "I just told you. If that's what you want, I'm happy for you."

"No," he said impatiently. "About coming back."

Kurt set his cup down. "I've got my business here. I bought this house. I can't leave Bridgeport."

"Your business is barely off the ground. You can sell the equipment and the house, too. Why, probably make a profit. Then, with my seniority, I could get you on at the mine. You'd be set."

There was no way that was happening. "Dad, even if I wanted to do that—which I don't—you're forgetting something. I moved here for Sam. He's been working hard. Real hard. You know that."

"If that boy is as smart as everyone says he is, he'll finish high school back in Spartan and be just fine."

Remembering Emily's sweet words of wisdom, Kurt shook his head. "No, he won't. Moving here has been hard on him. It turns out that as good as the school was back in Spartan, he's got some gaps. Too many to do well in college. Sam's even been getting tutored some to make sure he's ready for the scholarship applications."

"The boy's been having to get tutored? Who's paying for that?"

"I am."

"You're probably wasting your money, Son. I mean, if Sam is having to get spoon-fed, he's obviously not as smart as he's been telling us. He needs to come on home."

"And do what?" he asked sarcastically. "Hope he gets a ride to a local community college for a couple of years?"

"There's nothing wrong with that. Shoot, it's more than either of us had."

Kurt didn't want to argue anymore. Didn't want to discuss things that weren't going to happen. All it was doing was making him want to start yelling. "I'm not going back to West Virginia. Neither is Sam."

"He needs to. Living here is obviously not working out."

"It is. He needs to stick this out. He made this decision. You were there."

"You encouraged it. He wouldn't have come here if you wouldn't have pushed it."

All of his good intentions flew out the window. "Hell no, he wouldn't have come to Bridgeport if I hadn't pushed it, because you didn't even want to talk to the school about him. You didn't want to listen to the counselor's advice. You didn't want to do a thing for him."

"That's because there was no reason for him to go getting airs."

"Getting airs?"

His father waved a hand. "I've looked around. It's fancy here. Far too high-class for the likes of you. Sam, too. He doesn't belong here."

Kurt shrugged off the insult. He knew he wasn't anything all that special—just a normal guy who was trying to do right by his brother. But hearing his father put down Sam? It riled him up like nobody's business. "That's where you're wrong," he retorted. "Sam fits in just fine around here. He's made friends. He's got a girlfriend, too."

"She's going to soon want something more, Kurt. She's going to want someone else."

"Who? Like a man with a college education?"

"Someone with money. Someone whose brother was something better than rich people's lawn boy."

Kurt didn't want to admit it, but his father's words cut like a knife. All at once he realized that his father hadn't really listened to his dreams about his landscaping business. Hadn't wanted to understand that his company was already handling some corporate jobs. That he'd had to hire more guys. That he'd done a lot of things that his father should be proud about.

He'd never listened.

Exhaling, he forced himself to say the words one more time. "I'm not going to West Virginia. I'm not going back. Sam needs to stay here, too."

"Don't you see that you're trying to make that boy follow your dreams? You want him to achieve the things that you were never capable of."

Boy, that hurt. "Maybe Sam is. Maybe I really did want to go to college. Maybe I did want to have someone help me get out of that town. Maybe I would've given almost everything I had to have someone believe in me like I believe in him."

"You aren't him, though. If you aren't going to do what's right, I'm going to ask Sam to do it."

"Dad—"

"Let's get one thing straight," his father interrupted, his voice hard and filled with a mixture of impatience and contempt. "As much as you might like to pretend otherwise, you aren't Sam's father. I am."

"Yes, sir," Kurt said through gritted teeth.

"I might have given you some rights, but you are not his parent. You certainly weren't around when he was just a kid and was crawling on his hands and knees."

"No, sir." Each word felt bitter in his mouth.

But, as hard as it was to hear, he couldn't deny it. His father was right. He definitely had not been around when his brother was a baby. But what he also knew as clear as day was that his father hadn't been around, either. He'd been working in the mines or sleeping or hanging out with his buddies watching sports. Mom had been the one who had raised them both.

"I'm glad you finally understand. I know what's best for Sam. Not you."

"No, you don't," Sam said from the doorway.

Kurt whirled around. "Sam. I thought you were still asleep."

Pure pain was etched in his little brother's face. "Nope." Straightening his shoulders, he faced their father. "What were you talking about?"

Before Kurt could speak, their father walked toward him. "There are rumors that the mine is going to start up again. I'll be going back to work."

"Oh." After darting a look at Kurt, Sam smiled. "That's real good, Dad."

Some of the tension in the air dissipated. "I thought so, too. It's real good. 'Cause I'm telling you what. Once I start getting a steady paycheck again, things are going to be different for us."

Sam froze. "What do you mean, 'for us'?" He darted another look in Kurt's direction before staring at his father.

"I mean that it's time for you to come on home."

His brother shook his head. "No. No, way."

"As hard as it is to hear, you need to remember who you are." Their father's voice lowered. "What you are."

"What's that supposed to mean?"

Kurt stepped forward, "Sam, don't worry. I'll take care of this."

"No." He straightened up. "I mean, we're talking about me, right?"

Kurt swallowed. Feeling choked up, he nodded.

His jaw jutted out. "Then I have a right to know. And to say something about it."

Kurt's heart broke for the kid. Both for what their father was saying to him, and what it was doing to Sam. Right before his eyes, Kurt was watching the last of the adoration that his little brother had felt for their father get stripped away. In its place was the knowledge that their dad had faults.

Maybe it was time. After all, Sam wasn't a kid anymore. He was on the edge of manhood. He was having to make grown-up decisions and those choices were going to influence the rest of his life.

He raised his hands in acknowledgment. "You're right."

"Dad?" Sam finally said. "What did you mean when you said, 'what' I am?"

"It meant exactly what you thought it did. You don't belong here in Bridgeport. You don't belong in that school. You need to get on home." His voice softened, sounding almost upbeat. "You need to move back home, get back to your friends."

"But what about those test scores?"

"You don't really think a bunch of fancy government tests really mean all that much, do you?"

For a minute, Sam's whole persona deflated. Kurt realized then that had happened to him, too. Back when he wasn't talented enough or smart enough to get a free ride into college, their father had made sure that his dreams evaporated. He'd made Kurt feel that since he wasn't Troy, he wasn't college material. Kurt had believed him, too.

It was only now that he realized that he could have still gone to college. Oh, he would have had to pay, and get loans, but he could've done it if he'd wanted to.

But he hadn't thought he was smart enough to deserve that option.

Sam turned to him. "What do you think, Kurt?"

"I think you are the smartest man to come out of Spartan in years. I think it would be a shame not to do whatever you can to see where that brain of yours can take you."

"D ... do you mean it?"

"I wouldn't have brought you here if I didn't," he said, feeling like his heart was in every word. "But listen, it isn't just me who thinks this. All those teachers back in Spartan did, too. Miss Springer is your advisor and she says you're brilliant. You're going to be somebody special one day. I promise."

Their father scoffed. "Pretending that all your hopes and dreams can come true ain't no way to live, boys."

"I'm staying, Dad," Sam said. "I've got to see what's going to happen. Life's good here."

"Because of that school or your girl?"

"Because of both."

"If you don't come home, you're going to regret it."

"Yeah. I might. But I know I'll regret everything if I go back. Now, I'm out of here."

"Where you going?" Dad called out.

"Out. Bye."

Kurt leaned back and let Sam go, knowing he could text him later to see how he was doing.

"So that's how it's going to go," his dad said. "Can't say I'm real proud of you right now, Kurt."

For all his life he'd held his tongue, but the bitterness and disappointment burned so deep, he said exactly what was on his mind. "I'm sure as hell not proud of you right now, either. So maybe we're both screwed, Dad," he snapped before walking out to the back deck.

Breathing in the scent of the clean air with just a hint of a fall breeze in it, Kurt knew he'd just done the right thing.

But damn, had it been hard to do.

CHAPTER 31

"Poker is like life, most people don't learn from their mistakes, they only recognize them."
—C. AREL

Sam felt like a wuss, but he didn't care. All he knew was that if he didn't see Kayla right away and talk things over with her, he was going to ram his fist through a window or something.

It was either that or start crying like a baby.

He felt like such a selfish jerk. All his life, he'd taken his place in the family for granted. His mom had been so proud of him. She'd sat by his side at parent-teacher conferences and while it hadn't been her way to be real demonstrative in front of other people, there'd been a solid feeling of satisfaction coming from her so strongly that Sam could practically feel it.

Those nights, after they'd got back in the car, she'd reach for his hand and squeeze it gently. "You've done us real proud, Samuel," she'd say. "Real proud."

And he'd sit there and beam inside, like he'd done something pretty fantastic to deserve the praise.

But now he realized that he'd only been coasting. God had given him a really good brain and he'd taken it for granted. He'd never thought once about how Kurt had never been treated like that. Or how their father had given up so many dreams and filled up those gaps with bitterness and disappointment.

But even after his mom had died, he'd been sure his dad had been proud of him, too. But it turned out that it didn't matter what kind of grades he'd gotten or scores he'd achieved, Dad hadn't been on the same page.

When he got to Kayla's house, Ms. Everett opened the door right away. "Hey, Sam. I didn't know you were coming by today."

"I texted Kayla. She said it was okay if I came over. Is that all right?"

"Of course it is." Opening the door wider, she stepped back to allow him entrance. "She's in her room."

"Yes, ma'am." Sam stuffed his hands in his back pockets and prepared to wait. He knew from his previous visits that her mother liked them out in the open when he came over. He'd always thought it was kind of funny, because if he was going to try something with Kay, it sure wasn't going to be at her house with her mother in the next room.

"You know what? I think you should maybe go on back and see her there."

He was pretty sure his eyes had just bugged out of his head. "Ma'am?"

"She's had a pretty tough day, I'm afraid. I trust you with her, which is why I'm hoping if the two of you have some privacy, you might be able to get her to open up to you some more." Ms. Everett sighed. "Garrett Condon struck again."

Rage flew through him, burning his insides. "What did he do?"

"I'll let her tell you about it. I already called his parents, but Mrs. Condon hardly gave me the time of day." She shook her head. "I swear she thinks she puts her pants on differently than the rest of us poor souls."

He forced himself to unclench his hands. "Can I go see Kayla now?"

"She's the second door on the right."

He paused, feeling like an idiot but also feeling like he needed to say something. "I really like her, Ms. Everett. I ... well, I just wanted you to know that."

Reaching out, she squeezed his shoulder. "I know you do, honey. I just hope you can help her feel better."

Kayla, her mom, and her sister lived in a townhouse. It was about the same size as his house, but it was a rental. Everything about it screamed beige. It was all kind of cheap-looking, too. The first door on the right was open and it was obviously her sister's room. Across the way was a bathroom.

Making himself take a deep breath, he knocked on the designated door. "Hey, Kayla? It's me." Feeling foolish, he added his name. "Sam."

"Sam?"

"Yeah. Your mom said I could come on down."

"She did?" He heard a shuffling in her room. Drawers opening, the closet door sliding shut.

Her sister Brianna poked her head down the hall. "Hi, Sam," she said with a smile.

"Hey."

"Want me to go in there for you?"

"Nah. I've got it." At least he hoped so.

"Brianna, you come back into the kitchen," Ms. Everett called.

Rolling her eyes, Brianna turned and walked away. When she was out of earshot, Sam leaned toward the door. "Open up, Kayla. I don't care what your room looks like."

After another couple of seconds, she opened her door. She was dressed in a pair of boys' basketball shorts and a ribbed aqua tank top. Her hair was pulled into a ponytail on the top of her head and he didn't think she had a lick of makeup on.

Or, if she'd had on any, it might have already washed off. Her face looked blotchy and her eyes looked red. She'd been crying. "I can't believe you're here already," she said, her voice thick. "When did you hear?"

"I didn't hear anything. I came over to see you because my dad pissed me off."

"Oh. What happened?"

He shrugged. "It wasn't anything important. But when I got here your mother said something's been going on with Garrett." He stepped forward, deciding that he better not give her a choice about whether to let him in or about what they should talk about. If he did, it was pretty obvious that she would try to change the topic.

Looking ruffled, she stepped back.

If she hadn't been so upset, he would've teased her about her room. It looked like Kayla had a definite thing for Disney. She didn't have dolls or anything, but she had about seven or eight framed movie prints on her walls.

She had some kind of girly princess bed, too. It was white on white. All flounces and fluff.

All the girliness should have made him uncomfortable, but in a weird way it kind of made him like her even more. It was so unapologetically feminine. So different than what he'd become used to, living with his father and brother.

But it brought back a sweet memory of his mother, with her pink fuzzy slippers and her special bottle of perfume. She would've loved this room. Loved it like crazy.

Kayla was staring at him, a faint pink sheen lighting up her cheeks. "I bet you think it looks like a five-year-old girl sleeps here, huh?"

"Nope."

"Really?"

He didn't want to bring up his mother. At the moment he didn't think he could come up with the right words, make whatever he was trying to say sound like the way he meant it. He really did need help with his vocabulary. Instead, he grabbed her hands. Pulled her toward him.

Kayla edged closer easily, a curious expression lighting her face.

She was so pretty. He leaned down. Kissed her cheek, then kissed her again, this time lingering on the corner of her lips. "Maybe I think that my very own girlie-girl sleeps here. I like it."

Her lips curved into a full-fledged smile. "I like it, too. I kind of have a thing for Disney World."

Unable to help himself, he played with the ends of her blond hair. Liking how soft it was, how the ends had a curl to them. "Maybe princesses, too, huh?" he teased.

"Maybe. I don't know."

Though he was half afraid her mother was going to come in and kick him out, he led her to the edge of her bed and sat down beside her. "What happened?"

Her bottom lip trembled. "Garrett didn't delete all the pictures of me that he had. Some boys in the wrestling team told me he was showing them to a couple of guys in the locker room. They said he was laughing."

"Laughing?" He was going to kill him.

She pulled her hand from his clasp. "You know what's stupid? I don't know what made me more upset. The fact that he lied and didn't get rid of the photos, or that he thinks there's something wrong with me and he's laughing about it."

"There's nothing wrong with you."

She looked down at her hands. "Maybe there is and you don't see it. My boobs—"

"Are fine." He was pretty sure he was blushing too. But what else could he say?

She bit her lip. "Or maybe it was my bra or something. It's nothing special. I think I got it at Walmart."

"Guys don't care about stuff like that, Kay."

"Oh."

Crap. Now she was back to thinking something was wrong with her again. Anger rushed through him. He could feel his blood pressure rise as he thought of what a prick Garrett Condon was.

He had to deal with him. Take care of him so he would never even think about Kayla again. But first he had to help her.

"Kayla, look. I don't know what the right words are. I've been with some girls before but never had a girlfriend. Not until you."

She sniffed. "Is that what we are? Boyfriend and girlfriend?"

"Yeah. I mean, I had thought we were. I asked you to be mine. Remember?"

"I guess I just needed to hear it again." She groaned. "I bet I sound as childish as this room looks."

"If you didn't think I was serious about us that was my fault." Taking her hands again, he said, "I really like you, Kayla. I don't want to be with anybody else but you. I like you being mine … if that's what you still want, too."

She smiled. "I still want."

He leaned close and kissed her lips lightly. "Now, listen to me. I don't want to sound like a jerk, but back in West Virginia, back at my old high school, I played football. I was smart. My brother's name was plastered all over the old trophies and shit in the lobby. What I'm trying to say is that I was popular."

"And you dated."

"I did." Still not sure if he was saying the right thing or not, he plunged ahead, figuring it was better to sound like a conceited jerk than say nothing, because that hadn't been working for him. "I've seen a couple of girls without their shirts on, okay?"

Even though her eyes widened and she was staring at him like she was shocked, he barreled on. "They were pretty. Heck, all girls are pretty. But you … well, even if we never go that far, I can tell you for sure that you're beautiful. You've got nothing to worry about. Do you hear what I'm trying to say?"

Her lips parted slightly. After a couple of seconds, she nodded. Right then and there he knew he'd done the right thing. It was better to say something instead of keeping it to himself.

"Why do you think he was laughing, then?" she whispered.

"I don't know. But it doesn't matter, Kayla. No guy I want to know is going to do crap like that. Even if you sent me a picture of yourself half naked, I would never let someone else see it. That would be between us."

"I would never do that."

"That's fine. I'm not into that, anyway."

"What should I do?"

"About Garrett?"

She nodded. "My mom is so mad."

"I'm mad, too. But listen, I talked to your mom and she wasn't mad. She was worried about you. That's why she let me come into your room, Kayla. She was that worried about you."

"I'm glad she did." She drew in a deep breath, attempted to smile, but then it collapsed into tears. "I don't know what I did to deserve this."

"You didn't do anything. That guy is just a jerk. I promise what he did is going to last with him a lot longer than it will ever touch you. He's always going to be known as the loser who was reduced to gazing at pictures on his cell phone."

She tried to nod, but her bottom lip trembled again. He felt so bad for her. "Oh, Kayla. Come here."

She leaned into him, threw her arms around his neck, and started crying. He held her close, rubbed her back, and just let her cry. He had a feeling that's what she needed as much as anything.

And while she did that, he realized that he wasn't thinking about his dad anymore, all of his own insecurities about college or high school, or even about Bridgeport, Ohio. All he was thinking was that he was glad he was there for Kayla. Glad he'd found her, and glad that he hadn't messed things up between them by him saying the wrong thing.

After another ten minutes or so, she pulled back. "I'm sorry. I didn't mean—"

"Don't worry about it. I'm glad you cried."

She attempted to smile. "Boys aren't supposed to like girls tearing up."

"I don't like your tears, Kay, but I'm glad you weren't in here crying by yourself."

She sniffed. "I don't know what to do now."

He knew what he was going to do. But she didn't need to worry about that. "You know what? It'd be kind of a shame to waste a moment like this. Maybe you could kiss me a little."

She laughed. "You still want to do that, even though I just cried all over you?"

"Oh, yeah." He slid his hands down her sides, liking the way he could feel her ribs, the indention of her waist. The flare of her hips. Resting them on the middle of her lower back, he pulled her closer and brushed his lips against hers. Again and again, until he wasn't thinking about anything besides how good she tasted and she wasn't doing anything but gripping his arms like she was afraid he was going to let her go.

Then, all too soon, he stood up. "I've got to go. I'll call you later."

She climbed to her feet, adjusting her clothes as she did so. "Hey, we never even talked about you. Why did you come over? What did your dad do?"

"Nothing that matters. I'm better. Now, listen, you might want to splash some cold water or something on your face."

"Why?"

"You look like we've been making out in here."

Her eyes lit up. "That's 'cause we have."

"Yeah, but if your mom finds out, she's going to be mad at me and we'll never get to be alone again."

Looking amused, she nodded, "I'll do that."

"Okay. Later." He turned and walked out her door and went directly down the hall, going quick enough so that even if her mother was around she wouldn't be able to stop him and talk about Kayla.

Once he got to his truck, he scanned his friends and called up Graham. "I need to know where Condon lives."

"Why?"

"He's been sharing Kay's picture again. I don't think the principal's suspension did much good."

"You going to try to do something better?"

"Hell, yeah."

"Where are you? I'll come with."

"No need."

"Yeah there is. Someone's got to have your back."

Five minutes later, Sam was in a parking lot in the middle of town waiting for Graham. While he was waiting, he called Coleman and told him about both Kayla and what his dad had said.

As he'd hoped, Cole knew exactly how to respond. "Your dad's just jealous, Sam."

"Jealous of what?"

"Of you getting out. Of your brain. Of your future. But mainly of Kurt."

"Kurt? You think so?"

"Oh, yeah. Kurt wasn't afraid to do the right thing. Your dad was. That's why he was so ticked."

Sam knew he was going to have to think about that, but it could be true. "Maybe so."

"You going to go pound on that kid?"

"Yeah. I don't have a choice."

"Hell no, you don't. You might be living in the burbs now, but you're still from Spartan. We take care of our own. Can you imagine what all the guys would say if they found out you just sat there while some asshole was creeping on your girl?"

He didn't have to imagine what they'd say. He knew, and he would have deserved it, too. He was just about to answer when Graham pulled up beside him in his brand-new Explorer. "I've gotta go. Thanks, Coleman."

"No problem. Call me later."

"Yeah. Will do."

He got out then and hopped in Graham's SUV. "Hey."

"You ready?"

"Yeah."

It only took ten minutes for Graham to get to Condon's house. Only five minutes for Graham to text Garrett and convince him to come out and talk to him.

And only two for Sam to hit Garrett three times. Hard enough for his chin to split open. Hard enough for him to be crying like a baby. Hard enough for him to take the kid's phone, hand it to Graham, who then promptly backed up his new Explorer right over it.

CHAPTER 32

FROM LES LARKE'S
TIPS FOR BEGINNING POKER PLAYERS:

Have a purpose for playing. In other words, what do
you really want to win?

"Are you going to ground me?" Sam asked after he told Kurt about going over to Garrett's and hitting him.

Sam was standing stiffly in front of him. Kurt had just sat down at the table. They were in the small area that he supposed house wives or interior designers called a breakfast nook.

And because Sam had conveniently waited until morning to tell him everything, Kurt was in old gym shorts, an older T-shirt, and was barefoot. His coffee was still half-drunk on the table. An open bottle of orange juice stood next to it, along with a bunch of bacon that he'd cooked in their mother's old cast-iron skillet. He'd just eaten two strips and had picked up a third when the kid had begun his confession.

Now even the thought of food sounded bad.

Kurt stood up, turned away, and walked to the window. He didn't know what he was staring at, all he knew was that he needed a minute so he wouldn't wring his brother's neck.

Or give him a high five.

SHELLEY SHEPARD GRAY

That was the state he was in. He had no earthly idea how to discipline a teenage boy. Worse, he wasn't even sure if he wanted to.

For a brief moment, he allowed himself to feel resentful. He should've been worrying about work, his buddies, and Emily. His mother should've lived and his father should've agreed with the counselors and him about school and college. Shoot, even if Dad hadn't wanted to move here, couldn't he have even started Face-Timing them a couple of times a week? Even picked up the phone?

Then Sam would be having to face their father and Kurt could simply be the older brother.

Then, just as suddenly, all those negative thoughts dissipated. It was what it was. And as things went … sure, this wasn't easy.

But he and Sam had certainly weathered worse watching their mother waste away from cancer. They would get through this, too.

Now he could practically feel Sam staring holes into his back, waiting for Kurt to respond in some appropriate way.

"Kurt?" he asked hesitantly. "I'm sorry."

At last he turned around. Sam was still standing in front of him. Looking almost like a man. He hadn't filled out yet, but practically overnight he'd reached Kurt's height.

His brown hair was in need of a trim. His T-shirt was a little too tight. His arms had become thick from all those years of football. Now the muscles came from all the work he'd been doing with the lawn service.

But there in the blue eyes that were so like his own, something shined in their depths that looked like trust. And, perhaps, something that he was pretty sure the kid hadn't actually felt in a real long time. Innocence.

The kid still thought Kurt had all the answers. He was gazing hard at his big brother, sure he would know what to do. Help him.

And that pretty much gutted him. Sam was waiting for him to help.

"I know you're sorry," Kurt said at last. "But, just to make sure I know what you're talking about, what are you sorry for?"

"Hitting Garrett."

"Okay. That's a start. So, if you really feel bad about it, what do you think would have been a better way of dealing with him?"

Sam looked dumbfounded, which, on a smart kid like him, was kind of a new look. "I don't know."

"Really?" Kurt sat back down and gestured for Sam to do the same. "All right then. Let's do some thinking." He kicked out his legs. "Do you think you could have talked to him? Had a little heart-to-heart? Told him that he shouldn't be looking at pictures of your girl?"

Sam sat down but he didn't look happy about it. "No."

"No? How come?"

"Come on, Kurt. You know why. He and I already argued about it, so he knew how I felt. And his parents probably talked to him. Shoot, I know Principal Hendrix did. Kayla told me that her mother even called his mom! It didn't help."

Kurt took another sip of coffee, pleased that the temperature hadn't turned lukewarm yet. "So, talking didn't help. I guess suspension didn't either."

"None of that helped, Kurt. When I went over there, Kayla was crying. Like, a lot." Sam glared at him like it was his fault.

Though he was trying real hard, Kurt's insides clenched. He'd always hated tears. Their mother wasn't a crier, but when she did, something inside of him always went into panic mode.

"Do you think beating the crap out of him helped?"

"I didn't beat the crap out of him. I just hit him."

"Three times."

Sam shrugged. "I figured it couldn't hurt."

Kurt bit his lip so he wouldn't smile at that. "Did Kayla tell you to go beat on him?"

"No."

"Did you tell her you were going to go do it?"

"Of course not. She would've said not to, 'cause she wouldn't have wanted me to get into trouble."

Still feeling his way through the conversation, Kurt got up and got himself another cup of coffee. "You already told me how Graham got involved. You already told me that you called Coleman."

Sam's chin lifted. "Dad was here so you know I couldn't call you."

Kurt nodded, replaying the memory of their father gathering up his stuff and leaving not thirty minutes after Sam had stormed out of the house. Claiming that there hadn't been a reason to stay.

And him? Well, he'd let his dad go, then had opened a beer, sat outside, and tried to calm down.

"It sounds like you did what you thought was best, Sam. And while I wish you hadn't gone off half-cocked, I can't say that I wouldn't have done the same."

"So, you're not mad?"

"No. I'm not happy, but, like you told me a couple weeks ago, I'm not your father."

"So, you're not going to ground me?"

He sounded so disappointed, Kurt almost smiled. "I'm thinking whatever happens next is going to be tough enough."

"Do you think I'm going to get suspended now?"

"I don't see why the school would want to get involved. But who knows how they do things here? I guess we'll find out."

"Yeah." He leaned back in his chair.

"Now what can I do? Do you want me to call Garrett's parents?"

"No. You already hit his dad."

The kid probably had a point. "Okay. Should we get Miss Springer involved? She is your advisor."

Sam shook his head. "I don't want you or her to do anything unless you have to."

"Then I won't." He picked up another slice of bacon. "Now, um, about everything else ... you okay?"

"I'm not really sure. When I got home last night and saw that

Dad had left, I was kind of upset … but I was kind of glad, too. Is that bad?"

"I hope not, 'cause I felt the same way. I love our dad, but I don't always agree with everything he says."

"I don't either. I don't want to move back home. Not yet."

Just as Kurt was about to nod, the right words finally came to him. Leaning toward Sam he said, "For what it's worth, I've learned something lately that might help you, too."

"What?"

"Every once in a while, a man has to do something that he feels is the right thing to do. Maybe it isn't what the rest of the world calls right. Maybe it even hurts other people's feelings or makes them feel bad. But if you can live with the consequences, then you need to make peace with that and move on." Looking a whole lot more grown up than he had fifteen minutes before, Sam looked straight at him. "I can live with the consequences."

Thinking about the move and their father's hurt feelings and even about trying to do right by a little brother, Kurt realized that he could live with them, too.

Feeling a hundred pounds lighter, he pushed the plate of bacon toward him. "Then have a piece of bacon," he said.

Better people could have probably come up with something better to say. But when Sam grinned and did just that, Kurt knew everything was going to be okay.

CHAPTER 33

FROM LES LARKE'S
TIPS FOR BEGINNING POKER PLAYERS:

Win graciously. A broke loser always
appreciates a free beer.

When Kayla had hesitantly peeked into her classroom barely five minutes after her last class of the day ended, Emily had been fairly sure that the girl's reason for being there had nothing to do with school.

When she'd closed the door after Emily invited her in, she'd been sure of it.

But though Emily had been around a lot of kids in her four years of teaching, never had such a chain of events hit her so hard.

Poor Kayla had poured her heart out—and had done so not because Emily worked at her school, but because she was dating Kayla's boyfriend's older brother.

It was a little mind-blowing, if she was honest. It made her relationship with Kurt—which she'd been trying to both keep private and come to terms with—seem more real. It was all connected.

When Kayla finished her story with a hiccup and couple of tears, Emily was wishing that she had a lot better idea of how to help her than she did.

All she knew to do was help Kayla make the right decision for herself. Reaching out, she curved a hand around Kayla's. "I really am sorry all this happened."

"Me, too." After taking a shaky breath, the girl continued. "I can't believe that this whole situation will never end."

Placing both hands in her lap again, Emily said, "It really is too bad. However, no matter how much we wish otherwise, we can't get rid of the past. What's done is done."

"That doesn't help me, Miss Springer."

"No, I guess it doesn't. How about this? How about we do our best to try to figure out what to do about this latest development?"

"Okay …"

"What's really bothering you? That Sam beat up Garrett in order to defend your honor and got called into the office because Mr. and Mrs. Condon called the school? Or is it that you suspected Sam was going to go after Garrett after he visited your house and you let him do it?"

Kayla paled, but to her credit, didn't try to pretend that she didn't know what Emily was talking about. "Maybe both. Or, maybe that I wanted him to beat up Garrett because he was such a jerk and it didn't seem like anything bad was happening to him."

"At least you're taking responsibilities for your actions and saying the truth. I would have been pretty disappointed if you were sitting in front of me pretending you didn't know what was going to happen with Sam after you told him everything and started crying in his arms."

"That's all you're going to say?"

"What did you think I was going to say?"

The girl's eyes widened. "Something about how I should've been thinking better things about Garrett. Like I should forgive him."

"Not at all. He did some pretty stupid and mean things. Of course you're going to be angry. I'd have a hard time forgiving him, too."

"But just because I wanted him to hurt a little more didn't mean I told my boyfriend to beat him up." She blushed. "I promise I didn't tell him to do anything."

Noticing the fresh burst of pink on her face, Emily smiled. "Your boyfriend, huh? It's official?"

"Yep. We just made things official." Looking pretty darn adorable, Kayla lit up. "Oh, Miss Springer. You should have seen Sam. He looked kind of worried that I was going to say no."

"That's very sweet."

"It was. It really was. He's the best."

"I've heard he thinks pretty highly of you, too."

After smiling again, Kayla said, "What do you think I should I do now?"

Emily shrugged. "I know what I should tell you as a teacher and an advisor."

"That I should have tried harder to stop Sam," Kayla supplied.

"That's what I should be telling you. But to be honest, if I were in your shoes I would've been really mad, and I probably would've wanted somebody to make him stop."

"I think his brother's upset with him."

"I think Kurt is worried about him. He's had one goal in mind, and that was to get Sam a scholarship to college. To a really good college. He's afraid Sam's lost that chance."

"Do you think he has?"

Emily shrugged. "I don't think so. Not to get into college. Maybe it will affect some people who are in charge of scholarships, but I hope not."

Kayla looked near tears again. "If he doesn't get his scholarships it's going to be all my fault."

"Definitely not. Sam made that choice."

"But—"

"No buts. He's seventeen. He really cares about you. I also know from Kurt that Sam doesn't regret hitting Garrett one bit."

"I hope Kurt doesn't hate me. If Sam wasn't seeing me, he wouldn't be in this mess."

"Kayla, if you and Sam weren't together, I don't think Sam

would be as happy. And believe me, Kurt wants his little brother happy." She winked. "One more thing. I can promise you that Kurt would've hit Garrett, too. Those brothers are more alike than they realize."

Kayla smiled at last. After giving her a quick hug, the teenager walked out the door.

Leaving Emily to stare at a pile of essays that needed grading, lesson plans that needed to be finished, phone calls that needed to be made, and even more paperwork that needed to be filed.

But instead of doing any of that, she walked out to her car. She had somewhere more important to be.

***

An hour later, she juggled two shopping bags and a purse as she walked up the sidewalk to Kurt's house.

He answered as soon as she knocked, but instead of pulling her into a kiss, he looked a little weary. "Hey, Em. Did you text me and I didn't see it or something?"

"Nope. I decided to come over and cook you boys some supper. Is Sam around?"

"Yeah. He's had a crappy day."

"It's that bad, huh?"

Kurt shrugged as he took one of her bags and led the way down the hall to his kitchen. "You probably know as much as me."

"I heard Garrett's parents called the school."

"Yes, they did. After Ryan Condon called me."

She set her purse on the kitchen table. "Oh, my gosh! What did Mr. Condon say?"

"About what you'd expect. This wasn't his kid's fault. Sam was just being a redneck and needs to learn how to behave. I should be teaching him how to control himself better." Kurt rolled his eyes. "I could hear his wife egging him on as he said all that."

"Oh, my word."

Kurt laughed. "I had a couple of better words to tell them. Which, unfortunately, is why they called the school."

"What did Mr. Hendrix do?"

"You don't already know?"

Emily shook her head. "I went right to the parking lot after school."

"Well, Sam got suspended for two days."

Emily felt her heart sink. "Really?"

"Mr. Hendrix said he had to do something, otherwise the Condons were going to call the police."

"I guess you're pretty upset."

Kurt shrugged. "I'm upset at the situation but I'm not going to dwell on it. Sam did what he felt he had to do and now he's paying the consequences." He paused. "The only good thing is that Mr. Hendrix had some choice words for Garrett and his parents, too."

"Good." Feeling like they might as well get everything out in the open, she said, "Kayla stopped by my classroom after school. She feels like it's her fault Sam got into trouble. And that you are mad at her because Sam's dating her in the first place."

"What? Of course I'm not mad at Kayla. She sure didn't get Sam in trouble either. She's the victim. She hasn't done a thing wrong through this whole adventure."

"Maybe one day you can tell her that."

Kurt nodded. "I will."

Looking at him carefully, she said, "You know, I have to tell you that I'm pretty impressed. I didn't expect you to be this calm about everything."

"I wasn't this calm yesterday, but I've come to the conclusion that there's nothing to do. Yeah, I wish Sam could've stayed away from Garrett, but I can't really blame him."

"Something else is bothering you, isn't it?"

"Yeah." He walked to the refrigerator and pulled out two beers. "Want one?"

"All right." After taking a sip, she said, "What happened?"

"It turns out that my dad didn't just come to Bridgeport to see Sam and me. He, uh … well, he said he thought the mine was going to reopen and he wanted me and Sam to come back."

Though her insides were clenched at the thought of him moving away, Emily did her best to keep her expression impassive. "Are you going to?"

"Hell no. I couldn't even if I wanted to. I borrowed money to pay for my building and my equipment. I just hired two guys to help me with a new account. I can't just walk away like none of that even matters."

"What you've accomplished so quickly isn't easy. He should be proud of you."

"Yeah, it doesn't work that way in my family. I didn't have any problem telling him no. What did happen is that Dad started talking about how everything we'd always had and done was always good enough." Looking pained, he continued. "That I shouldn't start wanting things that were too far above my station in life."

Emily couldn't believe it. "He said that?"

"Pretty much."

"I bet that hurt."

"It did. So much that I didn't even try to tell him that I loved growing up in our town. I liked our neighbors, my friends, and my school. So, it wasn't any of that stuff, it was that ever since the mine closed, it hasn't been the same place."

"And that your brother needed something more."

"Yeah." He grimaced. "Then my selfish father started talking all about how maybe Sam wasn't actually all that smart after all."

"Ugh."

"Uh-huh. But here's the best part. Sam heard it and took off."

She pressed her hand to her mouth. "Oh, that poor kid."

"Yep, he went right from that nightmare to holding Kayla while she was crying."

"That's a lot to handle in one day."

Kurt nodded. "This move has been hard. I know it has been. Any move for a high school senior would be. But added to it, he's got a lot of pressure on his shoulders ... which I probably put there."

"And now he's overheard your dad say that maybe he can't even handle it."

"Yep." He sighed. "My father said something to me that I can't seem to shake as well."

"What was that?"

"He mentioned that maybe I've been trying to make Sam into something out of my dreams. That maybe I've been trying to make him achieve things that I never was able to."

"Do you think he's right?"

Kurt stared at her for a moment, then shook his head. "No. I mean, I really don't want that to be right."

"He's not, Kurt. Your father was hurting and wanted you boys to hurt, too."

"If that was his intention, he succeeded."

Kurt looked so down, Emily was even more thankful that she'd come over.

Which reminded her that she had things to do. Reaching into one of the paper bags, she pulled out a package of chicken. "It just so happens that you're in luck, Kurt."

"Because?"

"Because I'm about to make you and Sam my famous broccoli, pepper, and chicken pasta."

His lips twitched. "It's famous, huh?"

"Okay, it's not all that famous, but it is pretty good. Go get Sam."

"Why?" He looked at the packet of raw chicken. "Supper's not going to be for a while, right?"

"I didn't come here just to cook for you Holland boys. I came to cook dinner with you," she said as she pulled out the rest of the ingredients. "Go get Sam."

Kurt looked doubtful, but he did as she asked. And before long, all three of them were working on dinner together. Sam teasing Kurt about his knife skills and Kurt teasing her about the dishtowel she'd tied around her waist.

But when the three of them sat down to eat and both men's expressions were at ease, Emily knew that everything was going to eventually be just fine. The three of them were beginning a life together. It was imperfect and full of mistakes. But it was also full of laughter and warmth.

And yes, maybe even love.

CHAPTER 34

FROM LES LARKE'S
TIPS FOR BEGINNING POKER PLAYERS:

*Smile at the table. Don't waste your time off work
turning poker into another job.*

ONE MONTH LATER

"Did you know you've been staring at your toenails for the past
five minutes?" Campbell asked. "That color pink looks fabulous,
but even so, I don't think they're worth that much contemplation."

Realizing she was right, Emily looked up with a start. "Sorry."

"What's going on? I thought you wanted to come over here for
a girls' night."

"I did."

"But ..."

Emily sighed. "I don't know. Maybe staying in on a Saturday
night, watching old movies and painting our toenails isn't really
cutting it anymore."

Campbell frowned. "I know what you mean. We used to crave
these evenings. But now, even with a bottle of wine, it doesn't seem
all that exciting."

Her glass of wine was still half full. "You're right. Even the
wine isn't making things better. No offense, Camp. It's not that I

don't love your company or anything."

Campbell stretched out her legs on her beige suede ottoman. "None taken." She pursed her lips, then said, "If I tell you something, will you promise not to be offended?"

"Promise."

"Well, while you were eyeing your toes, I was doing some thinking. About five minutes ago, I came to a conclusion."

Emily took a sip of her rosé. "And what was that?"

"I think our Girls Nights In leave a lot to be desired." Lifting one foot, her toes a freshly painted teal blue, she said, "Actually, I think they kind of suck."

Campbell was practically a Southern belle. She didn't use words like suck. She didn't use them ever. Because of that, Emily was having a hard time not gaping at her. "How come?"

"Because you and I are sitting here at my house because our guys are having a poker night."

"Well, yeah."

"Kurt's hosting, Troy's there. So are two of his buddies."

"So is my brother and my brother-in-law, and one of my brother's neighbors."

Campbell waved a hand. "I think Ian might even be there."

"Wait a minute. Ian, like Ian the basketball coach?"

Slumping back against the cushions, she nodded. "Yep. Even Ian."

"That's not very fair. Ian's a nice guy. I bet he's getting along great with Kurt and Troy and the other guys."

"I bet he's having an awesome time, Emily." Bitterness oozed through every word.

"I'm sorry, but you've lost me. What's the problem?"

"The problem is that our idea of fun is sitting home—or going to hot yoga," Campbell complained. "But the guys are having a party in Kurt's garage."

"Uh, they're playing poker," Emily corrected her. "They're sitting in a garage. They're drinking beer, eating crap, and no doubt talking about sports and who-knows-what-else."

"I drink beer. I've seen Kurt Holland's garage and I kind of liked it. And I've eaten plenty of crap right here by myself."

"So, what are you saying? That we need to learn how to play poker and start our own club?" Emily tried not to sound too appalled, but she kind of was.

"I already know how to play poker." She paused, then said, "And what I'm trying to say is that we should go over there tonight."

"You want to crash poker night." She was kind of flabbergasted. But, strangely, not completely.

"I don't want to crash as much as join in," Campbell said. After pressing one fingertip to a couple of her toenails, she said, "Why couldn't we do that?"

There were about a dozen reasons that came to mind right away. The first and foremost being the most obvious one. "We're not men."

"I know that. But before you get all excited, remind me what the name of this poker club is."

"The Bridgeport Social Club."

"So, it's not the Bridgeport Men's Social Club?"

"No. But that doesn't really matter. It's understood."

"If we go, do you think the guys will kick us out?"

"Maybe not exactly. But they might not be happy about it."

Campbell was on her feet now. "I've only had a half a glass of wine. You've had even less. We can drive over there, no problem." She looked over Emily's outfit with a critical eye. "How soon can you be ready?"

"I'm in yoga pants and a tank top."

"You can borrow a shirt to put over it and you'll be great." Already walking to her bedroom, she said, "Come on in and pick out something to wear. I'm going to put on a pair of jeans."

"Can we just point out that I never said I would actually go?"

"You're not going to make me go by myself, are you?"

Emily barely stifled her groan. "No, but if my boyfriend gets mad at us, this is all your fault."

Campbell's eyes shone, accompanied by a very happy smile. "Understood."

Reaching into Campbell's closet, she pulled out one of her friend's favorite navy linen shirts and slipped it on. "Give me five minutes to fix my hair and face. And brush my teeth."

"This will be fun. You'll see."

All Emily could think about was Kurt's reaction. She really hoped he didn't break up with her over this. Because she had a feeling it was a foregone conclusion that it wasn't going to end well.

***

"Girls are here," Ace said as he walked toward Kurt. "And one of them is your girl. Did you invite her?"

Kurt turned away from the grill, where he'd been grilling a mess of hot dogs for all the guys.

They'd gotten off to a slow start, given that another three guys had shown up, which meant they needed to get out a second table and carry in the chairs from the back of his hall closet. Then, of course, had been the forty-dollar buy-in. Troy had taken over that job, and he was collecting the money, writing down a record of everyone's name, and passing out chips.

Given all that, Kurt was a little bit distracted. Okay, a whole lot distracted. And that was why he was pretty sure he had misunderstood Ace. "Say again?"

"You heard me. I just went out to the courtyard to pour myself a beer when Emily and some pretty teacher friend of hers showed up." He scowled. "What's going on with you? Your girl is real nice and all, but no one wants to play poker with girls."

"I didn't invite her."

"They're acting like it. They went right over to Troy with cash in their hands, man."

He was fairly certain this new development wasn't about to end well. Tossing the tongs to Ace, he said, "Here. Deal with the dogs."

"They're done. Where's a plate?"

Kurt waved a hand. "Over there somewhere. Figure it out." Before Ace could both complain and ask another question at the same time, he went into the garage.

And, sure enough, there were Emily and Campbell. Each had a red solo cup and forty dollars in their hands, and were wearing skin-tight yoga pants, of all things. And Em was even wearing a black tank top, too. Sure, she was wearing some kind of loose shirt over it … but it wasn't good. She looked way too hot.

He'd just caught Brenden's neighbor checking her out. Next thing they knew, the guy was going to saunter over and try to offer her poker tips.

Honestly, this was why guys played poker on their own. It wasn't because they didn't think women were good at cards. It wasn't because they thought they didn't want to lose to a woman.

It was because girls like Emily Springer were a distraction.

Fuming, he strode to her side. "What are you doing here, Emily?"

That dazzling smile faded. "Well, um, Campbell and I were thinking maybe we'd join in the game tonight."

Ignoring all the other men's interested stares, he wrapped a hand around her elbow and pulled her to one side. "I don't know if that's such a good idea."

Hurt flashed in her eyes. "You don't want me here?"

No. No, he did not. But not for the reasons she had obviously jumped to. He leaned closer. "Baby, it's not that I don't want you here, it's that it's kind of a guys' night. They're going to be cross and do all kinds of gross guy things that men do when women aren't around. I promise, you aren't going to want to witness it."

But instead of taking the hint, she giggled. "I have a brother, Kurt. I teach high school. Believe it or not, I've witnessed my fair share of icky male behavior. I'll be fine."

Now what? He scanned the room, looking for her brother and brother-in-law for help. But instead of marching over to lend a hand, Emily's brother just was standing off to the side grinning at him.

"We've got to get started, Kurt," Troy said.

Campbell looked around the room. "Any special place you want me?"

This was getting out of hand. Kurt inhaled. "Actually, I don't think y'all should stay."

"Why not?" Campbell asked.

It was obvious Campbell had entered with an attitude and intended to put any dissenters firmly in their place.

Pulling out the last of his patience, he attempted to scoot them out unobtrusively one last time. "Because—"

But before he could finish that thought, Campbell drove on through, like a freight train running in the middle of the night. She held up a yellow plastic cup that Troy had ordered and given to him the other day. BRIDGEPORT SOCIAL CLUB was printed in bold letters on the sides. Below that was a drawing of a deck of cards. Kurt had thought they were awesome.

Until this minute.

"Scc," Campbell said, pointing at the words with a red painted nail. "It doesn't say *Men's* Social Club, does it?"

"No. It doesn't. But it's understood."

"Not to me."

Now he was getting irritated. "Listen—"

Emily raised her eyebrows. "Listen?"

He realized right then and there he needed to pull it together. "Sorry. What I'm trying to say is—"

"Oh, let them stay," the guy who'd been ogling Emily called

out. "I can take their money as easy as any of you guys'." Looking around the room, the guy grinned broadly. "Besides, I'd rather look at them than at the rest of you idiots."

A couple of men even clapped.

Crap.

Which was exactly why Kurt didn't want them to stay.

Looking into Emily's eyes, he realized that he really had no choice. If he pushed the fact that he didn't want her there, things were going to end badly with him.

And as much as he liked the Bridgeport Social Club, the club with the understood "men," he liked his relationship with Emily better. He waved a hand. "Have a seat anywhere you like," he said. "And good luck."

She smiled brightly. "Thanks, Kurt."

"Just, ah, be careful, okay?"

"Don't worry about me. Just worry about your chips, cause I'm about to take them all."

When some of the other guys moaned, Brenden grinned. "Sorry I didn't warn you about this earlier, Holland. But my sister? Well, she really hates to lose."

She lifted her chin. "You ready?"

"Absolutely." Raising his voice, he said, "Tonight's tournament will start in two minutes. Clock is on."

They were going forward, whether anyone was ready or not. Huh. Felt a lot like life.

CHAPTER 35

FROM LES LARKE'S
TIPS FOR BEGINNING POKER PLAYERS:

*It's always good idea to play with new players from
time to time. Don't get in a rut.*

Emily might have eaten nails before admitting it out loud, but after about an hour of play, she was secretly thinking that Kurt had been right. These men were gross. And yes, her brother and Chris were included in this assessment.

Some of them were sore losers, too. When she'd raised the bet and won the hand while bluffing on a pair of twos, one of the men had thrown down his cards and muttered something under his breath that was really not nice.

Usually, she would have pulled out a bucket of five-star words and put him in his place. But tonight? Sitting at a table in Kurt's garage? It felt like any comment she made would be misconstrued.

While she was waiting to be dealt the next hand, she began devising ways to get herself out of there. Unfortunately, Campbell, who the men had made sit at a different table, was lit up like a Christmas tree and didn't seem to be having any reservations at all about staying as long as she could.

"What are you going to do, Em?" Troy asked.

"Hmm?" Belatedly she realized she'd let her mind drift. She had a four of hearts and seven of spades. "Fold."

Kurt met her gaze. She smiled, then sat back, drinking her water bottle while the rest of the men played around her.

Two hands later, she was out. Three hands after that, so was Kurt.

While some guys were eating cheese coneys that someone's kid had brought over from Skyline, Kurt looked pleased to be standing next to her.

"How you doing?" he murmured. "Are you mad at me?"

"For not wanting me at your boys' night?" She shook her head. "No." Lowering her voice, she said, "I'll deny this until my last breath, but I would have had more fun watching old movies and drinking wine."

Relief entered his eyes. "I promise, it's not that I don't like you."

"I get it. You just don't want me here. I'm not upset."

When one of the guys got a straight flush, he cheered. A couple of guys around him made good-natured comments. Some of the talk got even louder.

Kurt leaned close. "Step outside with me?"

Her eyes widened. "Is that allowed?"

"Yeah." Wrapping an arm around her shoulders, he guided her out the door and into the cooler air. Street lights, combined with the lights shining from the garage door illuminated Em's face enough that he felt like he could read her pretty well.

Her expression was easy, but she looked relieved. "It's certainly quieter out here."

"Yeah, it is."

Just that moment, he heard a rustling in the bushes on the side of the house. Afraid that it wasn't a stray cat but one of the guys who didn't feel like running into his house to pee, he steered her the opposite direction, toward the small park that was at the end of his block.

Emily walked by his side. Halfway there, she wrapped an arm

around his waist and stuck a finger in his belt loop. He liked that. Liked that a lot.

"You know, I've passed this park all my life, but I've never actually stepped foot in it. It's nice."

"When we first moved here, Sam was disappointed that there weren't basketball courts and stuff, but now I think he likes it. I might be wrong, but I'm pretty sure he's taken Kayla here once or twice."

She smiled. "And now you're taking me. I guess you brothers aren't as different as you'd like to believe."

It was on the tip of his tongue to point out that he hadn't brought Emily there to make out. But, seeing the way she was looking up at him? Well, obviously he wouldn't be opposed to do a little teenaged necking there.

If the timing was right.

If he ever got the nerve to actually talk to her about his feelings.

She sat down on the top of the metal picnic table. "Kurt, what's on your mind?"

He sat down next to her. "A lot. Sam. The poker game. Work. But mainly you."

"What about me?"

"Meeting you, getting to know you … dating you, well, it's been pretty unexpected. I didn't count on getting in a relationship when I moved here. Then there's the fact that you've got everything together. You have a nice place. A good family who you are close to. A good job. Multiple degrees. You've done so much with your life, Emily. While I … well, I'm still trying to figure things out."

"I think you realize by now that I've got plenty of things that I'm struggling with, too."

"Look at tonight. Based on what you told me, you would have never gotten out of your comfort zone six months ago."

She brightened. "You're right. I wouldn't have." She leaned into him. "Kurt, I'll tell you this over and over, until you don't need me to say it anymore. But I don't care that we have different back-grounds. I don't want a man who is just like me."

"Do you want a man who will appreciate you? Who wants to take care of you?"

"I do. If you'll let me do the same for you."

"I guess we have a plan then." He shifted so he could pull her into his arms.

When she leaned closer, he smiled slightly before at last taking her lips. Once again, he was struck by how soft they were. How soft her skin was. On her cheeks, on the small of her back where he'd just tucked his hand under her shirt.

He ran his fingers along the indention of her spine. Then flat-tened his palm so he could press her closer.

She moved toward him easily. Eagerly. Opened her lips. He gently bit on her bottom lip before deepening the kiss.

And then it continued.

Before long, their breathing turned ragged, and an ache had formed inside of him. He wanted her closer. Just as he wrapped both of his hands around her waist, intending to lift her so she could straddle his lap, a car drove by.

The lights shined on them and it honked, followed by laughter.

Emily pulled back with a start. "Oh, my word! We just got caught making out on a public picnic table."

Finally releasing her, he got to his feet and held out his hand so she could do the same. "Yeah, next time we should probably choose someplace more private."

"I'll remember that. But for now, I better go see how Campbell is doing. If she's done, then we'll get on home."

"Sounds good. Want to come over in the afternoon? I'm going to be pretty busy in the morning, cleaning up."

"I've got church, and then lunch with my family. How does four o'clock sound?"

"I have a better idea. How about I go to church with you."

Her eyes widened. "You would want to?"

"Yeah. I would. I want to know all of you, Emily. I want to hang out with you in the evenings, volunteer in the park when I can, make out with you on picnic tables … and worship by your side."

She smiled, then bit her lip. "My mother is going to want to invite you over for lunch. Sam, too."

He smiled. "It sounds perfect, Emily. Better than that."

They held hands back to his garage. When they arrived, the poker game was still going strong. He looked along a side wall, sure to find Campbell frantically texting Emily to see where she was … but instead she was one of the last players still playing.

"Uh oh," Emily said. "I think you're stuck with us for a little while longer."

"Don't you worry about a thing, Em," Troy said as he approached. "That girlfriend of yours is taking everyone's money hand over fist. She smiles, bats a couple of eyelashes, then goes for the kill."

"Campbell really likes playing poker."

"I think we all figured that out," he said dryly.

CHAPTER 36

FROM LES LARKE'S
TIPS FOR BEGINNING POKER PLAYERS:

Take winning or losing like a man. Recognize that poker is full of life lessons. If last night's game gave you lemons, deal with it.

It was the next morning. Early. Way too early. Eight forty-five. The poker game the night before had gone late into the night. To Emily's amusement and Campbell's pleasure, Campbell had come in third.

After they'd left, the other guys had, too. After kind of half-heartedly offering to help Kurt clean up, Ace had stumbled upstairs. Kurt had thrown out a load of trash then turned off the light and fell asleep on the couch.

Now he and Sam were in the garage and cleaning up the last of the mess, though he was tired, a little hungover, and would have rather been sleeping. Later Sam was going to hang back with Ace and look at houses while Kurt went to church and lunch with Emily.

But for now? Even though they were working in a hot garage, he was enjoying spending time with Sam. So far, they'd discussed his college applications (he'd now sent off four), the interview he'd had yesterday with someone from the Rotary Club (they were considering him for one of their three scholarships), and Sam's buddy Coleman (who'd recently broken up with his girl).

Actually, Kurt hadn't said a whole lot. He'd just been listening to the stories, nodding when it was appropriate, and laughing at Coleman's new take on love.

"Sounds like Coleman's gonna be okay after all."

Sam grinned. "Yeah. I keep trying to tell him that he should apply to OU, but he says he doesn't want to live in Athens."

"He'll find his place. Everyone does."

Sam looked up at him. "I guess that's true, huh? We ended up being happy here, haven't we?"

"You know what? Yeah."

"I'm glad you took me here. Even though Dad is still grumpy with us, I'm glad."

"Me, too." Feeling like now was as good as any to say what had been on his mind of late, Kurt put down the towel he'd been wiping the table with.

"Sam, I'm thirty-one years old. I've got my own company but I'm not all that. I've never been as smart as you. I've never been that great an athlete. And half the time? Well, I'm sure I'm saying the wrong thing with Emily, and I like her a lot. But I've learned something from being here in Bridgeport. Maybe even from being in this very room."

Sam stilled.

It was obvious that his little brother was listening hard. Glad that he hadn't lost his attention yet, Kurt kept talking. "I've learned that life is a lot like playing poker."

"Yeah, right."

"No, I'm serious. When you get started in a game, you're stuck with a bunch of different people. Some might be good friends. Some aren't." He paused, thinking on it. "Shoot, some might even be people who you'd rather not see again for the rest of your life. But still, you play."

Seeing that he Sam was staring at him hard now, he continued. "You get chips. Sometimes more than you need. Sometimes they're never enough. But usually you make do. And you get dealt in."

"Then you either win or lose," Sam said.

"Yeah. You do. But it ain't that easy. Shoot. Sometimes it isn't even that quick. But before you win or lose a hand, you start talking to the guy beside you. Maybe you talk about his kids or his wife or that last trip he took to the beach. You laugh a little louder than usual. Maybe cuss and swear a bit more than you should. Hours pass."

Kurt paused, thinking about last night's game. "Some guys take chances. Others play it real safe. Sometimes people play it smart. Or they get impatient, or they make stupid decisions." He grinned. "And some players? Well, they place too much emphasis on the wrong stuff. Eventually, everyone goes on home."

Sam looked at him curiously. "That's what's supposed to happen, right?"

"Right." Kurt nodded. "But here's the thing. Every single time, after I've been sitting in this old garage for a couple of hours, I start to realize something."

"What?" Sam asked.

"That these nights really aren't just about cards and chips and bets. Not really."

"That's because it's about winning."

"No, it ain't." Looking at Sam directly in the eye, he said, "These games, this Bridgeport Social Club? It's about being around friends who matter. It's about relationships. It's knowing that for a couple of hours, I did something for me. It's about knowing that even if I go all in or fold too early—or even if I win it all, what matters is that I did it."

He stared hard at his little brother. "Do you understand what I'm talking about, Sam? I didn't stay home. I didn't stand still and wait for something to happen to me. Even if I lose a couple of bucks, I didn't sit around and wish for something to happen. I tried to do something. I tried to accomplish something."

Sam nodded slowly. "Because you took a chance."

"Yep. Because we took a chance. Because we took a chance coming to Bridgeport." Clasping him on the back, Kurt continued. "I hope I make a ton of money landscaping office buildings around this town. I hope some school offers you a ton of money to be smart for them. But even if it doesn't happen, at least we'll have tried. And that is why I'll never regret moving here."

Sam's eyes widened. "Do you really mean that?"

"Yeah. Absolutely. It's fine with me if you don't get all the scholarships that you want. It's okay if you decide you don't want to go to Harvard or Yale or even Ohio State. What matters is that you're happy and you're at peace with your decision."

"What about you?"

"This conversation isn't about me, Sam."

"Sure, it is," Sam countered. "It's as much about me as it is about you. What if your business fails and Miss Springer breaks your heart?"

"Well, that's going to suck."

Sam's lips twitched. "I know. But will you wish that we never came out here?"

Kurt thought about it, then shook his head. "Not at all," he said with complete honesty. "Look at all that's happened here. You and I got closer. I met Emily. I actually *tried* to accomplish my dream instead of only sitting in my living room thinking about it. I can't regret any of that."

Sam studied him for a long moment. Looked down at his feet. Then, to his surprise, smiled broadly.

Now Kurt felt completely confused. "What's that smile for?"

"'Cause I may be real smart, but you just taught me something that's going to get me through the rest of my life."

"And what was that?" He really had no idea.

"That no matter what happens in our lives, we've already done something pretty good, Kurt. No matter what we do, we're not going to have to worry about failing. When it comes to trying our hands at things that matter? I figure we've already won."

Slapping his kid brother on the back, Kurt felt that ball of worry that had taken place in his chest for the last year fade away. "You're right, kid. Me and you? We've already won."

An Excerpt from

All In

THE BRIDGEPORT
SERIES
SOCIAL CLUB
BOOK 2

CHAPTER 1

FROM LES LARKE'S
TERMS FOR POKER SUCCESS:

All In: When a player bets everything he's got. Be advised that this can be a risky undertaking. If you lose, there's nothing left.

The shove came out of nowhere, hitting Meredith Hunt hard on her shoulder and knocking her down onto the paved walking path. Feeling both shocked and confused, she threw out her hands in a weak attempt to break her fall. But instead of helping the situation, a sharp, fierce pain reverberated along her right hand. Pebbles tore into her other palm, her knees, and parts of her thighs. She felt dizzy. Stunned. Half in shock.

What the heck had just happened?

Panic overtook her as she realized that whoever had just rammed her to the ground had taken off with her backpack.

Just like that, a dozen images of what was stashed in there flitted through her head. Her wallet. Her phone. Her keys. Her address. The idea of any of that coming into a stranger's hands was enough to make her jump to her feet.

Well, she would've jumped—or simply sat up—if she hadn't been feeling so dizzy.

"Hey. Hey, are you all right?"

Opening one eye, she realized a man was kneeling next to her. He had short black hair, matching eyes, scruff on his cheeks, and a very concerned expression.

"I think so," she muttered, horrified to realize that she sounded gritty and hoarse. Like she was barely hanging on. Which, unfortunately, pretty much summed up exactly how she was doing.

The guy's expression grew more concerned. "I saw some punk push you down. Looks like you hit the ground hard, too."

Hating that she was still sprawled out in front of him, she stretched a leg experimentally. "I need to get up."

"Hold on. What hurts, darlin'?" he murmured. Actually, he drawled. Though Meredith knew better than to be taken in by a southern drawl and a cast-off endearment, she felt herself responding to him. "I'm not sure," she murmured. Good Lord! Even to her own ears she sounded like a wannabe damsel in distress. She really needed to get a hold of herself.

But instead of being turned off, the man looked even more concerned. He leaned closer. Slipped a hand under her head. "Is your neck okay?" he asked, staring at her intently. "Can you move your head?"

She nodded experimentally. "I'm all right. My head kind of hurts, but I'm sure it's fine. I've got a hard one." At least, that's what her mother had always told her.

After studying her a moment longer, he took a knee. "Ma'am, I'm going to take your elbow, okay? We need to get you sitting up."

Ma'am? She swallowed. Did she really look that old?

"Dad, what are you doing—" A voice called out. "Oh my gosh. Miss Hunt?"

Surprised, Meredith focused on the person just beyond her rescuer. Finn. He was a sophomore at Bridgeport High. One of the kids she helped out when she volunteered in her friend's class once a week. Finn was fifteen, muscular, almost six foot, and a little on the chunky side. He was built like the football player she'd recently learned he was.

However, in spite of all that brawn, there was still a sweetness to him. His face still had a touch of peach fuzz that most underclassmen boys at the school had. He also had dark brown eyes and dark hair, making him pretty much the spitting image of the man who was still kneeling by her side.

"Hey, Finn," she said, glad she'd at last found her voice. "Fancy seeing you here." Inwardly she winced. Had she really just said that?

Finn blinked, then grinned, like she'd really amused him. The man by her side, the one whose hand was now curved protectively around her elbow, looked confused.

No doubt it was not only because the kid knew her but that she spouted such an idiotic phrase while lying on the ground. When she noticed that his free hand was hovering in her general direction, but that it seemed he didn't want to manhandle her without her permission, she tentatively smiled at him.

That was all he needed to press that hovering hand around her side. A little above her waist. A little below her breast. Not that she should be noticing anything like that. After all, she was a Pilates instructor. She, of all people, knew that positioning other people didn't always mean anything personal. Sometimes it really was just an offer of assistance.

But still, she was aware of his touch as she moved to a sitting position. She breathed deeply, hoping that a good dose of the crisp January air mixed with the scent of pine would help her get her bearings. But all she smelled was soap and tobacco and peppermint. It shouldn't have been a good combination. Nor should this man's underlying scent—the one that signaled he was all man.

She really needed to get herself together. Like, immediately.

"You all right?" he murmured.

"Mm-hmm," she whispered back, though why she was whispering, she didn't really know.

Finn peered down at her. "Miss Hunt?"

She summoned what she hoped was a sunny smile. "I'm going to be just fine."

The man looked from her to the boy in confusion. "Looks like y'all know each other."

"I help out in one of his classes," she replied. "Finn, well, he's currently my favorite sophomore."

Blushing, Finn ducked his head as he dropped to one knee next to his dad. "You tell everyone that."

"Maybe. But right now it's true." Looking at his dad, she attempted to act like the situation was normal, even though she was on the ground in the middle of the bike trail. "Hi. I'm Meredith Hunt."

"You work at the high school?"

"Work? No, not really. I'm just a volunteer."

"She helps out in Miss Springer's classroom, Dad," Finn explained before turning back to her. "Miss Hunt, are you really gonna be all right? That guy who shoved you was really big."

"It sure felt like it." Remembering the reason for the shove, she groaned. "He stole my backpack."

Finn frowned. "I thought that was what he did. Sorry I wasn't close enough to tackle him."

Even imagining Finn getting tangled up with the man who'd shoved her made her tense up. "I'm glad you weren't any closer! You could have been hurt. No backpack is worth that." She shifted, ready to get to her feet and figure out what to do next.

"Hey, take it slow," Finn's dad said softly, that thick drawl accentuating every word. "You're bleeding pretty good."

She looked down at her bare legs. In spite of it being January, she'd decided to wear shorts to run. The sun and fifty-degree temperature were too welcoming to ignore. But now, seeing the scrapes, she was coming to regret that decision. They did look kind of bad, but there wasn't that much blood. "My knees will be fine."

"I was talking about your hand, Meredith."

She watched him pull out a worn, soft bandanna from his jeans and press it on her hand. Right then and there a sharp, slicing pain entered her wound. She sucked in a sharp breath.

Finn's dad curved a palm around her shoulder. "Easy, now. It's deep. You need stitches." Still looking at her hand, he frowned. "It's swelling, too. You might need an X-ray."

Shifting, Meredith looked down at the bandanna, which was quickly turning red. "Gosh. You're right. I guess I better go—" Her memory suddenly returned, bringing with it the knowledge that everything she'd been carrying had been stolen. "Actually, I don't know what I'm going to do. I don't have my license or keys." Or her insurance card. Or any money. Or her phone.

Crap!

Panicked, she struggled to her feet. "I need to—"

Resting both hands on her arms, Finn's dad held her steady. "Hold on, now," he drawled. "You're gonna hurt yourself."

"You don't understand. My phone was in there with my wallet." Which, for once, was full. Plus it had all her credit cards.

Crap again!

Oblivious to the minor meltdown she was having in front of them, Finn said, "Dad's right, Miss Hunt. You need to be careful. Sorry, but you look pretty bad."

She felt pretty bad, too. Though she was feeling fuzzy, she had recovered enough to start making sense of the situation. "Do you think that guy might have only taken the cash then ditched my bag or something?"

"It's worth a try. Finn, go look up ahead. Maybe go a couple of hundred yards or so. What color is the pack, Meredith?"

"Teal blue."

"I'm on it." But just before he turned away, he looked back at her. "You gonna be okay?"

Everything inside of her turned to mush. Just mush. In the

three weeks since he'd arrived at the school, Finn Vance had been kind of hard to read.

At first she'd thought it was simply because he was the new kid. That would be hard for anyone. But then she heard from one of the coaches she worked with that Finn was destined to be a starter on the varsity team in the fall. She'd also heard from her friend Emily that he seemed to be struggling in school. Meredith had also noticed that he never looked all that happy when he was in class, either. Always serious.

That serious attitude, combined with his fake diamond earrings, faded jeans, and collection of black concert T-shirts made him definitely stand out in the school.

But though he also seemed tough, he behaved well and always watched her like he was trying to figure her out. Just last week, when her arms were full of notebooks and she was having trouble managing them all, he'd helped her carry them to her car.

She'd suspected then what he was proving now. Underneath all those muscles, T-shirts, and attitude was a kid who'd been raised to be something of a gentleman. "Finn, I wish every kid in Bridgeport was like you. Thanks."

The blush that reached the roots of his hair made her smile. When he trotted off, she turned to his father. "I think I can stand up now."

He nodded, but looked at her steadily. And, if she wasn't mistaken, in a completely new way. "Careful, now."

Feeling awkward, she stood up, accepting his hands on her elbow and waist again. Once they were both on their feet, she blinked as she had to lift her head another couple of inches to meet his gaze. "Thank you again. And, um, I guess we should probably introduce ourselves a little better. As I said, I'm Meredith Hunt."

"And I'm Ace Vance, Finn's dad."

His voice was serious, gravelly. Meredith thought that it went well with his eyes, which looked like they saw too much and were ready to take on anyone's burdens. "Thank you for coming to my rescue. I don't know what I would have done if you two hadn't arrived."

His dark eyes turned stormy. "Don't thank me. I haven't done anything yet." Before she could refute that, he visibly scanned her from top to bottom. "We need to get that hand taken care of."

Looking at the bandanna that was now very soaked, she resigned herself to the fact that he was right. "I guess I better call the police. Maybe they can help me?" Of course, that was going to be kind of hard to do, since she no longer had a phone. Thinking of all she'd lost, the panic started to creep back in. "Could I borrow your phone for a minute? Would you mind?"

"If you need the cops, I'll call. But give Finn a sec, okay? I think there's a good chance he might find it nearby. Most muggers are only after cash, not backpacks and keys."

Imagining the worst, she said, "I hope that mugger isn't nearby. I'd hate for Finn to get hurt."

"He already weighs one-eighty. He's played football since he was six. No backpack-stealing punk is going to get the best of him."

Releasing a ragged sigh, she knew he was right. One step at a time. Seeking to take her mind off her misery, she said, "Um, your son is really great."

"Thanks," he said offhandedly.

"No, I'm not just saying that. He helped me carry some equipment from the field to my car the other day. Half the kids I work with wouldn't do something like that. That's how we met."

His eyebrows lowered. "They should."

"What I'm trying to say is that he's really composed and mature for his age. You should be proud of him, Mr. Vance."

A reluctant smile appeared on his lips. "Thanks." This time it sounded sincere. "Finn's not much of a student, but he's a good person. At least, I've always thought that. You know, when he's not being a teenager with a chip on his shoulder."

She laughed. "I'd guess half the kids at Bridgeport High have chips on their shoulders. My friend Emily says it comes with the territory."

A reluctant smile crossed his features. "Why don't you call me Ace, Meredith? I've never been the type of guy to be called a 'mister' anything."

"That's reserved for your father?" she teased.

"Nah, he ain't that kind of man either." Looking bemused, he said, "Now that I think about it, I can't think of a single person to ever call my dad anything but Buck."

Buck. Ace. Finn. Interesting names. Country names. "All right." She smiled slightly, thinking how odd it was that she felt so at ease with a man who looked so different than the majority of the men she hung out with. He had to be at least six or eight years older than her and he seemed to favor black as much as his kid. Plus, he wore earrings in his ears, as well. Two tiny silver hoops. And one of his arms had a bunch of tattoos, all inked in black.

Startled by the direction of her thoughts, she held up her bleeding hand and pretended to be completely fascinated about the way blood was oozing out of her palm.

"It'll be okay," he said in a soothing tone. "I bet you won't even have much of a scar."

She was an adult. She'd had CPR. She'd had extensive training when she became a certified Pilates instructor. She dealt with clients recovering from injuries on a daily basis. She definitely did not need some strange man coddling her and murmuring sweet things in her ear.

So why did she kind of feel giddy around him? Why did she feel like maybe he was even making her feel better?

She turned to stare at the path behind her. Maybe if she stared down the empty path long enough she could suddenly will this episode to be over.

And then she saw her savior. Again.

"Here comes Finn!" she called out like he was returning from battle. "And he's holding my pack." Relief flooded through her.

Ace looked in that direction as well. When Finn got within speaking distance, he grinned. "Good job, kid."

Finn smiled broadly. "It weren't nothing. It was laying on the ground just around the bend. I didn't see the guy who took it, though."

"S'okay. You got her bag," his dad said quietly, in that same soothing tone that she found so mesmerizing. "That's most important."

Finn nodded before turning to her. He said, "It was already opened, Miss Hunt. "I didn't open it."

"Of course you didn't." Impulsively, she squeezed his hand with her good one. Before she thought the better of it, she waved her fingers toward the zipper. "Well, go ahead and check it out. What's inside?"

He opened it. "Keys," he said, pulling out her heavy Minnie Mouse key ring. "And your phone."

"That's a relief. Do you see my wallet?"

Ace frowned. "Nope. Sorry."

"Thanks, Finn." She held out her good hand to take the pack. "That's too bad about my wallet but at least I can get home now." Already making plans in her head, she said, "I'll cancel my credit cards when I get home. And if I get pulled over for driving without a license, I'll just have to explain to the policeman what happened. He should understand, right?"

Finn was staring at her like she'd grown another head but nodded. "Yeah, maybe."

But Ace frowned. "You need to get to the doctor first before you do anything. And you shouldn't be driving. Not until you get checked out."

"That's sweet advice, but I don't really have a choice."

Ace sighed. "Why don't you let us take you to urgent care?

There's one of those doc-in-the-box places in the center of town. After we get you seen to, I'll drive you back to your car."

"I couldn't let you do that."

Studying her hand, he nodded. "Would you rather go to the hospital? We could do that …"

Cutting him off, she said, "I hate to point out the obvious, but I don't have any money on me. I can't pay right now."

"If they charge you something up front, I'll pay it."

"I could never ask you to do something like that."

He raised an eyebrow while his son remained silent. "You didn't ask. I offered. Right?"

He did have a point. But how could she take advantage of him like that? It wasn't even like she knew Finn all that well.

Then there was the little matter that he had also just spent the last half hour getting her on her feet and retrieving her backpack. That was more than enough good works for two strangers. "I'm sure you've got other things to do. This isn't your problem."

Finn lifted his chin. "We don't have anything else to do, do we, Dad?"

"Nothing as important as making sure you are okay," Ace said. "You don't want to drive if you're woozy. Trust me on that one."

"I hate to impose. I mean, you've rescued me, found my backpack, and gave me your bandanna to ruin."

Finn smiled. "My dad doesn't take no for an answer real well. You might as well give in now."

Glancing at Ace, Meredith saw a new light shining in his eyes. He was pleased about his son. Pleased about how the boy had reached out to her. Glad he was joking around a little bit.

That, in the end, was what did it. Sure, she was still a little shaky on her feet. She also needed help paying for the clinic visit. But what mattered most to her was the sense that Finn seemed to need to help her as much as she needed a helping hand.

She could ignore a lot of things, but she could never ignore that.

"In that case, thank you," she said finally. "I really do appreciate your help."

Acknowledgments

I've often said that there's usually a team of people behind each one of my books, and that has certainly been true with both *Take a Chance* and the whole premise of the Bridgeport Social Club series. With that in mind, I'd like to thank some of the people who were so instrumental in helping me bring it to life.

First, I owe a great deal of thanks to Tony Westley, who started a poker club in his garage, which became my inspiration for the series. Tony, thank you for your friendship and for making so many of us feel like we're part of your extended family. We're all better for having known you.

I also am indebted to my agent Nicole Resciniti. Nicole not only didn't laugh at me when I pitched this idea but encouraged me to get started on it! I'm blessed beyond words to have an agent who believes in me the way she does. Without Nicole, this series wouldn't have seen the light of day.

Along those same lines, I'm extremely grateful for the enthusiasm and support of Blackstone Publishing, especially my editor

Vikki Warner. Vikki, thank you for believing in the Bridgeport Social Club enough to take a chance on me. I hope the books do you proud.

In addition, I want to thank Brian and Amy Salzl. What a team! Though both Brian and Amy are so busy with two careers and four kids, they took time out to help me make this book better. Brian patiently described the ins and outs of owning a landscaping company and Amy read the manuscript very quickly (three days!) and offered suggestions. Believe me, Team Salzl, y'all helped so much.

Last but not least, I'm so grateful for my critique partners Heather Webber, Cathy Liggett, and Hilda Knepp. They not only joined me on a very long and crazy writing retreat, they read and reread (and reread!) multiple sections of the book. They are wonderful women, friends, writers, and editors—and yes, my very own social club.

Everyone should be so blessed to have so much support.

Reader Questions

1. So much of this novel is about finding a place to belong and fitting in. What are some groups in your life where you have found a "home"?

2. What do you think about the dynamic of Kurt and Sam's relationship? What did you like about their bond? How do you think it might grow and change over time?

3. Though Kurt did move for his brother's future, he never thinks of his actions as a sacrifice. What do you think? Do you know of anyone who would do something similar for a family member?

4. Why do you think Emily Springer was the perfect match for Kurt? How do you think her character will grow and change in the future?

5. Sam's girlfriend, Kayla, was one of my favorite characters in the novel. Though she was made out to be a victim, I think she was also a source of strength for Sam. How do you think Sam's adjustment to Bridgeport might have been different if he hadn't started dating Kayla? What do you think will happen in their future?

6. Each character had to "take a chance" in the novel in order to find happiness. When have you had to take some chances of your own?